I.R. VASQUEZ

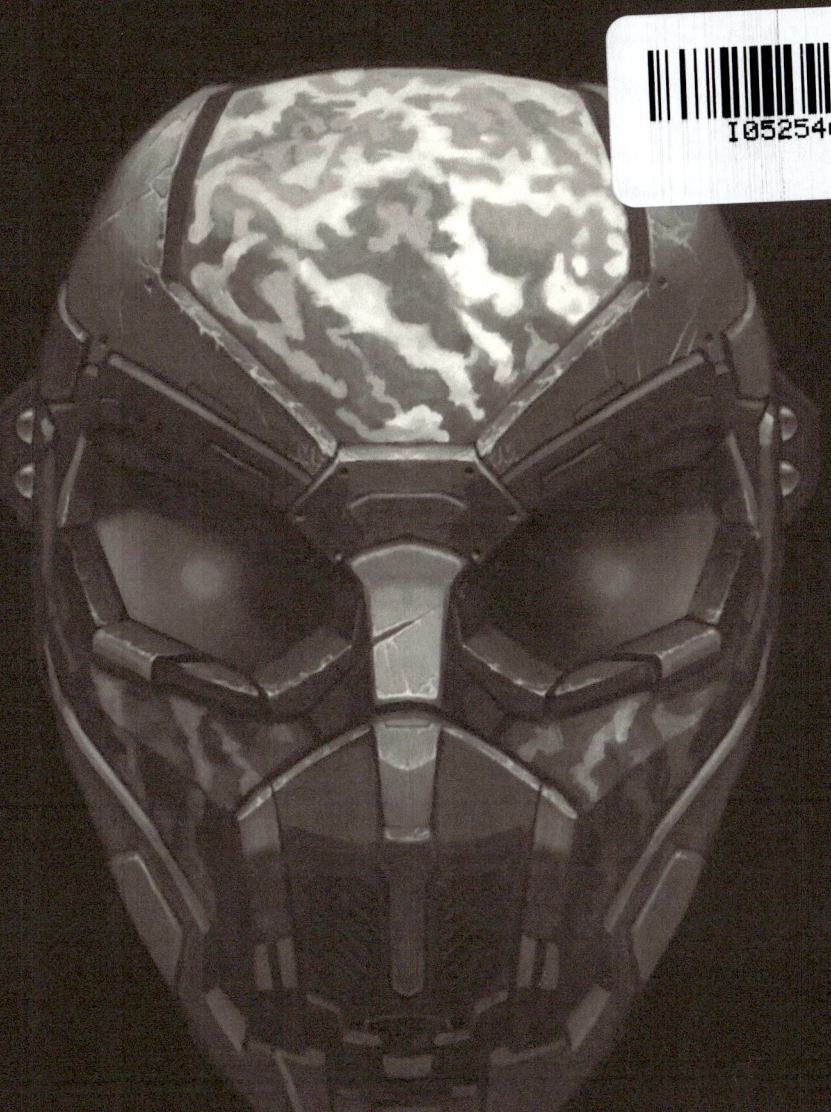

SITCH
GHOST IN THE SHADOW

SITCH
GHOST IN THE SHADOW

I.A. VASQUEZ

To request permissions, contact the publisher at
I.R.Vasquez@outlook.com

ISBN: 978-1-7354762-1-6

Edited by Tochi Biko and Lidice Valdes
Cover art by Yuri Chuchmay
Layout by Laura Perdomo
Book blurb and definition by Jessie Cunniffe

Printed by Lulu Press in the USA.

Lulu Press
627 Davis Dr. #300,
Morrisville, NC 27560

CONTENT

CHAPTER 1

Fort Pierce, FL.

The morning is bright and warm, with the smell of saltwater filling the air. A light breeze is blowing in from the ocean. The city is quiet. There is a war raging that has wiped out most of its population. A war that has been raging for 40 years.

Florida is no longer a part of the United States at this point. It, and a number of other states, separated from the U.S. seven years after the great invasion from Russia. Texas, Florida, Louisiana, Alabama, Mississippi, and Georgia formed what became known as the "Freedom States", with rumors of more states wanting to join. The fear of retaliation from a government that has fought the Freedom States for the past 30 years has, so far, been enough to stop them. There is an old fashioned cafe called Mitch's Landing, right on the beach, where you can find an old man that loves to spend his time sitting crooked and telling stories of his journies. He is a little overweight and has snow-white hair, a goatee, a wrinkled face, and half shut bluish-gray eyes. At the café, there is just one waitress. She is always dressed up in a red, plaid, 1950's style dress with a white apron. Her brown hair is always pinned up, she wears red lipstick and speaks in a thick southern accent. She has a soft, round face, and wears a constant smile. The waitress is soft-spoken, and a sweetheart to most people. She looks to be constantly moving, with a red pen over her right ear. The café sits facing the beach, with sides painted yellow and light blue, and white trimming on the outside. On the inside, all-natural wood planks are visible, and there are hand-drawn paintings of beaches from all over the country. On the side of the cafe facing the beach, there is a deck with seven tables and foldable umbrellas that are all different, vibrant colors. The old man always sits in the same spot and the young lady knows exactly what to get the old man. To most, the old man is known as Taavet the Wise.

Ten years after the great war, the ISA, or the Islamic State of America, as it is now known, is more organized and established than its former self, ISIS. The ISA did what ISIS could not. It did what every terrorist organization had tried and failed to do; it succeeded in infiltrating the United States.

That morning, a troop from the ISA government walked into the café. It was, of course, unusual for ISA troops to be seen so casually in a Freedom State, because of the ongoing war against the ISA. But these troops had been allowed to cross the established border separating the Freedom States from the ISA. Their instructions were to search for a mythical individual known only as Sitch. This is a man some ISA troops don't even believe exist. He has not been spotted for five years, but the President of the ISA declared a nationwide manhunt for Sitch and convinced the President of the Freedom States to let them search their country for Sitch in exchange for a cease-fire. The hunt went on for seven years with no clue where to look, until calls began to pour in. All of the information pointed to Taavet's knowledge of Sitch's location.

The commander of the troop; a tall, strong man with a full, long beard, leads a troop of fifty men, every single one looking every inch a troublemaker, into the café. Each man is wearing green camouflage and a black mask. The Commander walks straight up to the waitress and snarls his demand. "Where is Taavet?"

The waitress looks directly at him with no fear in her eyes and asks, with a big smile on her face, "How may I help you?"

"Woman, do you know who I am?" The Commander is suddenly

screaming. "At the snap of my fingers, I can turn your little hole in the wall into a mountain of rubble. I will teach you your place and where you belong!"

He raises one hand, ready to strike, and grabs the waitress's arm with the other. The waitress reaches behind her and grabs hold of a knife, but at that moment Taavet speaks. "I am Taavet." Taavet has not moved his eyes from his breakfast. He is in the process of cutting his pancakes and eggs. The Commander turns to Taavet with his arm stretched out, still ready to hit the waitress.

Taavet speaks again. "I suggest you lower your hand, young man. You don't want to do something you'll regret."

The Commander lowers his hand slowly, pushes the waitress away, and walks toward Taavet with a grin. "Oh yeah?" He sneers. "What are you going to do about it?"

Taavet pierces a tomato before he replies. "Have you heard of the Legend of Sitch?"

"Sitch is nothing but a criminal." The commander retorts. "And he must be brought to justice. Where is he?"

"I will tell you in time," Taavet responds. "But first, let me tell you a story about this so-called criminal."

Taavet puts his knife and fork down slowly as the Commander and his troops take seats. The troops seem motionless and cold. The waitress tries to take orders, but the men remain as motionless as statues.

"October 24, 1945," Taavet begins. "The United Nations was established to prevent future wars. But changed sixty-nine years ago, when the old United States declared war against Russia. The U.N. had no say in a fight between the two greatest powers in the world, and other countries took advantage of the war. Japan and a United Korea invaded China. Israel took the Gaza strip. Lebanon and Pakistan held ground as Egypt and Syria persisted in a relentless attack. And Jordan allied with Israel. Saudi Arabia was in shambles, and their broken economy sparked a civil war. Iran and Iraq joined forces and were abnormally quiet. Turkey was almost nonexistent. Germany stayed away from a war between Great Britain and France. Spain allied with France. Ireland, Wales, and Scotland became one big country, and no one messed with them."

The Commander interrupts. "I know the history. Now tell me where Sitch is."

"Patience, Commander. You've been searching for Sitch for five years, what are a few more minutes? Besides, history is good to learn and know. Let me continue."

The Commander is frustrated, but he rolls his eyes and waits.

Taavet continues. "The President of the old United States ordered the invasion of Russia over the rights of oil that Russia had taken from Saudi Arabia. American soldiers began Operation Ares: the invasion of Sochi. Operation Ares would be the biggest United States invasion in history. One million men, two hundred and fifty thousand A-1 Abrams tank, ten naval fleets of battleships, submarines, carriers, one thousand experimental submergible landing boats, and ten thousand submergible amphibious Buffalo were parked in the Black Sea, fully cloaked and ready to enter the Black Sea undetected."

"When the invasion began, the Russians were caught off guard. To accomplish this, the Americans pulled a trick from the past. They set up a fake outpost with fifty thousand men in uniform, one thousand outdated A-1 Abrams (painted and disguised as modern A-1 Abrams), one broken-down naval fleet, and one hundred old F-22 raptors. Forty thousand troops were criminals, ten thousand were guards. The criminals were ordered to march around at certain times of the day with fake guns and move fake cannon ammo around."

"The Russians moved a massive part of the army to the east, putting most of their defenses in the east and north, but leaving the west vulnerable to an attack. Russia figured if America intended to attack from the west, they would have to go through Finland, and Finland was on nobody's side."

"Soon enough, at the break of dawn, shots began to ring out from the fake outpost, the ships, and some cannons. The Russians took battle positions and started to return fire. A boarding party of criminals, taken from the prisons, were forced to rush to the beaches near Naukan, Uelen, and a land bridge south of Naukan. After serving five years, the criminals would be freed in return for the success of the invasion. But the chances of taking the beaches were zero. It was a suicide mission. That attack was just a diversion for the real invasion from the Black Sea, an invasion that took, in one day, Sevastopol, Anapa, and Sochi. They took every city from Shakhty, near the border of Ukraine, to El'ton, the border of Kazakhstan; the whole Southwest area of Russia. The invasion was successful on both counts; the true invasion and the suicide mission."

"The suicide mission was led by a Captain James Walker. Walker was not an old man. He was a six-foot, one-inch fellow with a well-groomed goatee, brown eyes, and short, salt and pepper hair. His long face ended at a round chin. He kept his camouflage pressed, and he loved that his wife said he looked good in the uniform and helmet, with its new design. The helmet was similar to desert storm helmets. It was made of a material called 'indomitable' that was thinner, lighter, and stronger than traditional Kavala.

James was a fighter. He was the first one on the battlefield and the last one to leave. James was also a Special Forces officer, but this was supposed to be his last mission. The success of the suicide mission made James a legendary captain and an honorary general. He was sent stateside to live out his days."

"The war progressed, but too many men were dying. So the government initiated its first draft since January 27, 1973. The draft called upon every man between the ages of eighteen and forty, calling James back to the front lines, after being home for four years. The draft lasted for five years and ended when disaster struck in the form of a massive counterattack that killed more than half of the army. The United States was so enraged it lowered the call-up age to sixteen and raised the cut-off age to fifty.

They drafted five hundred thousand men and women. It took the government nine weeks to put them through basic training and send them straight to the front lines."

"Three years later, there is no advancement in the west. The United States was stopped just outside of Moscow in a city called Kaluga, where the US army met the Spetsnaz. For a few months, America tried to break through the Spetsnaz's front line to no avail. The troops from the east, meanwhile, made a lot of progress, marching the thousand five hundred miles into Russia. Leading them was Captain James Walker, not yet a

General, but at that time in consideration to be promoted."

"James began a new fighting style that became known as the rushing ambush. The strategy is a full-frontal attack no one sees coming. Even when there was an ambush set, it was almost as though James knew where they were and their plans before even they knew their plans. One fateful day, as James set up another attack on a town called Nyurba, he came face to face with a troop of Spetsnaz. He and his troop held their own and took the city, but as the Russian army began their retreat, James was hit by a stray bullet and then taken. The troop looked for James for a few months before reporting James as missing in action on the day he was promoted to General. A small group of ex-criminals that had fought beside James in the invasion went on the search for James and were never seen again."

"The United States suffered massive casualties after that. In the confusion that followed, the President pushed for a third draft with the support of the Vice President and Secretary of Defense. The House was not convinced, because they had already asked so much of their people and left their country wide open for an attack. But behind everyone's back, the President ordered immediate implementation of the draft. He widened the age bracket again, to a call-up of everyone between the ages of fourteen and sixty-five. The Secretary of Defense said to his men, 'You do what you have to do to put bodies in the front lines. If they run, shoot their legs. As they recover, everyone else goes through boot camp. At the end, you put the recovered person in the front line of the biggest battle without a weapon.'

"This is where our story begins."

CHAPTER 2

Hampton, VA.

J ames was home with Sarah, his childhood sweetheart. She was a woman of petite stature with big, round eyes, a gentle face, and a flawless smile. Her eyebrows - as stunning as National Park arches in the winter – were complemented by blushing red cheeks, and her rosy lips finished off the masterpiece.

Sarah's hair was brownish red, and she liked to wear it in bangs. She was skinny enough to seem fragile and delicate, but her constitution was firm and healthy. Her hands were bigger than average, but this was what had won James over on their first date in a Thai restaurant, where she had spilled soy sauce all over the table. James, unable to help himself, had burst out in laughter, and immediately thought he had completely screwed his chances of being with her. He was wrong.

Every time Sarah smiled, James was convinced God had let an angel dwell among fools. He was 27 years old the year he married her, and by then he was already in the military. His career was hard on the relationship for the longest time, but Sarah clung to a certainty that one day he would come home and finally stay for good.

She hated every time James had to go. Sometimes he was gone for several years at a stretch, and she would not stop praying until he returned. One year, after they thought James had finally come home to stay, Sarah found that she was pregnant. They had been trying for years with no success.

The due date started like any other day. It was quiet, with a brisk chill in the air. James and Sarah were just cold enough to wear a light jacket. The day was still young when her water broke. They were out, in the middle of a pirate festival, but James Walker took the news calmly. He found the nearest ambulance and asked if they could borrow a wheelchair for there was quite a distance to their vehicle and his wife's water just broke. The paramedics were more frantic than James. They grabbed a wheelchair from inside the ambulance and began barking out orders, trying to get Sarah to sit down on the wheelchair.

Sarah, refusing to sit, was grunting and yelling "Where is my husband?" until James' deep voice cut through the chaos and deafening noise with an unnatural calm.

"Honey, I'm here. Don't worry, no one is going to hurt you. Please. Sit down, and let's have our handsome baby boy." Still grunting, but now cooperating, Sarah sat in the wheelchair and the medics moved to rush away. But James grabbed the medic pushing the chair and pulled him back.

"Medic?" he asked. "Would you please let me push her?" The medic did not want to let go, but the pressure of James' grip increased until the medic reluctantly released the wheelchair.

James took over and said, "Please follow me closely and keep up." Then he took off running. He ran fast and smooth; so swift it was almost as though his feet were not touching the ground. The medics were soon left behind. It was a spectacular thing to see. James sang as he ran, and as he bundled his wife into the car. He didn't stop singing until they arrived at the hospital.

"Be gentle and kind,
don't look for a fight,
but if one finds you,
you do what is right.
Stand straight and upright,
with God by your side,
that is the way to live your life."

It was a Jewish hospital, painted orange and brown, with white letters on the front that spelled 'Mount of Olives Hospital'.

James had called ahead while searching for paramedics at the festival, and attendants were waiting for him and Sarah at the door. He parked their blue 2019 Dodge Ram 4x4 in the valet parking, handed the keys over to the drivers, apologized for coming in so fast, and thanked them. Even then, minutes away from his wife delivering a child, James remained calm.

Sarah called out her husband's name. His composure may have soothed her nerves, but she still had a baby on the way. "Would you hurry up and thank them later, I'm giving birth!"

James grinned down at her. "You're right honey, forgive me, I did not want to be rude."

The nurses took her straight in. Doctor Clay Jordan, a woman Sarah had known since they were kids, was expectant. As she prepped to help to deliver the child, she sang praises to the Lord. "Thank you Jesus!" she sang. "For a new life and peace over Sarah."

The doctor Dr. Jordan was olive-skinned, with straight jet-black hair and a voice that could start a church revival. She looked, saw the baby coming out, and said: "Jesus! Help me catch this baby."

The baby slipped out and Dr. Jordan caught him by his leg.

She lifted the child high.

"Yup, it's a boy." She declared.

Then she put the child on Sarah's chest.

James dropped to his knees and turned his face to the ceiling. "Thank you, Lord, for a strong healthy boy."

At that moment, James' eyes were opened. Angels in battle armor, carrying swords of fire, had surrounded the small group that was helping Sarah deliver her baby.

The nurse asked, "What are you going to name him?" Sarah and James stared at their son. In unison, both parents replied "Mitch."

The name meant "Who is like God?'

The nurse smiled. "It's a beautiful name," she said.

When they brought Mitch back in from the nursery, Sarah was sleeping, so the nurses put Mitch in his father's arms. James was nervous at first, because he had never held a newborn before. But he embraced

Mitch, and as he looked at his son, he began to sing.

"Be gentle and kind,
don't look for a fight,
but if one finds you,
you do what is right.
Stand straight and upright,
with God by your side,
that is the way to live your life."

While he was singing, Sarah woke up. She lay there, watching her husband and her son with a smile as James swayed Mitch around the room.

Three years later, a military truck rumbled down the dirt road and through the oak canopy that led to James' and Sarah's half-built home. James was working on the second floor of the house. When he saw the truck, he climbed down to meet it and asked Sarah to stay in the house.

The military truck came to a stop. James stepped toward it.

"Hi," he said. A soldier stepped out of the truck and saluted James smartly. "Captain."

James saluted back. "At ease, to what do I owe the pleasure?"

"Sir, your presence is required on the front lines of Russia."

"There must be a mistake," James replied. "I was discharged four years ago."

The soldier shook his head. "Sir, there was a draft and the United States chose to bring you back. Please report to the nearest outpost by sunrise." He stepped back into the vehicle as briskly as he had stepped out and the truck pulled away, leaving a devastated James in its wake.

Sarah approached slowly and touched her husband's shoulder. "It's okay my love. We will survive. Go. Do what you have to do."

James hugged Sarah and broke down crying. "I thought this was it. I thought that-" He held Sarah tight and cried. Sarah kept her face blank as she held on to her husband. A single tear rolled down her cheek. James packed up, got in his car, and never returned.

Two years later

At the age of four, James' son met David, an orphan who had lost his parents in a bizarre car accident. The two met in a church known as The

Called and soon became best friends. David - old enough to be troubled but not quite old enough to understand the full gravity of his loss - was downcast and withdrawn for some time after the accident, but he soon learned to trust Mitch and his mother. Gradually, he grew to consider them his family.

Now in the custody of his grandfather, an Afghanistan veteran, David went over to Mitch and Sarah's house often to escape the old man's violent tendencies. Every Sunday and Wednesday, the three went to church, where Sarah served in the praise and worship group.

The Chosen Community Church was a building two stories high and ten feet tall, made of solid concrete walls that had been painted gray with blue trimming. Light, tinted windows displayed the church insignia - two hands caressing a dove that held an olive branch in its beak. The insignia was all white. The symbols sat above the church name, and both name and symbol were in a circle.

The parking lot could fit up to 55 cars and the sanctuary up to 200 people. Next to the parking lot, there was a junkyard with a dog that did not seem aggressive until you touched the chain link fence. Then, the dog would let out a series of growls and barks to warn. The children at church knew not to get near the fence.

The church was also next to an old, red-brick bank that blocked part of the view of the building and the road to the church. Next to the bank was a strip - a half-abandoned mall that they needed to pass to get to church. It was not the best location for a church, but the pews filled quickly on Sundays.

At church, Mitch's family always stayed behind to either help clean or practice as members of the praise and worship team. After they cleaned, everyone would leave. However, sometimes all the leaders of the church would go into the head pastor's office - a room that, although not that big, could fit about seven people comfortably. There were twelve leaders. They would tell all the children to go play outside but not leave the parking lot. On Sundays like this, the children would play hide and seek. On one of those Sundays, something happened that would remain seared in Mitch's memory forever.

It happened when Mitch was 5 years old.

Nissi Montana, 4 years old, was one of the other children in church.

She was a sweet little thing, with eyes as sweet as honey and eyebrows like two young caterpillars. Her face could break out in the most amazing smile, and she had a soft square jaw. Her brown, wavy hair fell to her shoulders and caressed her face in a way that made it shine. She was the most kind-hearted little girl you could have ever met.

That day, the children were playing hide and seek as they used to. The weather was warm and sunny, and the air smelled like car grease and gas. One of the other kids started counting to one hundred. Mitch decided to hide in the parking lot, and Nissi hid amongst the cars parked on the side of the road. As the child that was seeking got closer to him, Mitch began to move towards the side of the building where Nissi was hiding. Mitch did not know she was there. Out of fear of the seeker finding him, Mitch jumped behind a car and to his surprise, discovered Nissi crouching right next to him.

The seeker passed through the cars and did not see them. Mitch and Nissi ran to another car. They had been crouching together for about five minutes when, all of a sudden, Nissi began to reach over - as if uncertain of what exactly she was doing - and touched Mitch's hand.

Her touch was as gentle as if she were petting a soft puppy. She touched the palm of his hand with her fingertips, then moved them across his palm like a dancer in ballet. Then, she leaned over and kissed him.

It was just one small kiss on the lips, but Mitch's heart was beating extremely fast. Time stood still and he felt like he was flying. Seconds felt like hours and minutes felt like days. Mitch did not know what to do. It was so sudden. The whole thing caught him by surprise.

A few minutes later, Nissi's father was barging through the glass doors of the church building, shouting something. Mitch could barely hear or understand what the elder was saying. He flew so fast across the yard.

He yelled his daughter's name, and Nissi shot up out of their hiding place. When her father saw her, he grabbed her roughly by the arm, and the dreamy expression in Nissi's eyes cleared swiftly. Nissi's father was not usually aggressive, but he was in a rage about something today. He bundled her into their gray, 1993 style Toyota Camry and drove off, leaving skid marks behind.

This whole time, Mitch had said nothing, because he did not know what to say or do. He was in shock, afraid, and shy, all at the same time.

It was the last time he saw Nissi. But the memory of that warm Sunday and that soft kiss would forever haunt him, no matter what, because it was Mitch's first.

Mitch prayed for many years that he would see her again. After that day, she was the last and only person he ever wanted to kiss. He wrote letters to her often, telling her of every good and bad thing that happened after that last day he saw her. He put his letters in a wooden box, hoping to see her again and deliver every single one. Hoping to show her that he had never once forgotten her all these years.

All the letters remained in the wooden box except for one he kept in a necklace he had made. It was like a locket, but it seemed impossible to open unless you knew there was a hidden button.

Another five years went by and suddenly the letters from James stopped coming in. Sarah was sad. She guessed that James was on a top-secret mission because he had gone on missions like that before, but never for so long.

One day, Sarah had some friends over for a bible study. It was warm and bright outside and the children were playing in the yard. David, age 9, was now a short and slender child with darker skin than the others. He looked more Hispanic, like a typical Mexican boy, with a round face, long and sleek black hair, and dark brown eyes. Mitch, 10 years old, was tall for his age. He had short, brown hair and a slender body. His face was long with a round jawline and light brown eyes.

They were outside when Mitch spotted a car coming down the dirt road toward their two-story American Craftsman-style house. The 2020 Hummer, made in the style of the old Humvee, was an unwelcome sight.

Mitch ran inside and told his mother there was a car coming.

Sarah got up from her chair to see who it could be. As soon as she got to the door, she spotted the messenger beside the dreaded vehicle and her knees began to shake. She walked to the end of the porch and waited. She and the man were now face to face.

"Are you Sarah?" He asked.

"Yes."

"I'm so sorry," he said. It was all Sarah needed to hear. She dropped to the floor and began to weep. The man continued. "He was the greatest man I knew. I served with him and he saved my life." Sarah was still sobbing.

"We can't find him," the stranger said. "But we will."

Sarah collected herself enough to thank him, and the man gave her an awkward hug, then walked back to his vehicle and drove away, leaving Sarah now curled up in the fetal position. Mitch and David tried to go to her.

The other women grabbed the boys and held them back. "She needs some time to mourn," they said.

"Why? What happened?"

One of the ladies squatted, looked Mitch in the eye, and told him the truth. "Your father is not coming home."

"But why?" The little boy was confused.

"He's with Jesus and we will all see him again, but not for a while."

"Okay."

"You have to be strong for mommy now, okay?"

"Okay."

Later that week, a cold frost passed through that dropped the temperature to a pleasant 57 degrees Fahrenheit. Mitch went up to his mother. Her eyes were puffy and red from crying herself to sleep every night since the messenger had brought her the news. She wanted to stop going to church.

Mitch spoke gently. "Mommy, me and Jesus love you," he said. Then he walked away to clean his room. Sarah found him kneeling at his bedside a few minutes later, praying. She leaned on the doorpost and listened.

"Dear Lord," he whispered. "Please help my mommy. I don't know why she does not stop crying. I miss my dad, but I know you need him more now and that is why he is with you. Help me to help mommy be happy again. In Jesus name, Amen." Then, he got to his feet and started playing with his cars.

Sarah let him play for a while, then walked into his room, dropped to her knees, and spread her arms. "Come over here and give your mom a hug." Mitch left his toys and embraced his mother. Sarah kissed his head and said, "Thank you." Then she put her chin on Mitch's head, looked up, and said once more, "Thank you."

When she let go of her son, she looked him in the eye. "You are meant to do great things for God," she said.

David walked in shortly after, all bruised up and bloody, with a fresh black eye on the left side of his face. He had a big book bag with everything he could fit in it. When Sarah saw him, she was livid. "You stay here," she said to David. To Mitch she said, "Keep an eye on David." The she drove to David's grandfather's house.

She pounded on the door as if she were going to break it down. David's grandfather opened the door and looked at Sarah. He was a six-foot, seven-inch, hunched over old man, with long, messy white hair. The man looked and smelled like he had not showered or shaved in years. He was completely drunk, high on who knows what, and extremely aggressive.

"Well, hello there beautiful," He slurred.

"Don't you beautiful me!" Sarah all but screamed. "I'm taking David. And if I see you anywhere near any one of us, I will have the army throw you in the streets to rot like the pig you are, then have you arrested for child abuse!"

The grandfather squared up to Sarah and tried, unsuccessfully, to get his footing straight so he could move closer to her. "You can't do that!" He blustered. "I am his legal guardian and the only family he has."

Sarah drew herself up to her full height. "That, sir, is where you are wrong. He has a better future with me. I'm going to give you till tomorrow to sign him over to me. If you do not, expect the police and my lawyer at your door. Either way, he is going to end up with me." The grandfather tried to grab Sarah by the shirt, but Sarah deflected his lunge and the old man ended up on the floor.

"Until tomorrow," Sarah said to him.

"You can't do this!" The old man screamed, rolling uselessly on the ground. Sarah got in her car and drove away, leaving David's grandfather on his cold concrete driveway floor. The next day, he signed David over to Sarah.

Now with full custody of David, Sarah treated him no different from Mitch, just like a son from her own womb.

CHAPTER 3

Sarah, Mitch, and David spent each day trying to live every moment to the fullest. The boys were homeschooled. They learned about Yorktown in Yorktown, Virgini, the Alamo in San Antonio, Texas, and other historical locations. They learned battle strategies and found an appreciation for science, economy, mathematics, and English. They were taught five languages including English, Spanish, German, French, and Russian. Four years passed.

One September, on Mitch's fourteenth birthday, things went awry.

It was a cool, quiet morning. The boys were still asleep when Sarah called some friends to help decorate the house and a part of their fifty acres for a party. The theme was Mad Scientist. Most of the props were made of wood so the children could play with them: test tubes, an Erlenmeyer flask, beakers, and syringes.

For Mitch, Sarah bought all of the actual equipment and hired a lab scientist to do the experiments and show Mitch how to handle chemicals correctly. Just as they were putting the finishing touches on the setup, David snuck out of his room.

He appeared beside Sarah and she jumped when he touched her arm. "Sarah, what can I help with?"

Some years before, David concluded he was cursed and everyone he loved was either going to die or be hurt. Perhaps in an attempt to keep her safe, David had never called Sarah 'mom'.

Sarah smiled at him and ruffled his hair.

"Try to keep Mitch in the room until we're done."

David did a salute and nodded his head, then ran into Mitch's room.

He took a position at the foot of the bed and stood there, staring at Mitch.

Mitch's eyes were still closed a few minutes later when he asked "Why are you being a creeper?"

He cracked one eye open and looked over his left shoulder at David.

David's face broke into a big and slightly disturbing smile.

"Happy birthday bro, you want to play a game?"

Mitch rolled over. "No. I want to sleep."

David got on the bed and began to jump.

"Come on bro, time is wasting! This is going to be the best birthday ever!"

David threw himself backward and landed right next to Mitch.

Mitch turned and accidentally hit David in the face. David, exaggerating, grabbed his jaw and rolled around groaning. Mitch, on realizing what had just happened, rolled frantically out of bed. He hit his head on the floor but jumped up like nothing had happened and ran to the other side of the bed where he dropped to his knees and begged.

"I'm sorry… please don't tell mom."

He tried to shush David, but David groaned even louder. Pleaseee, shush!" Mitch pleaded. "We can play mad scientist and you can be the scientist."

Right after David heard that, he snapped out of his dramatics, but held on to his jaw as he sat up. Sniffling, he pretended to concede.

"No, you can be the scientist, why don't you put your coat on?"

"It's our coat," Mitch said. "And I'm sorry, please forgive me." He hugged David.

"It's okay, I know you did it on purpose." David giggled.

Mitch giggled back. "I would never hurt you on purpose, I promise."

They did their secret handshake.

Mitch put on his lab coat, which was blue - his favorite color. Then he grabbed his play lab equipment and turned to David. "So, what are we going to discover today?"

David rubbed his jaw and grinned. "Well, let's find a way to heal my jaw."

Mitch walked up to David and laid his hand on David's right cheek, praying like he had been taught in children's church.

"In the name of Jesus, we come in agreement for David's healing. Father, you said we would lay hands on the sick and they would recover, and that by your stripes we are healed. So I come now claiming healing in Jesus' name. Amen."

David opened his eyes wide. He was amazed by the words of Mitch's prayer but even more so by the results. Even though he had been exaggerating about the pain, it had hurt a little bit when Mitch hit him. Now he felt no more pain.

"Thank you," he said, still in awe.

Mitch grabbed his big round goggles, snapped them onto his face, and announced; "We are going to study microorganisms."

He grabbed a microscope from under his bed.

David asked, "How are you going to look through the microphone with your goggles on?"

"You are too funny! It's called a microscope and the goggles are for our adventure."

"Adventure... Where? Today?"

"In the Amazon!" Mitch declared.

The room changed as a palm tree sprung up from the wood floor and grew rapidly, followed by another, and another, until there was an entire forest in their bedroom.

Mitch was in his blue coat and David was in an explorer's outfit complete with a safari hat, holding a red spiral notebook and a matching mechanical lead pencil. They set out on a search to find the mythical waterfall of Amar in the deep jungles of the second floor.

They journeyed miles, searching high and low until they found it; a roaring waterfall that was 500 feet tall and 10 feet wide.

Mitch stretched a hand, palm out, to David. "Test tube!"

Mitch put one hand behind himself as David handed him a test tube.

Mitch filled it halfway, then pushed a cork in to seal the top.

"Time to head back to base," he told David. "You ready?"

David was practically hopping from foot to foot at this point. "Definitely!"

They were headed back to base camp (or Mitch's room) when they began to feel small tremors beneath their feet. They looked around, trying to see where or what it was coming from.

A familiar female voice called out: "Mitch! David! Where are you?"

The jungle disappeared, the muddy ground became wood again, and by the time Sarah came up the stairs, Mitch and David were standing in the middle of an ordinary hallway.

"There you two are!" Sarah said. "Thank you, David, for helping. And happy birthday Mitch. Are you ready for your birthday breakfast?"

"As long as we have enough for all of us," David replied.

"We have more than enough," Sarah said.

"Good... I don't want special treatment for my birthday."

Sarah turned and began to head back the way she had come. "Okay, well, let's go down and see what that noise is."

David nudged Mitch. "Yeah bro, let's check it out!"

Mitch nodded. "Alright, let's see."

Sarah led the way down the hallway, and then down the stairs. As Mitch reached the last step facing the front door and the porch of the house, he heard a ridiculously loud "Happy Birthday!" followed by cheering. The sound startled Mitch, not only because it was the sound of several people yelling at once, but also because the scene that greeted him in their front yard was something he had never experienced before.

For some time now, they had been living off widow's pay from the army, and Sarah had not been able to find work. It was the support of their church members that had made the food and decorations possible.

After the setup was done, everyone had stayed to make Mitch feel special. There were one hundred plus people and enough food to feed three hundred people. The church rented a bounce house and the church band showed up to play a few songs on a black mobile stage that was two feet tall with four standing speakers facing different directions. It was all good, clean, fun. The whole thing touched Mitch so much, he decided to give a speech of thanks an hour into the party.

The band stopped playing and the main singer announced "Mitch would like to say something." When he handed the microphone to Mitch, everyone stopped to listen to what Mitch was going to say.

"I want to thank everyone for coming," Mitch began. "I am both honored and humbled by everything you've done. W-we haven't had a lot and you have gone above and beyond what was expected."

A tear ran down Mitch's left cheek.

Sarah and David were tearing up as well as the band began to play background music to accompany Mitch's speech.

Mitch continued. "We are in gratitude to the Lord and the church. I would like to thank all the ministries represented here, including our pastors. Will you please raise your hands?" Ten people raised their hands.

Mitch, completely unaware of the maturity in his voice, went on.

"I want to give all the glory and the biggest thanks to our Lord and Savior Jesus Christ for moving on your hearts and blessing my family today. I will never forget this day or the people who came today… God bless all of you and please enjoy."

A great noise of clapping and shouting praise to the Lord rose. The cacophony was almost deafening. And it was all because of a few words of thanks. The band began to sing worship songs. The worship songs attracted bystanders who came in and joined the party. Sixteen people accepted the Lord that day. The crowd stayed for two more hours before the crowd began to dwindle. A few close friends and church members stayed behind to help clean.

Mitch walked up to his mother. "What can I do?"

"You can help by playing with David in the cornfield." Mitch ran off.

Sarah stopped to look at her son as he raced off with David, and for a moment she was stunned at how much he had grown.

Half an hour later, the rest of the guests left, and Sarah was left alone on her rocking chair on the porch. As she rocked, she put her left hand on the adjacent chair and cried out from the weight of the moment.

"Oh James, we did a good job! I miss you and wish you were physically here, so I can hold you in my arms again, kiss you, feel your warmth and see your smile. I wish I could watch you and the boys play. I wish I could see you teach Mitch and David how to be good men like you."

A tear found its way out of the corner of her eye as she rubbed the arm of the rocking chair.

"Lord, please. Help my heavy heart, because I miss my husband. Give me the strength to keep pushing and don't forget Mitch and David. I know what you told me in secret about how great they would be. Please, guide them and protect them, in Jesus' name. James please, don't forget me, my love. I'll see you soon. Amen."

The distant hum of a diesel generator broke the silence and began to grow. A dust cloud appeared on the dirt road - the one road that led to the Walker's home. Mitch had heard the sound as well. He and David were trying to find their way out of the cornfield.

Mitch said, "There's something wrong." And he was sure of it.

An army Humvee became visible through the cloud of dust, and it was followed by seven Oshkosh MTVR (Medium Tactical Vehicle Replacement) military trucks, tailed by another green camouflage Humvee. As they approached, Sarah stood, puzzled. The caravan stopped, but no one stepped out of their vehicles until the dust had cleared.

The tension and uncertainty in the air thickened.

After the dust had settled, a captain stepped out of the front seat of the lead Humvee. A Lieutenant stepped out of the back seat and ten fully armed troops with old M-16's in army green camouflage stepped out of the lead Oshkosh. The other trucks were parked in a way that made it impossible for Sarah to see inside.

The captain walked up to Sarah. "Hello. Tell me where Mrs. Walker is."

"Why?"

"Do you know her or not?"

"I may or may not."

The captain pulled out his handgun and pointed it at Sarah's head. The frustration in his voice was potent. "Tell me where she is woman, or you will die."

Sarah got close and pressed her forehead against the barrel of the gun. She looked the captain in the eye and said, "You pull that trigger and you will never find her."

The captain, extremely angry at this point, had begun to press on the trigger when Sarah suddenly snatched the gun out of the captain's hand and side-swept the captain underfoot with her left leg. She stood straight up again so fast, no one was able to react.

Now she had the gun pointed at the captain. The look of fear in his eyes scared his troop.

After a few moments, Sarah spoke. "The next time you pull out your gun, make sure you pull the trigger fast and aim right, because you're not going to get a second chance."

She pushed the magazine release and a full magazine fell to the ground. She cocked back the gun, removed the bullet from the chamber, and threw the gun in the opposite direction. Then she turned her back on him and began to walk back to her chair. The captain pulled a small revolver from his boot, but as he took aim, his lieutenant stepped in and kicked the gun out of the captain's hand. "Captain, you're out of order."

The lieutenant turned to the stunned troop. "Restrain him!"

As they restrained their captain, the lieutenant got on one knee and said, "I am relieving you from duty."

The captain, who had been in some kind of shock up until that moment, began to struggle and kick. "You can't do this! You can't!" he yelled, until he was pulled into a vehicle and a car door muffled the noise.

The lieutenant walked toward Sarah, who was now sitting on her rocking chair. He got on one knee in front of her, and with his head bowed to the earth said; "It is an honor to meet you, Mrs. Walker. Your husband saved my life in Russia and he spoke highly of you. I apologize for captain Aline. He is a hothead and I came to pacify his temper, but if he stepped out of line, I was to relieve him as you saw."

Sarah cut him off. "What are you doing here?"

"I'm here under orders of President Jerry Schultz to execute the draft order 35-50."

"What are you talking about? My husband is dead, and my son is not old enough to be drafted."

The lieutenant looked into Sarah's face and glanced away. "The President passed a new draft order a week ago. All men from the ages of fourteen to sixty-five."

Sarah was on her feet in an instant. "This is outrageous! First, you took my husband and killed him, now you want my son!"

"Ma'am- ma'am, I'm just following orders."

"I suggest you leave before something bad happens."

"Ma'am, I can't leave here without Mitch and these troops are here to make sure he's brought in.

Sarah turned around. "I will not give him to you. Now LEAVE!"

"Ma'am, we've been ordered to bring him at any cost, even killing the opposition and shooting any who try to escape."

Sarah, standing with her back to the lieutenant in the doorway of her home, froze and looked over her left shoulder. In anger, she conceded.

"Come inside, please. But only you. Leave your troops outside and we will talk."

At that time, Mitch and David came out of the cornfield fifteen yards away. They paused for a moment and looked at the troop, but then ran into the house.

A few moments later, Sarah and Mitch walked out of the house alone. Sarah kissed his head, looked Mitch in the eye, and whispered, "You come back to me either in this life or with God."

They hugged and tears came out of Sarah's eyes.

She released her son and Mitch began to walk toward the troops by the Oshkosh.

The lieutenant emerged from the house, and a series of gunshots rang out.

Mitch hit the ground looking for cover.

Sarah dove into the house, tackling the lieutenant as a bullet grazed his hat.

Much to their surprise, they heard Captain Aline's voice call out.

"Cease fire!"

The shots stopped and the captain continued. "You should have made sure the troop was not loyal to me before you started a mutiny. Now, come out and face me like a man!"

"Alright!" The lieutenant called out. "Just don't kill the others."

The lieutenant stood up, but just before he showed himself at the doorway, the deafening bang of a Remington 810 shotgun sawed the silence. It came from the window next to the front door and killed two soldiers. Sarah cocked her gun for a second shot and the remaining troops returned fire.

A second, third, and fourth shot rang out and took out four more soldiers, including the captain. After that, everything went quiet. The lieutenant stepped out of the house and on to a splintered porch. He looked around and saw four soldiers hogtied and gagged. Then he turned around and saw Sarah walk out of the door resting a shotgun on her hip.

"I pray you were worth it," she said. Then she collapsed. The lieutenant caught her before she hit the floor and laid her down on the porch.

There was a bullet hole in her chest.

David ran out of the house yelling "MOM! NO!"

Mitch, with his face on the ground and arms over his head, looked up and saw Sarah on the ground. Time slowed down.

Mitch ran to Sarah and slid to his knees. He was already crying.

"Mom everything is going to be okay." He grabbed her head from the lieutenant's arms and laid her on his lap, stroking her hair.

David was on his knees, rocking back and forth and sobbing.

"I'm sorryyy mom. I love you! Don't goo. Somebody get a medic!" he screamed.

Sarah, choking on her own blood, tried to speak in a singing tone. "Be g-gentle, b-be k-k-k-k-"

Mitch finished for her. "Kind. Don't look for a fight." Sarah nodded her head and Mitch continued. "But if one finds you, you do what is right." Sarah looked out into the clear blue sky. "Stand straight and upright with God by your side."

Sarah gave her last breath and the tears were pouring out of Mitch's eyes as he completed his father's song. "That is the way you live your life."

Mitch hugged Sarah tight and the lieutenant closed her eyes.

David screamed. There was loathing in his voice. "Why God? Why did this happen?... I HATE you!"

Mitch was still stroking his mother's hair. "Don't blame God for what happened, God spared her from what's to come."

David turned to Mitch. "And what is that?" he asked quietly.

"Hell."

The lieutenant was on his feet. "It's time to go!"

Mitch was still holding his mother. "Can I stay I little longer?"

"If we don't leave now, the United States will send a greater army to destroy the town and find you. It is best you come now if you want to save this town."

Mitch laid Sarah's head on the porch, stood, and turned to walk away, but David reached over and grabbed Mitch's arm. "What are you doing? Why do you have to go?"

Mitch was staring at the ground. "To save what I have left." He paused, then turned to David and looked his friend turned brother in the eye. "I will see you again, sooner than we think."

There was a desperate confusion in David's eyes. He searched Mitch's face. "Why do I have to lose everything to be safe?"

"You're not."

"Please, don't go!" David screamed.

Mitch, chin up, and with tears streaming down his face, began to walk toward the Oshkosh. David cried out again.

"Please. Don't leave me!... Please!... I have no one! Mitch! MITCH!"

CHAPTER 4

Fort Pierce, Florida. Back in the café.

Taavet is staring at the epoxy wood table in front of him like he can see his recollections in the glass. "I know what it feels like to lose everything," he says.

He continues to stare at the table until the sound of dishes breaking snaps him out of his reverie. A sudden, eerie silence falls.

Then a stream of gunfire and bullets shatter the café windows.

The ISA troops dive to take cover, toppling tables.

Taavet just sits there, unflinching, as chaos descends.

He stands up, half hunched over, grabs his cane, and says loudly to be heard over the gunfire; "I'll be right back I have to pee."

The Commander tries to stand, but the buzz of bullets flying by his head sends him ducking back for cover. He yells at Taavet instead.

"Do you have a death wish or are you just crazy?"

Taavet begins to laugh. "Maybe a bit of both."

He walks across 30 feet of fully exposed windows without a single graze, almost as though there was some kind of smokescreen, or divine intervention, protecting him.

The ISA troops look on in shock.

The stream of gunfire lasts two minutes, and then stops as suddenly as it started. The ISA soldiers cautiously begin to come out of cover. They see that the ISA had very few casualties and Taavet is now sitting at the table without a worry in the world.

Taavet turns to the Commander. "They are gone, you're clear. Let's continue."

The Commander is shaking from fear. "W-wait, h-how did you do that?"

Taavet smiles. "If I can finish my story, I will reveal the secret."

** **

Somewhere on the east coast of Virginia.

It was hot. There were light screams in the distance, the constant hum of diesel engines, and the crying of young voices.

The back of the Oshkosh was lit a dim red. Mitch was staring at the metal gridded floor with tears still snaking down his cheeks, trying to understand what had just happened, struggling to cope with the loss of his mother.

An hour later, the caravan suddenly stopped.

A drill sergeant's voice broke through the depressing noise.

"Welcome new draftees! I am Drill Sergeant Peterson of the great United States Army. Listen up closely, because I am NOT going to repeat myself. From now on you belong to me. And you will only respond to me with 'yes drill sergeant' and 'no drill sergeant', do I make myself CLEAR?"

Everyone in the truck yelled "YES DRILL SERGEANT!"

"Some of you were brought here forcibly. Now if you try to run away, we will shoot your legs. At the end of boot camp, you will be put on the frontlines of the biggest battle we can find, without a weapon, and you will have to fight. If you retreat, you will be shot. Do you understand?"

"YES DRILL SERGEANT!"

"If you get injured in basic training, you will not go home. You will recover, a weapon will be put in your hand and you will still go off to war, do you understand?"

"YES DRILL SERGEANT!"

"When these doors open, you will have two minutes to get out of these trucks and make five lines. The women will be in one line to the far left, the men will form the rest. UNDERSTOOD?"

"YES DRILL SERGEANT!"

"One last thing. You will stand at attention at all times. You will not look me in the eyes, you will not talk, and you will not show any emotion. I am not your barbeque buddy, I am here to train you to survive and to kill. UNDERSTOOD?"

"YES DRILL SERGEANT!"

The doors of the truck flew open and everyone began to fight and push, trying to rush out, but Mitch stayed seated until the chaos had left the truck. Then he stood up, calm and collected, and walked slowly out of the truck.

They were parked in the middle of a giant dirt field. Visibility was low. It was dark and dust clouds swirled in the air.

United States troops had surrounded a big area.

They had on black bullet-proof vests on top of their army green uniforms and every man was fully armed.

Under four brown canopies were four long connected tables. Eight soldiers sat at these tables with stacks of papers in front of them.

Drill Sergeant Peterson squared up to Mitch for being the last one out of the truck, even though he had been right behind the prior person.

Sergeant Peterson was a slender, blue-eyed man with well-defined muscles. He stood seven feet tall. His head and face were clean-shaven, and he was dressed in green Army camo. On the right side of his chest, there was a strip of cloth engraved with his name, 'Peterson'.

In the middle, he had his rank of Master Sergeant and on the left side, there was the 'U. S. Army' sign. He was also wearing a brown Smokie the Bear hat with the US army seal - a medallion with an eagle clutching arrows in one talon and an olive branch in the other. In its beak, the eagle was holding a ribbon with 'E FLURIBUS' on the left and 'UNUM' on the right. Above the head of the eagle, there was a wreath with thirteen stars in the middle. The entire pin was 2 inches wide and solid gold.

"Glad you could join us, your majesty!"

Peterson did a long, exaggerated bow, then continued.

"What is your name son?"

Mitch just stood still. Peterson got closer to Mitch's face and asked again. "I asked for your name boy!"

Mitch remained motionless.

"Oh, I see you think you're better than us?"

"NO DRILL SERGEANT!" Mitch yelled.

"It speaks. Now, what is your name?"

Mitch remained motionless.

Peterson began to yell in Mitch's face.

"What the hell is wrong with you, boy?! Are you stuck on stupid?!"

Mitch yelled too. "NO DRILL SERGEANT!"

"Then speak plainly and tell me! What the hell is your major malfunction??"

Mitch was motionless again.

"You said to only respond to you in 'yes drill Sergeant' or 'no drill Sergeant'."

Peterson put on his best sneer.

"Oh, so you're just being a good soldier?"

"NO DRILL SERGEANT!"

Peterson moved in another inch and put himself nose to nose with Mitch. Then, he began to yell at the rest of the draftees.

"Thanks to this cherry, your new leader, you are all now enlisted in airborne training school. I will make sure I drop you in the biggest hell hole I can find. Your training begins NOW! Drop and do push-ups till I'm TIRED!"

Mitch dropped to the push-up position with everyone else. Peterson called down to him. "Not you! You're going to stand at attention with that stupid look on your face as we become true killers."

Mitch stood. Peterson put his mouth in Mitch's ear and whispered. "I have just made you the most hated boy in the group." He smiled. "You better watch your back."

Mitch's face was placid. "YES DRILL SERGEANT!"

Peterson stopped smiling and anger grew in his eyes. He lost it and punched Mitch in the stomach so hard it sent Mitch to one knee and took the breath out of him.

Mitch knelt, gasping for air.

Then he stood back up at attention.

Peterson's blood began to boil. He struck Mitch again, but this time, under the sternum. The punch took out whatever little breath Mitch had left and dropped him on his side. A young woman from the draftees jumped up and rushed Peterson. When Mitch saw this, with the rest of his strength, he quickly got up on his hands and knees and tried to get between the woman and Peterson. Peterson was unaware of the impending danger and continued to kick Mitch over and over again.

Mitch looked behind Peterson and said, "Hold yourself."

Peterson looked behind him but saw nothing. He turned his attention back to Mitch and asked, "What happened?"

Mitch said nothing so Peterson turned to the draftees and said, "Who was trying something behind my back?"

"Drill Sergeant..."

Peterson looked down at Mitch. "What?!"

Mitch was clutching his stomach. His face was full of dirt and dust. With tear-filled eyes, he said: "My name is Mitch Walker, son of James Walker and Sarah Walker - who was murdered - leaving my brother orphaned again by your people. If you want to take out your frustration, take it out on me."

Peterson grabbed Mitch by his shirt and picked him up.

"How dare you speak to me! I don't care who you are or your history! All I care about is getting bodies to throw at the enemy! And I will gladly feed you to the Russians now!"

Peterson put Mitch down. "But out of respect for your father, I will train you enough to survive for five seconds."

Peterson turned his back to Mitch and barked, "ATTENTION!"

Everyone stopped doing push-ups and stood at attention.

"You are standing in front of tables where you will fill out paperwork. After that, you will proceed to get on to the bus. AM I UNDERSTOOD?!"

"YES DRILL SERGEANT!"

The draftees, covered in dirt, looked at Mitch laying on the floor and grunting in pain. As they got their paperwork and walked by him to get on the bus, no one but one young woman stopped to help him. She was five feet tall plus an inch. A slender, almost fragile woman with skin so beautiful it was almost as if she was glowing in the dark.

Her hair was long and dark brown with naturally forming waves. She had a small, round face, her light brown eyes were oval, her eyebrows were well taken care of, and her nose complimented her bone structure beautifully, leading an observer's eyes to cherry red lips.

Her natural smile lit his face.

She knelt and touched Mitch's right arm. Mitch flinched a little, expecting more pain. The girl took her hand off Mitch for a moment, then laid it back on his arm. In her softest and most gentle voice, she said, "It's okay... I'm not going to hurt you. I'm here to help."

He realized she was the woman who had tried to rush Peterson. Her smile grew wider. "That was either really brave or really stupid."

Mitch couldn't help smiling back. "Maybe a bit of both."

The girl giggled. "Why did you do it?"

"I didn't want special treatment because of my name."

She looked at Mitch and stroked his hair with a puzzled smile. "Who are you, Mitch Walker?"

Mitch smiled. "The son of a legend."

The girl smiled back, then she looked up. "I have to go."

The girl gave Mitch a kiss on his forehead and lay his head down on the dirt. As she walked away, Mitch rolled over and asked, "May I have the pleasure of your name?"

She turned to look at Mitch and giggled. Then she continued to walk away until she had disappeared in the crowd of people entering the bus. Mitch found enough strength to get himself back on his feet and walk towards the line. Someone came up behind him and made to push him down. As the boy lunged at him from behind, Mitch stepped to the side and the boy fell on his face. He did not get back up. Mitch did not acknowledge him. He continued to walk toward the line.

From the ground, the boy yelled. "You coward, you will never be my superior! The first chance I get, I'm going to kill you!"

Mitch did not react. Two soldiers grabbed the boy and pulled him onto the bus. The boy yelled. "You're a dead man!"

Mitch straightened himself up although he was still in pain.

He did not reach the table for about another hour.

When it was his turn to grab paperwork, the soldier at the desk was an older, muscular man with salt and pepper hair. The left side of his face, ear, and head were covered with pink, deeply carved, and callused scar tissue. His jaw seemed like it was barely hanging on to his mouth. The right side of his face was untouched. He had half a beard, blue eyes, and a short square jawline. When Mitch saw him, he thought to himself; This man must have gone through hell.

The man was looking down at some sheets of paper. His mind seemed to be somewhere else. He looked troubled. When Mitch stood before him, he asked "What's your name?"

"Mitch Walker."

The man's right eye twitched as if he knew the name but was not sure. His blue eyes did not leave the paper. "What was the name?"

Mitch repeated his name slowly but respectfully. "Mitch Walker."

Tears pooled in the man's eyes when he looked up at Mitch. "My God. You look so much like your father."

Mitch's eyes lit up. "You knew my father?"

"He saved my life on Blood Mountain."

"Blood Mountain?"

"I'll make sure you hear my story. You should know the hero your father was. But we don't have that kind of time right now. This is your paperwork. Please fill it to the best of your ability, seal it in this envelope and write your name on the front. That is all, Mr. Walker. Make your father proud!"

"I already have by meeting you and shaking your hand. What is your name sir?"

"Lieutenant John Bradford."

"Thank you, Lieutenant Bradford. It was nice meeting you. God bless you!"

"You too Mitch."

Mitch smiled, waved, and headed to the last bus.

As Lieutenant Bradford turned away, he began to cry.

Mitch was the last recruit to get his paperwork. "I will see you again," Mitch said to himself.

When he stood at the front of the bus, every single recruit gave him a dirty look. All the chairs were taken except for two chairs all the way in the front. Mitch, unintimidated by the draftees, gladly sat straight in the front by himself.

He knew better than to fall asleep; besides the trained soldiers and the young woman, he was the most hated man on the bus.

Mitch could not stop thinking of the girl with long hair. His thoughts were not of love. He knew what that felt like, thanks to Nissi. It was that he felt sure, with an odd kind of certainty, that he knew her from somewhere. As Mitch pondered these odd feelings, he dozed off.

He was in an endless meadow, surrounded by brilliantly colored flowers that seemed to emit their own light. It was not blinding, but pleasant to look at. There were gentle rolling hills, all green, full of untouched grass as far as your eye could see. Mitch thought he was dead, so he decided to bend down and smell a red and blue flower, a tulip hybrid that he had never seen before. The smell was not like anything he had ever inhaled before, it was indescribable.

Mitch did not want to take a step because he did not want to ruin the beauty before him. As he looked around, he wondered how he had arrived here. He did not see any trampled flowers or a trail. Mitch raised a foot, and the flowers that had been underneath his feet seemed broken and dead, but a second later, the crumpled flowers had sprung back up like nothing ever happened.

Mitch's eyes grew in amazement. He put his foot back down and picked his foot back up. The flowers did the same thing, so he plucked a flower and sniffed at it. It smelled just as beautiful as if it never were trampled. The flower did not smell like mud and was not damaged in any way. Mitch placed the flower back on the ground and it took root where it was placed, a few feet away from where it was plucked. He smiled and began to run around the meadow like a prancing gazelle. Mitch threw himself into the flowers on the floor and spread his limbs up and down, making a flower angel.

He was having a good time when he heard a man's voice. "You're always welcome to come back here!"

Mitch, still on the ground, asked, "Can I just stay here?"

"One day. But you must go back."

"Back? Where am I?"

"The Mountain of the North."

"The Mountain of the North? As in the biblical mountain?"

The man laughed. "Yes! God's mountain!"

Mitch sat up. "Are you God?"

"No."

Mitch looked at the man and saw holes in the palms of his two outstretched hands. Mitch knew who he was and bowed down with his face to the floor. "My Lord, forgive me!"

Jesus reached down, touched Mitch's right shoulder, and laughed. "All is forgiven Mitch... Come walk with me."

"I am not worthy to even talk to you."

"I am not unreachable. I am in you and I will never leave you, nor forsake you." Jesus reached down. "Come, I need to show you something."

Mitch reached up and took Jesus' hand. Jesus helped Mitch stand up.

Mitch and Jesus were suddenly in a white and gold, open-air temple with white pillars. All the carving details were gold. Multicolored silk fabric walls were swaying in the wind. The temple was divided into three parts.

There was the outer court, where a massive altar made of solid gold sat. It looked like blood had been sprinkled on it.

Five wooden doors surrounded the perimeter.

The inner court had another small altar with the most beautiful smell wafting out of it and ten golden tables with ten golden candlesticks.

There were two giant wood and gold doors on each side, with two thrones in the middle.

The Most Holy place contained an ark each and five more doors of wood and gold. Each section was divided by a thin layer of a semi-transparent, leather-like material.

Jesus and Mitch were standing in the inner court. Mitch looked around in amazement. Jesus pulled back the veil that led to the Most Holy place and said, "I want you to meet some people."

Mitch, still looking at everything in amazement, entered the Most Holy place and saw one man.

"This is the Holy Spirit in you."

Mitch approached the Holy Spirit and shook his hand. "It's a real honor to meet and see you in the spirit."

"Now you know I am real and have heard my voice," the Holy Spirit said. "I've been there with you through it all. You're never alone." Then, the Holy Spirit vanished.

"I would like to introduce you to your guardian angel, but you two have already met."

"What?"

Mitch's vision began to fade as Jesus said, "Her name is Monica Luz."

"What? Lord wait..."

CHAPTER 5

Mitch woke feeling peaceful, feeling like he could win the world.

He smiled, but as his eyes tried to adjust to a new day, he realized someone was sitting next to him.

Mitch rubbed his eyes, but his vision would not adjust. It seemed like he was looking through a thick fog and all he could see was a silhouette. Mitch began to feel unsettled, but the raw power radiating off the figure was otherworldly.

When it began to speak, Mitch felt as if his head was ringing with a sweet melody. "Everything you saw and heard is a lie."

"What are you talking about?"

"You did not go to heaven."

The small still voice of the Holy spirit from inside of Mitch cried out. Don't listen to him!

Mitch was quickened. In a soft voice, he demanded; "Reveal yourself!"

The thick fog lifted and Mitch saw an angelic looking man. He was muscular with short, straight blond hair, and was wearing a white robe with a golden belt. His long face was clean shaven, and his eyes were a dark reddish-pink. He had a small hero nose that led to a close-pointed mouth and a rectangular jaw line. There was a white glow surrounding him.

The man looked straight at Mitch. "You will die at my hand."

He continued to speak, but Mitch zoned him out as he consulted with the Holy Spirit. "Who is this?" he asked in mind speak.

"This is Lucifer," the Holy Spirit replied. "He feels threatened by God's plan for you, because he knows through your life you will save millions. Now tell Lucifer that he is already defeated, to hold his peace and to get behind you; that he is an offence. Then, he shall leave."

Mitch said to Lucifer: "You are already defeated. My name is written in the Lamb's Book of Life. Hold your peace and get behind me Satan, for you are an offence to me."

Lucifer laughed. "You shall see me again very soon!" he said, then he was gone.

While Mitch was experiencing this vision, no one else saw anything.

Mitch sat with his eyes closed and his lips moving as though he were praying, but no sound came out of his mouth. He did this for two hours. If anyone had dared to disturb Mitch as he was praying, they would have seen a glow in the cracks of Mitch's eyes and mouth.

When Mitch finally woke up, he looked around him in the dark bus and saw silhouettes of people. He settled back in his seat and thought anxiously on what awaited them wherever they came to a stop.

Sum beams broke through the dark and the star filled sky turned clear blue. Mitch felt the bus slowing down and the sound of the turbo diesel engine going from a high pitch whistle to the gentle hum of deceleration.

He felt and heard the air brakes bringing the bus to a complete stop.

Two armed soldiers with M-16 style weapons, army green camouflage and the newly designed helmet walked up to the bus.

Their helmets were light, no thicker than a baseball cap, and flexible, but protected better than the old Kevlar helmets used in Operation: Iraqi Freedom. It engulfed the entire head, covering the back part of the neck and jugular. The helmet molded itself around the head, providing a snug fit.

Their faces were covered, exposing only the eyes and a two-inch line from the top of the nose to the chin. The entire exposed gap formed a T across the face that the military call the lucky shot area.

One of the soldiers walked on to the bus, grabbed the big stack of papers next to the bus driver, and left without saying a word.

Drill Sergeant Peterson walked on to the bus next.

"Welcome to my world, cherries! You already know who I am and what to do. We have already set up the leadership." He pointed at Mitch, then he looked around the bus and said, "No name here is your captain and that is the end of it. Now that we have established leadership, you will get out of this bus."

He looked right at Mitch. "As fast as possible. AM I CLEAR?"

"YES DRILL SERGEANT!"

"When you get out, you will line up as you did before and stand at attention, with the sealed envelope in your right hand. IS THAT UNDERSTOOD?"

"YES DRILL SERGEANT!"

"No one moves until no name here moves and you have one minute to get off my bus. UNDERSTOOD?"

"YES DRILL SERGEANT!"

Peterson turned around and walked off the bus. As Peterson took his last step off the bus, a boy jumped up and darted out like a scared rabbit before Mitch could react.

When he reached the last step of the exit, the boy was met with the butt end of a M-16 assault rifle to the face, breaking his nose and dropping a now bloody and crying mess to the floor.

As Peterson walked away, he called out; "Welcome to your first lesson! Pay attention and follow orders."

Mitch was not far behind the boy, so he grabbed him and moved him to the side of the bus to check him out as best he could.

"It's alright youngin, I'm here with you and I'm not going anywhere till you can move, okay?" The boy was crying hysterically but nodded yes. "So, what's your name?"

The boy's messed up nose made his voice sound nasal. "B-Bill Foster the Second."

"Hello Bill Foster, I'm Mitch Walker."

Peterson turned and saw everyone lined up except Mitch. All of a sudden he was fuming again. "WHERE IS NO NAME?!" He looked toward the bus and spotted Mitch with Bill. Now livid, Peterson stomped to the bus, murmuring the whole way.

When Peterson got within about fifty feet of Mitch, he screamed. "WHAT THE HELL ARE YOU DOING? I TOLD YOU TO GET IN LINE!"

"YES DRILL SERGEANT!"

Mitch reached down to help Bill to his feet. As Bill took Mitch's hand, Peterson pushed Mitch to the floor and yelled. "Worry about yourself no name!"

"NO DRILL SERGEANT!"

He stood back up and reached to pick Bill up again, but Bill did not reach out to grab Mitch and instead tried to get up by himself.

"What did you say to me?" Peterson asked.

Mitch did not respond but continued to try to help Bill get up.

Peterson pushed Mitch down again. Then he whipped out his Russian 1918 M1895 Nagant Revolver from World War II and pulled the trigger.

Mitch, with his face toward the ground, heard a loud bang then a moment of silence. He told himself, 'Jesus, I'm coming sooner than I thought.' But suddenly Peterson was whispering in his ear: "This one's on you!"

Mitch rolled and sat up to look at Bill. There was a hole between his eyes and and the bus had a giant red spot on its side. Tears formed in Mitch's eyes. Then something off to the side caught his attention.

When he turned to look, Peterson was pointing the same revolver at Mitch's head with his finger on the trigger. Two soldiers were pointing their M-16's at him too. Mitch remained motionless.

After a few tense moments, Peterson growled, "Now get in line!"

Mitch stood. Without losing eye contact, he walked over and joined the line.

"Welcome to hell!" Peterson announced. "If you survive here, congratulations! You will have progressed from the outskirts of hell and right into the fire. I will teach you how to survive in the wild. I will teach you to shoot, clean and maintain a weapon. I am your father, your mother, your lover, your God, I am your WORLD for the next fourteen weeks. There is no graduation, but you will be debriefed on where you will be shipped off to. Now, we're going to get you a nice haircut and a shave, after which we will proceed to the infirmary. After that, we will go to AONOTHER building where you will receive your United States issued uniform. Then you will be escorted to my barracks. UNDERSTOOD?"

"YES DRILL SERGEANT!"

Peterson continued. "We do things differently here. After you enter my barracks, you will wait there until your name is called, at which time, you will turn in your paperwork to the officer. AM I UNDERSTOOD?"

"YES DRILL SERGEANT!"

"Starting with the ladies, when the last person is at the front of the line, the first person of the next line will move. You will go line by line through the open-door. Head straight until you see another Drill Sergeant. You will enter the room and wait for further instruction. UNDERSTOOD?"

"YES DRILL SERGEANT!"

"Now, get a move on cherries. We are burning daylight!"

Mitch found himself in the middle of the third line. When he looked around, he found a twenty-five-acre plot of land full of armed soldiers, a giant training area, an enclosed shooting range full of men at target practice, and a bomb range.

The entire place looked like a bunker with a few yards of grass on the training areas only. Everything was surrounded by twelve-foot-tall chain linked fences with electric razor wire lining the tops of each fence.

There were four layers of fences.

Each layer contained four sniper guard towers on each side.

The place seemed more like a camouflaged prison than a military base.

Before Mitch's line moved, a young Asian boy ran out of the open door with a soldier right on his tail. The boy tackled a soldier that was not paying attention, grabbed the soldier's side arm, pointed the gun to his own head and pulled the trigger. The soldier that had been chasing him dropped to her knees when she saw his motionless body, then she took off her helmet and began to cry.

Peterson walked over to the female soldier and put his hand on her shoulder. The soldier that had been tackled was still sitting on the floor. Peter walked over to him, went down on one knee beside him and whispered something into his ear. Whatever he said made the soldier take of his helmet and get on his knees. Peterson stood up, whipped out his Nagant revolver once again, and pointed it at the bowed man's head. "I'm sorry," he said. And a tear broke out from Peterson's eye.

He pulled the trigger and the man's body hit the floor.

Then Peterson holstered his weapon and walked away.

He stopped for a moment beside Mitch and, looking straight ahead, said "We do what we have to do to survive. This is our life; you make friends and then you lose them."

Tears streamed down Peterson's face and Mitch knew that Peterson had just killed his friend but he did not understand why.

In a steady flow, like programmed robots, the draftees entered the building line by line until they were all in a big room with a red privacy table. The draftees lined up in front of it in attention.

Peterson barked out orders. "This is what we call a shake down. This is how it goes; you will take everything out of your bags, pockets, shoes, bras, underwear, and anywhere else you can hide anything. You will place everything on the table. UNDERSTOOD?"

"YES DRILL SERGEANT!"

"Good. You have one minute, starting NOW!"

Everyone rushed to the table and took everything out of their bags as fast as they could. Two more drill sergeants were yelling in the draftee's faces, but Mitch did not move. It caught Peterson's attention.

Peterson walked up to Mitch and yelled at Mitch. "DID YOU NOT HEAR WHEN I SAID TO EMPTY YOUR BAG AND POCKETS?"

"YES DRILL SERGEANT!"

Mitch's voice broke when he yelled. He did not move.

"WHAT IS YOUR MAJOR MALFUNCTION? MOVE IT!"

"YES DRILL SERGEANT!" But Mitch still did not move.

Peterson looked around Mitch, but did not find a bag. "Do you have a bag?" He asked.

"NO DRILL SERGEANT!"

"Do you have anything on you?"

"NO DRILL SERGEANT!"

"So you are telling me that if I strip you down butt naked, I will find nothing?"

"YES DRILL SERGEANT!"

Peterson pointed at an armed soldier. The soldier came to Peterson.

"Take him to the dressing room and search him."

The soldier took Mitch into an adjacent room.

As they entered the small room, the man closed the door behind them.

"Strip down to your underwear alone," the soldier ordered.

Mitch stripped down to his blue boxer briefs. As he stood, he placed both hands in front of him, covering his private parts. The faceless soldier frisked Mitch, then checked his clothes, but found nothing.

"You're clear, put your clothes on and get back to the room."

What the soldier did not know was that Mitch was hiding a letter. Every time the soldier walked in front of him, Mitch would flip the paper to the back of his hand, and when the soldier walked behind, he would flip the paper to the palm of his hand.

As a result of one of his boyhood fancies, he had learned sleight of hand with hopes of becoming a magician. Mitch went back to his position in front of the section of the privacy table he had been assigned to and stood at attention as Peterson continued barking instructions.

Every sound, every word, and every instruction became a muffled blur. A numbness fell over Mitch as he stood at attention watching the drill sergeants yell 'hurry up' or 'move it, cherry!' in draftees faces.

The smell of gun powder, bleach and iron from dried blood filled the air.

Mitch's senses faded, but he was fully aware of his surroundings. He snapped out of it when he saw people moving line by line out of the door, starting with the women. He searched for the lady that had tried to help him earlier but could not find her.

Mitch's line began to move, and Mitch followed the group as they walked out of the room then stood in line in a long, thin hallway.

The hallway was six feet wide, with a polished cement floor and walls that had been painted a faded antique white. The sound of a buzzing hair cutter and a vacuum came out of an open door at the end of the hall. Everyone had been walking in to half an hour sessions when it was

Mitch's turn to have his head shaved.

The hot, hard steel and vibration of the hair cutter startled Mitch for a moment. His flinched his head downward and the white haired old barber chuckled. "Don't move, it's cold," he said.

Mitch smiled and chuckled. "Thank you for my makeover sir."

"Anytime youngin." The old man shaved Mitch's hair in less than thirty seconds. "My masterpiece."

Mitch turned and asked, "Where is the tip jar?"

The old man laughed and pointed up. "With the big man upstairs."

Mitch nodded. "I will pray for you then."

The old man nodded back.

Mitch walked out the door and stood at attention in line again.

When every draftee was through, Peterson marched them toward a gray, five-foot thick concrete building. On the top of the eight-foot, green double doored doorpost was an old beat up wooden sign with a faded carved out medical red cross and grayed out letters spelling 'Med Bay'. It seemed as if the wooden sign had been made by hand and in a hurry.

As they walked into the building, the stench of rotting flesh and dried blood saturated the air. Peterson breathed deep. "Get used to that smell, cherries. This is the smell of war, this is the perfume of glory."

They walked past white walls and floors with a constant stream of blood and water flowing into a center drain. There were four rows of twenty old medical gurney beds. The sound of pained yells, crying kids and screeching tyres overwhelmed most of the draftees and a few kids peed in their pants, including the boy in front of Mitch.

Peterson stopped everyone to see the sick and injured. "These men, after boot camp, will be shipped off to the front lines with no weapons and no training. So I suggest you stay healthy, because your life depends on it!"

A feeling of dread fell on the draftees and even on Peterson. Peterson marched the group into another room full of chairs, in the manner of a waiting room, where beautiful young women were waiting.

These nurses were dressed in 1950's style outfits - short skirts and long socks. They seemed kind. The boys began to smile at the women. Mitch did not.

Peterson addressed the draftees. "You will meet one girl each in a room alone, you will give your paper to her and follow instructions. UNDERSTOOD?"

The responding yells were enthusiastic.

"YES DRILL SERGEANT!"

"Stay seated until your name is called. UNDERSTOOD?"

"YES DRILL SERGEANT!"

The draftees took their chairs, but as Mitch sat, everyone around him got up and moved away as if he had a contagious virus. All except one young man. He was already six feet and seven inches tall - a skinny red head weighing 180 pounds. Due to their new haircuts, the red showed only in his eyebrows. The boy had a deep voice.

"Aren't you going to run away like everyone else?" Mitch asked.

The young man looked at Mitch in a way that struck him as awkward. "Do I have to?"

"No," Mitch said, and then he smirked. "What's your name?"

"Dan Stone. Yes, as in a rock. At your service sir!" He did some crazy thing with his hands, slapping them together before he threw one hand at his forehead in something that resembled a salute. The palm of his limp hand was exposed and he had a stupid look on his face as he stared straight ahead.

Mitch giggled. "At ease."

Dan lowered his hand. "Thank you, sir!"

Mitch put his hand out and said, "I'm Mitch."

Dan shook Mitch's hand rapidly and said, "Everyone knows who you are!"

Dan got close and whispered, "Everyone secretly likes you," and nodded.

Mitch and Dan stayed speaking as the nurses kept calling names. After an hour, a beautiful young brunette finally called Mitch's name.

"Find me later," Mitch said to Dan, "and we can continue our conversation."

"Yes sir!"

"It's Mitch," Mitch said. Then he waved and said, "God bless!"

Dan waved back.

Mitch approached the petite young lady. She had a clip board pressed against her chest with her right hand and she gestured for Mitch to enter through the door.

"Hi ma'am, God bless." He smirked, but bowed his head almost immediately.

The nurse eyed him warily. "Is everything okay?"

Mitch began to cry, but managed to respond. "Yes, everything is alright."

At that point, Mitch dropped to his knees and began to cry hysterically.

The nurse knelt and put her left hand on Mitch's right shoulder. "It will be okay. Nothing I'm going to do to you is going to hurt that bad."

Mitch looked her in the eye and spluttered. "I've just lost everyone. M-my mom was murdered, now my brother is an orphan again. And I had to leave him! And my new f-friend. Bill Foster!" Mitch stopped and shook his head. It was too much for him to go on.

A tear fell out of the nurse's eye. She could see the pain Mitch was going through, but could do nothing about it. The nurse hugged Mitch and Mitch went limp for a moment.

As the nurse held Mitch in her arms, she spoke. "We have to get your shot done. Would you please give me your paperwork?" Mitch nodded and handed his envelope to the nurse. She took the papers from him gently, helped him to his feet and led him to the back of a curtain divide.

Mitch sat on a stretcher and heard all the other draftees yelling 'ouch', 'what the hell!'.

Once in a while it was just a scream followed by crying and the sound of a medical tool hitting a metal tray. A brutish woman with short curly hair whipped open the curtain divider and rolled in a cart with a tray full of plastic wrapped syringes and fresh needles. She sounded like she had been smoking for years when she barked at Mitch. "Drop your pants, turn toward the bed and bend over."

Mitch was still trying to pull himself together when he dropped his pants, turned toward the bed and bent over, but instead of feeling a big needle in his rear, he heard the woman and the young nurse whispering to each other. After a few moments, Mitch felt a gentle touch on his lower back and the young nurse's voice saying: "Hey darling, you need four injections. I will do them as gentle as I can, but one of them is going to burn, okay?"

Mitch nodded. "Ma'am, you do what you have to do."

The nurse smiled and grabbed a syringe filled with a clear liquid, then said, "This one is not that bad." Mitch giggled. She plunged the needle in one of his butt cheeks. The pain made Mitch cringe a little and the nurse said, "You have to relax."

"I'll try."

"By the way, my name is Mary Mills, but you can call me M."

Mitch relaxed a bit.

"My name is Mitch, but you probably already know that." At that time, Mary had stuck the second needle into the same butt cheek.

Mary giggled. "It is nice to meet you Mitch."

Mitch smiled at the bed. "It's nice to meet you too."

Mary plunged the third needle into his other butt cheek. "You know," she said. "If we got together, we would be known as M&M."

Mitch laughed. "That's true."

Before the last injection, she warned; "This is the one that burns, okay?" Before Mitch could say okay, Mary plunged the last needle into Mitch's butt cheek. That one REALLY made Mitch cringe.

"You have to relax!"

"I'm trying."

Mary saw that Mitch was not relaxing, so she leaned on top of his back and spoke softly into his ear. "It's alright." She kissed his cheek. "Find me in the mess hall. Tonight." Mitch finally relaxed and Mary finished.

"You're done," the other woman said. "Put your pants back on and head out the doors. Make a left and you will find your troop there. Stay there until further instructions."

Mitch pulled up his pants. "Thank you both, and God bless you."

Mary looked at Mitch and lowered her eyelashes. Mitch, still with sorrow in his eyes, looked at Mary, nodded, and walked out of the room to do as he had been instructed.

CHAPTER 6

Mid-day. Classified location in the mountains, Virginia.

Mitch was standing in line, pondering on everything that had just happened and everything that was going to happen, when he heard someone call out "Where is Mitch?"

"Here sir!" Mitch yelled, then saluted.

An average-sized man with white hair and a white and gray mustache walked into the room. His skin was wrinkly, dry, and honey-colored like a desert. He had a skinny and long, flat nose, giant white and gray eyebrows, and hooded eyes. The old man walked up to Mitch. "At ease. My name is Major General Jerry Horner. Grab your bags, you need to come with me son."

"Yes sir!"

Jerry began to walk, closely followed by Mitch. Without saying a word, Jerry led Mitch out of the Med Bay into a well maintained and guarded camouflaged air-raid bunker. The bunker had two green armored doors, 12 feet tall and several inches thick. Guarding the doors were four faceless soldiers fully kitted in black mechanical armor that covered every inch of their body. Jerry gestured at the soldiers.

"These are our captains' guards. They are mute and some of the best soldiers. They are ex-special forces who enjoy nothing more than they enjoy killing, so in honor of your father, they took a vow of silence and pledged their lives to provide protection and security to our captains.

We call them Zealots; when they've made a vow, they keep it till the death."

"Sir, did you personally know my father?" Mitch asked.

Jerry paused at the entrance of the bunker and turned around to look at Mitch. "He and his troop saved me more times than I can count. The Zealots fought with him till the day he died."

"So it's true he's dead?" Mitch asked.

"After another battle, in which your father saved me once more, we were celebrating your father. He pulled back to honor the fallen by taking a knee and praying. It was something he did often, and we always gave him some privacy as he did his thing. This time a sniper shot him and all hell broke loose.

We fought as hard as we could, and lost many men trying to recover your father's body, but after the dust settled, his body was nowhere to be found. The only sign of him we could recover was his dog tag."

Tears formed in Jerry's eyes and he cleared his throat. "He was the closest thing to a father this orphan ever had." He said, pointing at himself. "That's all anyone can ask for."

Jerry turned again and continued walking through the brightly lit hallway. There was a hint of lavender and orange in the air. "He was the best leader, best mentor, best friend. We were all criminals, orphans, street rats, homeless nobodies. But your father treated us like humans and gave us a purpose to fight for. That's why we honor him by living."

"He sounds like a great dad."

Jerry's voice cracked as he said, "I'm sorry for the loss of your father. But how is your mother? Your father spoke highly of her."

"She's dead. She was killed defending the lieutenant that came to get me."

Jerry stopped next to a door and opened it. "This is your room." He gestured for Mitch to walk in, and Mitch walked into a tiny room with one metal framed bed, white bedsheets, and a single pillow with a green blanket folded at the foot of the bed.

The bedsheet was so crisp it looked like it was ironed, and the covers were folded so tight you could bounce a quarter off it. "Observe how everything is placed and done because I will check twice a day to make sure everything remains the same way, we already have your uniform in the armoire, so get dressed in your PT uniform. We start in an hour, understood?"

"Yes sir."

Jerry headed for the door but paused as Mitch inspected every square inch of the room. Jerry broke his silence. "I'm sorry for your loss. They raised a good man." Then Jerry walked out, closing the door behind him.

Soon after Jerry left, Mitch fell to his knees at the foot of his bed and cried.

Flashback

Back on the Walker's ranch, their American Craftsman house is half-built and the night is cold and rainy. The sitting area has four rocking chairs sitting on wooden floors and a blue and white patterned trough rug all dimly lit by a stone fireplace. Three-year-old Mitch is curled up in a corner in the fetal position, crying. James puts his hand on Mitch's shoulder and sits next to him. A tear-stained Mitch looks at his dad and sees that James' eyes are puffy from crying.

James says, "It's okay to cry, son. It's normal. But when you stand in front of people, you never let them see you sweat. Do you understand?"

"Yes sir," Mitch sniffled. "But why do you have to go?"

"When you get older you'll understand. Just know that I love you son, and I will see you again in this life or the next."

James gave Mitch a big hug and then carried Mitch to his bed. "Goodnight son, I love you."

"Daddy please don't go," Mitch pleaded. "Please... please." James closed the door and shut it behind him.

Back in the Captain's Quarters

Mitch, after a few minutes of prayer, managed to pull himself together and wipe the tears from his red puffy eyes. He opened the armoire next to the door and found a pair of dog tags, a single set of ceremonial Army Airborne uniform, two sets of army combat uniforms with Mitch's last name and his rank on his collar, and five white t-shirts with five green camouflage cargo pants, a pair of old, beat up, black tactical boots for PT, a pair of tan combat boots, and a pair of dole leather black shoes with a note saying 'You better make it shine.'

Mitch pulled on a white shirt and camouflage pants, then wore his father's old metal dog tags and layered the new dog tags on the old.

Peterson barged into the room and saw Mitch on one knee surrounded by twelve, towering men in golden armor. Peterson stopped in his tracks and stood in dumb silence by the door, at which point he saw the men sheath their swords.

For the next two minutes, the angels maintained eye contact with Peterson. When Mitch was done praying, the angels suddenly vanished into thin air. Peterson, frozen with fear and shock until now, suddenly recollected himself and managed to blurt instructions to Mitch; "You must get a move on and prepare the troop."

Mitch, startled by Peterson's presence in the room, stood to attention and saluted Peterson. Peterson returned the salute. "At ease," he said.

With wide eyes, the drill sergeant asked, "Who was in the room with you?"

Mitch was puzzled by the question. "There was no one here with me sir."

Peterson shook his head violently, as if trying to wake himself up from a dream, and looked again at a still puzzled Mitch.

"Sir, are you okay?"

Peterson appeared unable to speak for a few moments before he finally snapped out of it. "Head to the barracks and prepare the men because training begins now."

"YES DRILL SERGEANT!"

Mitch left the captain's building and made a right. A handful of tents stood before him, and a big wooden sign displaying the words 'Barracks' was staked to the ground in front of the camp.

Mitch paused, closed his eyes, and took a deep breath. Then he walked into the barracks yelling. "ATTENTION!"

The men jumped from their bunk beds and ran to the front. The floor was orange-red and full of dust from the clay the barracks was sitting on.

There were a few holes and rips in the roof of the barracks and the beds were in really bad shape. Most of the mattresses were full of dirt, burn marks, and blood. The stench of sweat and body odor from badly maintained facilities had permeated the air.

Peterson entered the barracks and whispered in Mitch's ear, "Follow me and pay attention." Then Peterson began to walk back and forth, closely followed by Mitch. As he walked, he barked out instructions on the ways the troop would be expected to clean their living quarters, how to make their beds, and what their schedule was going to look like.

At the end of his address, Peterson re-introduced Mitch. "This man next to me is your captain. He will be the one to lead you to either victory or defeat, and you will follow his every order. Disobedience is considered treason, and you will be shot."

A group of boys threw disgusted glares at Mitch. Mitch saw but remained straight-backed with his head up before them. An eight-foot angel walked past each person, revealing everything about all of them, invisible to everyone except Mitch. As the angel walked past the group of men glaring at Mitch, he revealed that they were troublemakers. Then the angel stopped, looked straight at Mitch, and said, "I now leave this information with you. Do not misuse this information. Do not blackmail. This information is for you to understand your people. Now pay attention to what Peterson is saying, PT is about to begin."

The angel turned and walked out of the barracks.

As if on cue, Peterson turned to Mitch. "Captain, get your troops ready and be outside in five."

"YES DRILL SERGEANT!"

Peterson walked out of the barracks, and Mitch turned to address his team. "Alright, men! I want you out in THREE minutes. Let's move."

Draftees began to trip over themselves trying to rush out of the door.

The troublemakers remained standing.

Their leader, Leroy Henderson, a tall, blonde-haired, and blue-eyed muscular young man who towered over most of the kids, set squinty eyes on Mitch and stuck his narrow jaw out. He and his group walked very slowly past Mitch, giving him dirty looks. Mitch, holding Leroy's stare, thought to himself 'We have to organize this a little better because this is a disaster.'

It took ten minutes for everyone to get outside and into formation. Peterson was so mad he was ready to rip heads off. He soon had them all on the ground doing push-ups, but ordered Mitch to remain standing. Mitch disobeyed and dropped to the ground with everyone else. It won some people over.

Back at the café

A young soldier takes off his mask and interrupts Taavet in the middle of the story. The young man is no more than fifteen years old with mid-brown skin, dark brown hair, and peach fuzz where a mustache should be. His nose is slightly refined, his mouth is almost an overbite and a crackling voice speaks of puberty. He says, "Old man, we do not have time for this."

The commander's voice is stern. "Hold your tongue boy, or I will cut it off."

The boy is unrepentant. "Well I'm bored, and I don't want to listen anymore." He then turns around and comes face to face with the waitress. He grabs her. "Well, I think I just found my entertainment."

Taavet, still looking at the commander, speaks calmly to the boy, "I would not do that if I were you."

"Oh yeah?" The boy smirks. "What are you going to do about it?"

"I'm not the one you should be worried about," Taavet responds.

The young man chuckles. "I can handle myself."

The waitress looks at Taavet with wide eyes as the young man drags her into the kitchen.

"I apologize for my son's arrogance," the commander says to Taavet. "I am still teaching him to respect his elders."

Taavet chuckles. "He is going to learn one day."

A few moments later, the waitress runs back into the dining area. "They took him!"

The commander shoots up from his chair. "Took who? How is that possible? We have a parameter!"

Taavet chuckles again. "The city hides secrets; some you know, some you don't."

The commander pulls his gun of its holster, but before the barrel has cleared, Taavet disarms him. Then rests his arm on the table. He is now holding the commander's old 1911 .45 auto.

He points it at the commander's head. "Violence is not the wisest step to take," he says.

"Says the man pointing my gun to my head," the commander says. "By the way, at my word, you'll be dead before you pull that trigger."

"The giant red pimple, between your eyes tells me otherwise," Taavet replies.

A laser from a far-off sniper is centered on the commander's forehead.

"I am the only reason," Taavet says, "that you and your troop are alive." When he smiles and raises his hand, the red dot disappears.

Then Taavet releases his grip on the gun, lets it roll around his finger, and hands it back to the commander.

The commander reaches for the gun slowly, grabs it and holsters it, then gestures for the men pointing their weapons at Taavet to lower their guns.

The commander stares at Taavet as he begins to speak Pashto. "As I deal with this fool, I want five of you to take the waitress and follow the trail to find my son. Kill her when you're done with her."

Taavet, now looking down at the table, responds in Pashto. "As I have advised you before, that is not wise to do. You may take the cook, but the waitress stays here."

"How do you speak my language?" The commander demands in English.

Taavet smiles. "Know your enemy," he says.

"Love your enemy. Be your enemy."

The commander is confused. "What?"

"It's something I learned trying to hunt down Sitch."

"You tried to hunt him down?"

"I was not always in my right mind. But now that I am, the waitress is not to be touched or messed with."

The commander chuckles. "Take the waitress," he orders.

"Don't say I didn't warn you if the waitress comes back and your men don't."

"If I don't see my troop again, you will die," the commander says.

"Then you will never find Sitch," Taavet responds.

With reluctance, the commander orders his men to take the waitress but not harm her.

Taavet looks at the waitress and nods his head. The waitress smirks and willingly accompanies the five muscular masked men to the back room.

"Who are you Taavet?" the commander asks.

"You are not here to hear about me. You're here to find Sitch."

"And we are no closer to finding him," the commander retorts.

"Whose fault is that?" Taavet asks.

The commander and Taavet are silent and seated, staring at each other, when a child runs into the café, bouncing on his toes as if nervous.

The child is healthy. She appears to be about 5 years old, with sand-colored skin and a tall, soft nose. Her face is full of mud and grass and her squinty eyes look franticly around her before she makes eye contact with Taavet and runs to him.

The child whispers something in Taavet's ear that makes Taavet's eyes grow wide. Taavet whispers something back to the child and says out loud "Do you understand?"

The child nods and runs to the back room. Two ISA soldiers trail her.

Taavet says, "I have to urinate, please excuse me."

"What did the child tell you?" the commander asks.

Taavet smirks. "Nothing," he says, and then attempts to continue on his way, but a tall man steps into his path and takes off his mask.

The tall soldier has a full, white beard, scarred skin, and a fresh long cut that runs straight down from his forehead and through his nose before it ends at his upper lip.

He says to Taavet, "The commander asked you a question."

Taavet reaches up so fast, there is no time to react. He grabs a nerve located near the man's jugular. The pressure brings the man to his knees. Three more men jump out of their chairs and rush Taavet.

Taavet knocks out the man before him with a snap of his wrist and turns to face the others. He straightens up, gets into a fighting position, and as the three men reach Taavet, he hits one man on the side of the neck knocking him out cold.

Another man throws a punch that Taavet blocks before he delivers a forward kick to the man's knee, breaking his shin in three places.

The third gets on a table and jumps off it with both hands clenched together as if holding a sword. As he bears down, Taavet throws up a high kick that catches the man in the air under his bulletproof vest and stops his momentum.

The man falls back on the table he jumped from, shattering it completely. The rest of the troop jump out of their chairs and Taavet turns to face them.

The commander laughs. "Stand down," he orders. And he continues to laugh, approaching Taavet. Now before Taavet, he begins a slow clap. "Who knew you still had so much fight in you?" Taavet turns and walks into the bathroom, and the commander reaches out to grab Taavet's shoulder.

Before the commander can touch him, Taavet says, "I suggest you keep your hands to yourself and let me urinate."

The commander lowers his hand and begins his slow clap again. "Bravo, bravo."

CHAPTER 7

Café in Fort Pierce. Close to mid-day.

After half an hour, Taavet emerges from the restroom to see four men kneeling with hoods over their heads. He realizes they are the soldiers who attacked him. A soldier is pointing a black 9-millimeter gun to the back of each kneeling man's head. The commander, still clapping up until that moment, stops suddenly and gestures to the kneeling men.

"For your victory, you choose who lives and who dies."

Taavet is hunched over from pain as he walks towards the table.

Without looking at the men, he responds; "I would that all men should live as my God lives." Then Taavet turns to the commander and looks him in the eye. "But you are not as merciful are you?"

The commander smiles. "No."

The commander snaps his fingers. A loud and simultaneous bang rings out. There are now four lifeless bodies lying on the woodwork of the freshly blood-stained floor, and the commander is wearing a giant smile.

Taavet stares at the commander as he sits. Just then, the waitress walks out of the back room with a smug smile that disappears when her eyes meet that of the commander. The satisfaction in her face drains away as quickly as if all the joy in her life has just been sucked right out of her.

The commander asks, "Where are my men?"

The words tumble out of the waitress' mouth. "They found an underground tunnel so we jumped in and began to follow it, but they left me alone. When I heard something I was scared and ran here as fast as I could."

"Liar!"

The waitress begins to back up as the commander takes slow steps toward her.

"My men know to never leave a hostage alone." He continues.

"I'm telling you the truth—"

"Furthermore, if anything had been discovered, my men would have come to tell me straight away."

Now a considerable number of steps away from her original position, the waitress repeats, "I've told you the truth."

The commander now has the waitress' back to the bar. "Tell me the truth," he says.

In one swift movement, the commander has grabbed the waitress by the shirt and pulled out his weapon, pushing it into her face.

A dagger flies deftly through the air just then with such force and accuracy that it severs the commander's shooting finger and breaks the trigger of his prized silver 9-millimeter handgun.

Taavet sips his coffee and studies the table. "I told you to leave her alone."

The commander, now on his knees in pain, glares at Taavet with unadulterated hatred. Taavet looks back.

As the commander struggles to contain his anger under the blinding glare of a sniper laser, Taavet asks; "Do you have a medic?" The heavily breathing commander says nothing, but continues to stare at Taavet.

Taavet then gestures to the waitress to come.

The waitress leans over as Taavet whispers something in her ear, but pulls up sharply. "No I will not," she says in hot anger.

Taavet, still calm, answers softly. "Remember what I taught you."

The waitress rolls her eyes and stomps her way to the back room. Taavet stands up and walks toward the now surrounded commander. The soldiers around him point their weapons at Taavet as one.

"Can I stop the bleeding?"

Taavet's question is directed at the kneeling commander, who gives no response.

"Then he will bleed to death unless someone stops the bleeding. Good luck."

The soldiers debate amongst themselves before they move apart to give Taavet passage to Basser.

Taavet kneels and tries to grab the commander's hand, but the commander pulls away.

"If you die today, Taavet says, it is due to your arrogance and not my blade."

The commander finally gives his hand to Taavet. Taavet takes his belt off, puts it just behind the commander's wrist and tightens it to make a tourniquet. A few minutes later a medic walks into the café wearing a Freedom States uniform.

The commander, with puzzle and pain etched on his face, asks "Why are you helping me?"

"That you are barbaric and merciless does not exclude you from my help. I respect all men and women; friend or enemy. Everyone deserves a chance at life. Redemption is just one decision away and it starts with 'Jesus, come into my heart.'"

The commander begins to squirm. His eyes turn a solid black and with a deep growl completely different from the voice he has spoken with up until this point, he snarls. "Don't you dare say that name."

"Jesus?" Taavet asks innocently.

The commander's growl grows even louder. "Yes! This one belongs to me!"

Taavet now has a fire in his eyes. "We will see about that in Jesus' name."

The commander begins to roar and yell. "He's mine! He's mine!"

"Peace. Be still." The commander goes limp as if dead.

Taavet says, "Commander Basheer, wake up."

The commander opens his eyes. How do you know my name?"

"I know everything about you, and I will reveal everything in time."

The medic, now finished, makes his way to the back room, closely followed by two ISA soldiers.

As they reach the door, five Freedom States troops, one of whom is a Zealot, step out.

The ISA soldiers back off. Four of the Freedom States soldiers turn and leave with the medic, but the Zealot remains in the doorway, menacing in his mechanical body armor.

Zealots are usually armed with enough to destroy everyone present in the room three times over, and the ISA soldiers know it.

Taavet sits and the commander, with his bandaged hand, follows suit. Tears of fear, pain and anger fill his eyes. Taavet takes another sip of his coffee and speaks.

"Weeks passed by and Mitch's troop soon became the best of the 82nd airborne division and army draftees. Men and women had learned to trust Mitch. A group of restless dissenters grew nevertheless, and they plotted detailed schemes on the possible ways they could overthrow Mitch as captain, to put Leroy in his stead.

The Zealots kept a close eye on this group.

One week before graduation, an urgent message came in from the Office of the President of the United States, saying;

All troops, whether trained or not, are to be deployed immediately.

Classified Location. Virginia, Mid-Winter

Peterson gathers the 82nd Airborne Division and the Special Troops Battalion led by Mitch in front of the camping blocks and begins to address them.

"Today is a great day! Today is the first day of the rest of your life. It is both with a heavy heart and pride that I announce you are going to the front lines."

At that moment, fifteen brand new, modified C-17 aircrafts passed overhead in block formation and landed on a nearby concrete slab used for PT. These were new models, designed for stealth and vertical take-off. As the draftees gawked, Peterson announced, "You have three hours to gather your things and meet me at the PT court yard. UNDERSTOOD?"

A massive roar. "YES DRILL SERGEANT!"

As everyone marches into the barracks, there are whispers of both joy and terror. Mitch walks into his quarters and finds Monica Luz standing there. She is wearing army greens and her short hair is tied up in a ponytail.

Mitch says, "it's nice to see you again Monica." Monica nods. "How can I help you?"

"Your men are scared," she says.

"I am too."

"But you are ready, Mitch. And you must prepare your men as I have. Worry not, for God has blessed you to lead and will strengthen you to do what must shortly come to pass."

Mitch fell to his knees and began to pray. Monica turned around and walked through the solid concrete wall. Within half an hour, Mitch was sitting, packed, on his bed.

Peterson walked in quietly.

"Captain?" Mitch stood to attention. "Son, there's no need for that now. You've earned your stripes."

"Thank you, drill sergeant."

"I came to introduce you to your Zealot."

A five foot, eleven-inch armored Zealot walked in wearing a helmet with a tinted bullet-proof visor. You could only see the faded whites of his eyes. His uniform was a solid black, with three different rifles and a handgun on each hip. When he walked in, he dropped to one knee and bowed his head.

"This is your bodyguard. His name is Zealot Benjamin Brine and he is mute."

Mitch looked at the Zealot. "Thank you, sir."

Peterson handed a piece of paper over to Mitch and began to walk away. When he reached the door, he stopped and turned around.

"You are the best group of men and women I have had the privilege to train." Peterson saluted Mitch, then he walked out.

Mitch walked to Benjamin, grabbed his arm and helped him to his feet. "There is no need for that Benjamin, please. You are equal to me; you are not beneath. Do you understand?"

Benjamin turned his head, nodded a yes, snapped his head forward, and stood at attention.

Mitch tapped the Zealot's armor-plated shoulder. "We will work on that." He shouldered his bag and walked out the door but noticed that Benjamin was not following. "Come on, we don't want to be late."

Benjamin marched out the door and Mitch shook his head. Then he took one last look at his room, turned off the lights, and walked away.

When Mitch entered the barracks, a boy from the front of the room yelled. "ATTENTION!"

Everyone jumped up and stood at attention as Mitch walked in.

Benjamin stayed right outside the door because it was forbidden for a Zealot to enter a United States barracks unless there was an emergency. Zealot's had their tents.

Slowly, Mitch walked down the line of bunks. "At ease!" As one, the troop relaxed.

"I hear some of you are scared… And that is only natural. Today we will do what we have been trained to do. Today we will face the unknown… Not as individuals, but as the 82nd Airborne. Today we rise and become who we were meant to be! Warriors! Not just mindless soldiers."

He reached the end of the line and turned.

"Remember your training. When crap hits the fan, improvise and overcome. Take it one step at a time! A war is not won overnight."

Here, Mitch paused.

"It takes time."

His voice was softer now.

"I can't guarantee that I will bring you all home alive, but I will make sure you get home… Fight with courage, and we will survive."

Mitch turned around and walked out the door. A young man about the age of sixteen, five feet and nine inches tall; an African American with a wide, short nose and a pouty mouth sporting a gap between the center top front teeth, hurried after him. "Mitch!"

His voice was drowned out by a commotion in the barracks, so Mitch kept walking, but the man pursued him until he caught Benjamin's attention.

Benjamin turned, and in an instant, had put the young man in a headlock and lifted him off the ground.

"At ease, Benjamin." Benjamin paused for a moment and the young man stopped squirming.

"Let him down, please."

Benjamin released the young man.

"My men can come to me freely to talk. When they come, please let me know. Do you understand?"

Benjamin looked at Mitch and nodded, then stood at parade rest with his hands behind him.

"Hey, Jim. What's up?"

Jim was on his knees, rubbing his throat and struggling to draw in breath. "What the hell was that?" he wheezed.

"I'm sorry, tha's Benjamin, my guard. He's new. How can I help you?"

Jim began to rock back and forth, crying. "I-I am terrified, I-I d-don't what to die."

Mitch dropped to one knee, put his hand on Jim's shoulder and said, "It's alright Jim. I'm scared too, but I have an obligation to you and Sam and even Leroy to keep us alive for as long as possible. Courage does not mean you don't have fear, courage is facing your fears head on, but none of us will do it alone."

Mitch helped Jim to his feet. Then he wiped his tears, tapped Jim on the shoulder and kept walking, followed closely by Benjamin.

Mitch found a private area and asked; "Benjamin, would you guard the door please?" Benjamin nodded and Mitch said "Thank you." Then he walked into a janitors closet, knelt, bowed his head and began to pray. Mitch had been praying for about half an hour when Benjamin walked in, knelt and put his hand on Mitch's left shoulder. Mitch felt another hand on his right shoulder, it was Peterson.

Before he knew it, all the captains had joined in.

When the troops caught view of the group kneeling in the janitor's closet, they began to join as well. The chain soon spilled out and down the hallway, then it spilled out through the doors and into the courtyard where every man, woman and angel knelt praying.

Mitch prayed for another half hour. When he was done, he said "Amen."

The sound of ten thousand soldiers repeating "Amen" startled Mitch.

"Are you ready?" Mitch asked.

"All the way!" They roared.

Mitch and the 82nd Airborne Special Troops division were the first to board the C-17, destination unknown. Hour after hour passed to the sound of sniffling and snoring. Mitch took this time to write a letter to Nissi. They always all started the same:

Dearest Nissi,

I pray you are doing well. It's been so long since I've seen you, but I can still smell your sweet scent. I remember the taste of your lips and the way your hair flows in the wind. There was no sight greater to see. I long to see you and pray I see you soon...

Then Mitch wrote of everything that had just happened, from the President's orders to the praying soldiers. He spoke of how scared he was, and how he hoped to be the leader everyone expected him to be. He finished off with a poem he had written for her, and ended the letter with Yours truly, Mitch.

Eight and a half hours later, there was a beep and a voice came through the PA saying; "This is your captain speaking. I'm going to need everyone to sit still and not make a sound for the next ten minutes as we approach our destination. Thank you."

Mitch saw through the only window on the door that it was still daylight. The plane slowed to the point where it felt like it was hovering for a few minutes, then it descended, ever so slowly, until the window went dark and there was a light bump from landing. The engines powered down and the tail opened up. A man walked in wearing snow white camouflage, a Russian style fur hat and a full beard that made him look like he had come right out of the courts of Valhalla.

"Welcome, men, to the mountains of Russian Mission, Alaska. You have five minutes to get out of this plane and into block formation, understood?"

Everyone in the plane yelled, "Yes sir!"

The man turned, and by the time his foot hit the concrete, the soldiers were forming a block outside the plane. Mitch stepped out of the plane and looked up. The giant metal doors closed behind him. There was suddenly a plane beside the one he had stepped out of, and its tail began to open. Another appeared beside it, opening up its tail; and another, and still another. All fifteen C17 aircrafts emptied their contents onto the Alaskan plain.

The troops lined up in front of a seemingly ordinary concrete wall about two storeys tall.

One man sporting snow camouflage, a full, clean-cut salt and pepper beard and a Russian fur hat walked to the front of the fifteen battalions separated into fifteen blocks. He began to speak.

"Welcome to Russian Mission Alaska also known as tsa-ond. We are a secret base that has been hidden in these mountains from the world for fifty years. You were called here for a very secret and important mission. You have been called because you are our last resort in the fight against communism."

"Tonight, you will be sent to a town just east of Moscow called Kazan. You will take that town at all costs; you have half an hour. Intel shows that you will meet with little to no resistance. This door behind me will open, you will go through it, and you will walk onto a train. There, you will be equipped with your new uniforms, helmets and weapons. After you have received your equipment, you will sit and wait for further instructions from your captain. Captains, you will meet in the first cart half an hour after departure. Is this all understood?!"

"Yes sir!"

A massive bang followed their response, and then a click. The entire troop jumped back as the concrete wall began to retract from right to left, revealing an oversized bullet train. The stainless steel body of the train shone like polished mirror. Fifteen seamless doors opened wide enough to fit five men at a time. Within the train, lockers made of Plexiglas cylinder stood against the walls, with the soldiers' names displayed in lights on the glass. Inside each locker was a bullet proof vest, a snow camouflage uniform, a travel pack, a parachute, a modified Assault weapon with 5.56 NATO armor piercing rounds and collapsible stock, ten magazines, a handgun with five more handgun magazines, a camouflaged snow jacket and a T-style helmet.

On the other side of the train were chairs four seats wide, yet the space between the seats and the lockers was two seats wide. Mitch was the first to enter the train and grab his things in the third cart. He put them on and walked to the first cart, where a seat in the front of the cart had his name on it. The train began to move.

Benjamin stayed in the second cart with all the other Zealots. A General waiting in the first cart noticed Mitch as he sat. He recognized Mitch, because he looked so much like his father. The General had known James Walker when he was a lieutenant. He stood up from the dark corner he had been sitting in.

"Before anyone else gets here, know that you are going on a suicide mission," he warned. "You are a diversion for the real attack on Moscow. Find the shadows, then you will find what you're looking for." The General never revealed his face, but remained in the dark corner, and seemed to disappear into the shadows as the train began to move.

Mitch pondered on the strange man and his odd disappearance as other captains began to walk in, laughing and talking to each other.

All the captains took a seat, but the chair beside Mitch remained unoccupied. After a two hour debrief, they sent the captains back to their carts to debrief their troops. The captains had been shown the vital areas to take, and what targets they were to capture or kill.

Mitch debriefed his troops. "Intel was wrong," he said. "We are on a suicide mission. You are some of the best men and women I have had the honor to lead and I will not let you down."

CHAPTER

8

Mid-Winter. Just before sunset. Hidden underground is a bullet train. The drop-off point is Poligus, Russia.

They had been on the train for four hours, the windowless bullet was traveling at just under the speed of sound. Every hour, the temperature in the train dropped until it had reached the level of the climate they were headed to. The troops were slowly acclimatized to the harsh temperatures of a Russian winter. As they arrived, the PA system delivered one last detail.

"Welcome, 82nd airborne, to Poligus, Russia. The temperature is 19 degrees Fahrenheit, and you will have two hours to take Kazan after you jump. An ice storm is expected to hit. It will be the coldest in the last thousand years. If you fail, you will not only be fighting the enemy, but also the weather. Good luck, and God help you."

The train came to a stop and Mitch gave his battalion instructions. "When you leave this train, you will walk straight onto the tarmac and there form four lines. You will wait for further instructions, understood?"

"Yes sir!" His men yelled.

Mitch turned to face the closed door. When it opened, he saw a massive, gray, cement bunker. Benjamin was waiting for him at the right side of the train door.

With Benjamin in the lead, they walked to their waiting area; a twenty-acre, flat, clear area near a wall. The men lined up in the clearing.

"Sit," Mitch said. "You may talk to each other, but not loud enough for me to hear you. Too loud, you will lose all talking privileges. Understood?"

"Yes sir." The troops sat.

Daylight faded into night and the night brought a cold with it that made them anxious and restless. The later it got, the quieter it became.

Mitch was walking back and forth, checking on his troops, when Monica appeared right next to him.

Mitch glanced at her. "Hello, Monica."

She nodded. "What are your orders, sir?"

"What do you mean?"

"You are our superior. You tell us what to do, and we do it."

Mitch mumbled something under his breath and then, "What would you advise?"

"Have one company of angels hold the weather and the rest attack the hordes of darkness surrounding Kazan."

"I don't mean to sound rude," Mitch paused. "But what would that accomplish?"

"Fewer deaths on the battlefield," Monica replied.

"Will you lose angels?"

"Casualties are a product of war. Whether spiritual or physical. That is war."

"I don't want to lose anyone."

Monica smiled. "No matter what happens, God is in control."

Mitch pondered that for a moment. "Alright. When do you suggest?"

"Immediately."

"Go."

Monica nodded and shot up into a craft shaped like a giant triangle in the front with two swirling circles in the back. All you could see was a rainbow-colored outline. Mitch caught only a glimpse of it before it shot off without a sound.

Moments later, fifty shot up, burnt, hole-filled, and short-winged C-130's quietly appeared on the tarmac. Men ran into the aircraft and began to bring out dead, dismembered, and injured bodies.

The smell of blood, hot metal, burnt wires, sulfur, and rotting flesh filled the air as the screams of injured men and medics barking out instructions broke the silence.

The sight of fresh pools of blood from the burnt and dismembered bodies now littering the tarmac cloaked the troops with a heavy feeling of dread.

Mitch stopped a medic. "Where did these men come from?"

"From an outpost fifty miles east of Kazan. Kazan is a hell hole. We are all that's left of the first infantry. We never saw them coming. Their speed and ferociousness were overwhelming. We had to retreat and set up a temporary medical base when we got hit again. That was when the B-4 bombers began to rain down smoke and ash."

"What do you mean smoke and ash?"

"Bombs that explode so hot they leave nothing but smoke and ash. We thought we were clear when the C-130's showed up because no one survives smoke and ash. But they came like ants. Hordes of them. They took down five C-130's and damaged the rest of them. We were lucky we got out of there in time."

"My goodness, thank you for the heads up. Go rest."

"I want to go back in." The medic said.

Mitch studied the medic for a moment. "Okay," he said finally. "Restock, arm yourself, and get packed up. Then join the second wave of paratroopers and find me."

Mitch wrote an order requesting that the medic join the 82nd airborne special unit medics and signed it. He handed the order to the medic saying, "Welcome to the 82nd airborne. I will see you soon. My name is captain Mitch Walker."

"Thank you, sir, I am private John Edwards."

Mitch shook his hand. "Private, you are either really brave or really stupid. Either way, it is an honor to have you in our family."

The medic thanked him and ran off to prepare.

Mitch yelled, "Everyone up!" and everyone fumbled around but managed to get on their feet. Mitch ordered them into two different C-130's.

22:00 (10:00pm). D-Day.

Operation: Cold Lightning was a go. The C-130's took off. Both sides of the plane were packed with boys and girls about to be baptized by fire, being forced to become men and women in an instant. The C-130's had been modified to travel two times faster and one and a half times farther than older models. Mitch's heart was racing, he closed his eyes and breathed slowly, then began to pray under his breath. It was dark and cold outside, with only a dim red light in the plane. Almost everyone was writing a letter to a loved one.

Jim, sitting next to Mitch, handed his letter to him and said, "Would you please give this to my mom if I die?"

"I will hold it, Mitch said. "But you will give it to your mom yourself. You hear me?"

Jim nodded. Mitch tapped his helmet and nodded back.

02:15

The jumpmaster ordered everyone to stand. With hand gestures, he demonstrated how they were to hook their parachute line to a quarter-inch steel cable just above their heads. The silence was broken by the sounds of clicking.

The jumpmaster gestured to the troops to check their equipment from back to front. He went around inspecting. Two taps on the shoulder meant 'you're ready'. The doors opened five minutes before they jumped.

A deafening sound of wind filled the aircraft, and the sky was suddenly filled with exploding black clouds from flack guns and tracer rounds trying to shoot the plane down. The plane swayed from side to side and up and down, trying to dodge everything. The sounds of bullets tearing through the plane unsettled the men.

A massive explosion set their ears ringing, and it was quickly followed by the smell of sulfur. A more ferocious wind rushed through the plane. The C-130 began to pitch down and Benjamin, standing behind Mitch, unclipped himself from the quarter-inch line and ran to the cockpit. He unbuckled a motionless pilot and leveled the plane.

At the same time, a stray bullet hit the jumpmaster, killing him instantly. His limp body was sucked out of the open door. Mitch unclipped himself and ran to the front. He clipped himself to a pipe on the door and looked out.

Then he nodded, flicked the light green, and yelled "GO, GO, GO!"

Soldier after soldier began to run off the plane, jumping. When the last man had left, Mitch yelled at Benjamin. "Benjamin let's go!".

Another flack hit the plane and rocked Mitch off his feet.

Benjamin turned and looked at his captain.

Mitch saw that only half of Benjamin's helmet remained. The rest of his head had been blown off. Mitched looked for something to grab on to. "No!"

Benjamin rolled the plane and Mitch shot out of the plane door. A few eternal seconds later, he felt a jerk as his parachute opened. The world had not yet righted itself and he was hurtling through thin air, but at that moment, he could see the plane he had just been in.

It was now belly up and going into a nosedive with Benjamin still in it. The plane dived into the muzzle flash of a flack gun and was obliterated. Mitch looked around him and saw planes going down like flies. Some planes had giant gashes in their sides as if someone had slashed them with a sword.

Paratroopers were being pelted by tracer rounds and soldiers were plummeting all around him. Mitch was breathing heavily.

As he approached the ground, trees began to rush up at him. He managed to avoid them, then he hit the ground.

The sound of bullets whizzing past his head alerted him to a greater chorus of constant gunfire and explosions. It was the dead of the night and the only lights Mitch could see were the flashes of muzzles and grenades going off.

Another bullet whizzed past his head. Bullets were coming and going in all directions. Mitch ducked behind a tree. He closed his eyes for a moment and suddenly there was the screech of tank tracks and the giant creak and snap of trees breaking. When Mitch looked around his tree, he saw that there was a tank headed his way. He jumped out of cover and ran but tripped over the branch of a fallen tree. The tank turned towards him.

A man jumped out of a tree and onto the tank. He pulled the pin out of a grenade and threw it down the barrel of the tank, then lept off as fast as he had jumped on.

The tank exploded and swerved away from Mitch. Calm, and with no regard for the battle raging around him, the man reached down and helped Mitch to his feet. Then he disappeared into the dark without a word. A small still voice from within Mitch said to him: Move west and take the city.

Mitch checked his snow-covered compass, found west, found a few men, and told them to go west. "Pass it on!" He said. In a matter of minutes, all the gunfire was targeted in one direction. The troop shot flares to the west to expose the hidden city and a line of fox holes, and Mitch ordered the men to move forward. The men rushed into the fox holes and finally established a definitive area just outside the city. As the troops got into the fox holes, the gunfire stopped. They had been fighting for half an hour.

Mitch turned to the man beside him and saw that he was a scrawny kid. "I need you to do something for me, okay?" The kid seemed lost and confused. Mitch grabbed the kid by his bag straps and shook him. "Hey! Look at me."

The kid snapped out of it and focused on Mitch. "Yes sir."

"I need you to go from fox hole to fox hole, quietly. And see how many men we still have. Tell them we move in thirty. Can you do this for me?"

The kid nodded rapidly. "Yes. I can."

"Okay, go."

The kid rolled out of the foxhole and ran off into the dark. Mitch heard screams of pain and calls for a medic. Mitch yelled "Radio!"

Another man next to him said, "I saw him get shot when we landed."

Mitch turned to him. "What's your name son?"

The man was shaking. "Private First Class Jeremy Campbell."

Mitch stretched a hand out to him. "I'm Captain Mitch Walker. It's a pleasure to meet you."

"You too captain."

"Could you do me a favor and see how many men we have in this foxhole with us?"

"Okay." Two minutes later, Jeremy was back. "Captain."

"Yes?"

"We have five in our foxhole but seven next to us and another four next to them."

"Thank you private."

Five minutes before the attack, the skinny boy came sliding back into Mitch's foxhole. He was stuttering and shaking violently. "There are t-t-t-"

Mitch put his hands on the boy's shoulders. "Breathe. Calm down." The boy took a few fast, deep breaths. Mitch said, "Slow down." The boy slowed down his breathing. "Now, what is your report?"

"We have two hundred and seventy men ready to fight. I can't say how many we lost or were injured."

"That's alright. What's your name?"

"I'm Isaac Balsam."

"It's nice to meet you, Isaac. I'm Captain Mitch Walker. Find me after the battle."

Isaac nodded, and Mitch shot a flare into the air, signaling the troops to charge. His men rushed out of their foxholes.

The troop caught the Russians by surprise in the South East as they came up from Usady. There was little to no fighting, but in the north, troops coming down from Poselok had to fight for every inch. Mitch took Privolzhskiy with a hundred and twenty men. They were on the south side of the city leading to Vakhitovshiy. Mitch kept hearing heavy gunfire to the North.

"Isaac and Jeremy!" Mitch called.

Isaac and Jeremy ran to Mitch. "Yes sir."

"I am taking twenty men north, you two work together and take these vital targets in the south." Mitch pulled out a map with pictures. "Take these locations and meet me here." He pointed to a spot in the center of the city. "Understood?"

"Yes sir."

Mitch gathered his troops together. "I need 20 volunteers to help free the north." Ten men and five women stepped up. "We have no time. You fifteen, on me. The rest of you listen to Private Jeremy Campbell and Lieutenant Isaac Balsam. Understood?"

"Yes sir."

"Move. We have less than an hour."

Mitch and his fifteen volunteers moved north behind the enemy as they rained lead down on his troops. They snuck behind enemy lines and found two movable artillery units on a race track. They caught the men off guard and cleared the area without losing a single person. The ambush took fifteen minutes.

"Does anyone know how to use these?" Mitch asked.

Two men stepped forward. "Yes sir."

"How many men do you need?"

They smiled and spoke at the same time. "Three."

"I'm leaving four with you. Turn these guns on the enemy and wait for my signal."

"Yes sir."

"Good. The rest of you come with me, we have to save our men."

Mitch and the remaining nine found a trench system with explosive stock.

A female soldier walked up to it with a grin.

"You know how to use this?" Mitch asked.

"Oh yeah," the woman said.

"How long do you need?"

"Two minutes," she said.

"You have one."

She grabbed as many explosives as she could and began to set them up.

"We are going to walk to the top side of the trench and plant these explosives without being detected. Understand?"

The troop moved to do as Mitch had asked. They managed to cover a mile between the jam-packed troops in the trench. Then they headed back a safe distance and hit the trigger, burning and killing hundreds. The radios finally began to work and Mitch received a mess of gunfire and screaming men in his ear.

Mitch spoke into his radio. "This is Captain Mitch. We cleared an area at five, five, point, eight, zero, four, four, three, eight by four, niner, point, two, three, six, seven, three, five. All troops move in. Do you copy?"

There was a static mess of "Yes sir!"

One voice called for help. "We need backup at five, five, point, eight, one, two, niner, niner, one by four, niner, point, two, three, seven, four, five, eight."

"Artillery did you catch that?" Mitch asked. "Yes," a voice said. "Aim five, five, point, eight, one, zero, five, three, niner by four, niner, point, two, three, three, seven, four, zero." Mitch instructed. "Copy?"

"Copy."

Shells rained on the area and they heard cheering from the radio. "Good hit!" someone said.

"Come toward our location," Mitch said. There is a blue building where I and a few troops will meet you."

"Ten-four," a voice responded.

Mitch told the nine to move out. He and his men reached the dark blue doors and one of the men opened them quietly, then stood guard outside.

Mitch heard some rustling in the building and yelled "82nd Airborne!" One man yelled back "All the way!"

Mitch entered and saw about twenty-five men in US Airborne uniforms pointing their weapons at the door.

"I am Captain Mitch Walker."

The men lowered their weapons and one man came forward. When the soldier removed his helmet, Mitch saw that it was Leroy grinning at him. He reached out and grabbed Mitch's hand. "It's good to see you."

Mitch shook his hand. "It's good you see you too, Leroy."

"You saved our skins back there, thank you."

Mitch smiled and said, "You're welcome. Come on now, our new headquarters are not too far but we still have to fight." Leroy put his helmet back on.

"Travel by fives!" Mitch ordered. "But not too close to each other. Close enough that you have a chance if we encounter a counter-ambush. Understood?" The men nodded.

"Good. I'm going to need my nine to get ready for hell. The rest of you hit the opening. When when you reach the trench, head north. We will catch the enemy in a crossfire. Don't let up. We will do this for as long as we have to. Understood?" His men nodded again.

Mitch put his hand on Leroy. "I'm putting you in charge. Can you handle it?"

Leroy grabbed Mitch's hand. "Oh yeah."

"Okay. We go first. The rest of you follow Leroy's lead."

Mitch peeked out to make sure it was clear. The extra soldier was still standing guard. Mitch and his nine began to creep across a mile-long open field. There were dead bodies everywhere, and craters formed by artillery that had been aimed at the first infantry. The heavy silence was occasionally interrupted by a few pops in the distance. It was the dead of the night. Mitch ordered his men to split into three groups and get into the snow. "Pop your head out, pop three shots, get back down, and move slowly to another location to do it again. Understood?"

"Yes sir," the troop whispered.

"Move out!" Mitch said. He took a man and a woman with him and planted himself in the snow.

Then he aimed.

CHAPTER 9

The café. Just past mid-day.

Air raid sirens begin to blare and the ISA troops look around them frantically.

Basheer asks, "What's going on?"

"Your people are going to bomb us with you in the middle as a point of reference," Taavet replies.

"What?"

"Protocol seven, two, one, eight, niner dash zero, one states that if a Basheer has not checked in within four hours, HQ will send a question. If Basheer does not respond, they will try one more time, and if there is still no response, a distress beacon will be activated by a flashing green light like the one on your shoulder right now. This distress call will send bombers to drop fire and ash on your location. The intelligence you have on the back of your vest must be preserved. Have I left anything out?"

Basheer gawks. "How do you know so much?"

"I can answer that now and we all die by the planes that are on their way here as we speak, or you can give me the intelligence and my friend here will take you to our air-raid bunker."

Taavet stretches out a hand and Basheer ponders the wisdom of giving him the intel, but the sound of approaching planes breaks him. "There is no way to see it without me."

"Then there are no worries," Taavet replied.

Basheer reaches behind him and into his vest. He pulls out two thin, rectangular, metal rods and hands them over to Taavet. But when Taavet grabs one end of the rods, Basheer keeps a firm grip on them and asks, "How do I know you're not going to kill me?"

Taavet looks at him with an incredulous look on his face. "What movie did you get that from?" Then he yanks the intelligence out of Basheer's hands and leans back in his chair. He pulls and the sticks slide apart to reveal a translucent screen. Random words dart here and there across the screen and Taavet puts on his glasses to start reading. He goes "Hmm", looks up, sees Basheer still sitting.

"You can go now. Dozer, show them the way."

Basheer stands and stares at Taavet as he walks away. Taavet mutters under his breath. "I didn't know they knew this. Oh well."

As Basheer and his troop leave the café, the waitress sits in front of Taavet. An older woman approaches. She has a round face and a protruding jaw. Her hair is well taken care of; combed and swept neatly to the left. A big scar stretches from her ear to the backside of her jawline. Her eyes seem Middle Eastern but she does not have a tan.

Taavet looks up at her. "Call in the air defense and prepare the disrupter and the fire dome."

The older woman grabs Taavet by the shirt, pulls him close, and kisses him. "Consider it done."

Then she smiles and begins to walk away. When Taavet taps her butt, she looks back and tosses him a wink.

When the woman is gone, the waitress speaks. "That is both cute and disturbing, Taavet."

Taavet smiles. "Well, when you get to my age, this is one of the reasons you fight. Now, have you learned anything?"

"Yes."

"What have you learned?"

"No matter how many men you kill, they keep coming." The waitress giggles.

Taavet rolls his eyes. "That is not why I brought you here, what would your father say?"

"I think he would laugh."

"You are probably right, but what I need you to know is that when you walk, you see more than when you run."

"But running gets you there faster."

"And gets you killed faster too. Be patient. It is almost time for you to continue what your father started."

The waitress drops her head and tears fill her eyes. Taavet sends her off. An hour goes by and Taavet is still sitting at the table reading intel when he hears airplanes crash. Ten minutes pass and a voice broadcasts over the city-wide PA system. "All clear."

A few moments later, Basheer and his troop walk in and surround the cafe as before. Basheer sits across from Taavet and pulls the intel down.

"Tell me how you know so much?" Basheer asks.

"I used to be you." Taavet replies. "I will explain at the end."

A young soldier takes off his mask. He is twelve years old, with blonde hair, blue eyes, and a large hero nose. He looks like he has not seen a day of battle.

"What did Mitch see before he pulled the trigger?" The boy asks.

Taavet smiles but Basheer snaps, "Boy shut your mouth."

"It's alright," Taavet says.

Then Taavet looks at the boy and whispers loudly. "You can ask any question you like."

Kazan. Half an hour before the ice storm.

Mitch aimed and was just about to pull the trigger when he saw a black cloud like a shadow coming from the north. The black cloud filled his line of sight.

"Hold your fire," he called out.

Mitch listened. Suddenly there were screams of terror and gunfire erupting from the trench. The smell of burning plastic and gun powder filled the air and the temperature began to drop. Monica showed up next to Mitch, but there were no footprints in the snow.

"Tell your men to fall back to artillery. Call the nine and follow me. Quickly. Make a diamond."

The nine made their way to Mitch. "Get on one knee in diamond formation and wait for a retreat," Mitch ordered, then he spoke into the radio. "Leroy, fall back to artillery."

"Ten-four," Leroy replied.

A woman asked, "What direction are we going?" and Mitch pointed with his hand at the trench. The woman nodded. "Well, we haven't died yet so I'm in," she said.

Twelve angels streamed down from the sky in a beam of light and surrounded the nine in diamond formation.

"Move," Monica said.

"Move it," Mitch told the nine.

Mitch followed Monica into the cloud that led to the trench.

He ordered his men to stay together, for they could not see up to four feet ahead of them. They grabbed each other's backpacks with one hand and aimed their rifles with the other, constantly scanning as they walk through the black cloud. When they came out of the other side, Mitch and the nine saw a few Russian soldiers running. One of the nine opened fire but Mitch yelled "Hold your fire! They are retreating, save your ammo." The man put down his weapon. "Our objective here is to make it to the artillery and clear the stable or school next to it, understood?"

The nine responded, "Yes sir."

Mitch spoke into the radio. "Leroy, make your way to artillery. Make sure the stables on the way there are clear. Start in the far south in Codename: Coliseum and then hit the stables. The nine and I will start in the south. Copy?"

"Copy."

Mitch reached the overgrown metal brown gate surrounding the target area and noticed razor wire hidden in the bushes.

One of the nine said, "Cover me and I'll take care of the razor wire."

Mitch nodded and they hide in the bushes as the man pulled out bolt cutters and began to cut a path. When he had cut the last of the wire, he took off. Mitch yelled "FREEZE!" The man froze. "Don't move," Mitch ordered. "There is a mine right in front of you." The man stepped back. Mitch called out to him, "Follow me exactly, but don't get too close."

Mitch navigated through the minefield, closely followed by the nine. Then he found a hole in the barred fence and sent the nine through. When they entered, they found a training camp. Mitch's heart began to race and his breathing became slightly difficult. "Expect a fight," he said.

They marked out a small, light brown building with a dark brown roof and took positions. Mitch spotted two guards sitting by a fire in a barrel. He moved in with another man and signaled for the man to take the guard on the right. The man snuck around behind the guard and pulled his knife out. They each grabbed a guard at the same time and plunged their knives into the back of their necks where the skull meets the spine.

They dragged the bodies into the building and the nine moved in to regroup.

"Two of you take their place as if you were the original guards." Two men nodded and walked outside to sit where the guards had been sitting. They positioned themselves so the fire could cast a shadow on their faces. Mitch and the seven aimed down their sights and began to walk back into the dark. Mitch bumped into something that rattled. He reached out and felt a metal gridded gate, so he lowered his weapon and grabbed his flashlight. Then he put his hand over the bulb and turned the flashlight on slowly. Diffused light showed that they had stumbled onto an under guarded weapons depot.

"Check the guards to see if there's a key," Mitch said.

Two of the seven checked and found a key hanging on an identification card. "Here," one said. Mitch reached out. "Pass it here."

The woman passed the key and Mitch put it into the keyhole.

One of the men asked, "Why are you doing everything?"

"I don't want anyone to die because of me," Mitch replied.

"You can't keep putting yourself in danger like this. You're our leader."

The man took off his helmet and so did the rest of the seven. They were all Special Unit recruits; Terra, Joseph (the one that had been speaking), Jack and Jill (aka the twins), Tom, Alex, and Sheron. Their ages ranged from fourteen to sixteen.

"We were trained for this," Joseph said. "Let go of your fear, isn't that what you taught us?"

"You're right, Mitch said. "Go ahead and open the door."

"No it's okay, you already started."

Mitch laughed. "Where's your courage?" He finished turning the key and unlocked the cage door. Nothing happened. As he opened the door, however, the men outside began shooting and rushed into the building.

"What happened?" Mitch asked.

"There was a patrol passing by," one of the men said. "When the lights went off we managed to take out four but the fifth got away."

"What lights?"

"I don't know, a red light just started spinning and five men rushed our way, so we shot at them."

"Terra," Mitch called.

"Yes sir?"

"You're the explosive expert?"

"Yes sir."

"I need you to set up a plastic explosive in the center of the room. Jack and Jill will cover the door, the rest of you restock your ammo, and put the rest put on top of the plastic explosive so we can make a big boom."

"Yes sir."

They put their helmets back on and began to stack 7.62 rounds and grenades in the center of the room on top of the explosives. A hail of bullets began to rain down on Mitch's position.

Mitch yelled into the radio. "I need back-up at my position!" There was no response. As he returned fire, Mitch asked, "Do we have smoke bombs?"

"I do."

"How many?"

"Enough to kill the Pope."

"What?"

"Enough to make more smoke than a chain smoker."

"Can anyone translate?" Everyone shrugged their shoulders and Mitch said, "Just give me everything you have."

Tom gave Mitch ten smoke bombs and Mitch pulled two pins. Then he threw the bombs out the door and extremely thick smoke began to billow. Mitch yelled, "Head to the big building to the south!"

"What? That's where they are coming from!" One soldier shouted.

"Exactly! Pass it and get into the long building behind it, I'll keep smoking the area. When we're in, Terra, you know what to do."

"Oh yeah," Terra said.

"Move it!"

The nine rushed out, guns blazing. They ran through the door dodging bullets. Tom's helmet got hit. He stumbled but kept running. Jack got hit in the leg and his body armor stopped the bullet but the impact shattered his knee. Adrenaline kept him from feeling a thing. Mitch was struck in the shoulder but shot in the direction of the soldier that had shot him and kept moving. As they reached the big building, Mitch and the nine hugged the east wall. Joseph caught Mitch's attention and pointed up. There was an open window.

"Terra, do you have another bomb?" Mitch asked,

"Duh," she replied.

"Okay. Jason."

"Yes sir."

"Get on my shoulders and gently put the bomb in the window."

"Yes sir, one question sir."

"Yes?"

"How did you know it was me?"

"A good question for another time. Now come on."

Mitch leaned against the wall and put one foot on it. Jason, a tall, skinny man, climbed Mitch by putting his foot on Mitch's lap and lifting himself. Then he put his other foot on Mitch's shoulder, placed the bomb on the windowsill, and climbed back down. Mitch and his nine finally made it to the target building. When the last of the nine had stepped into the building, Terra hit the trigger and obliterated the brown building. The outdoor training area and all the windows within a quarter-mile were blown out. The explosion was so bright, it was as though someone had turned on a light then dimmed it down slowly.

Mitch, with his ears still ringing from the blast, heard someone ask "What was that?" on the radio.

Mitch shook his head to try to get the ringing out of his ear. "That was us," he said into the radio. "We need all available backup to clear buildings on the eastside of artillery. Do you copy?"

After a moment, a voice on the radio said, "Good copy."

"Leroy, what is your progress?" Mitch asked.

Leroy's voice came over the radio., "Not having as much fun as you, but we've already cleared the coliseum, the stables, and five hospital buildings to the south. We are close to your location."

"Good work. Leroy, regroup with the backup in the center-west building and clear that building, then press your attack on the remaining buildings. We are in the northwest building. We will clear and barricade until you are done and then wait for further instructions."

"Ten-four," Leroy responded.

Mitch and the nine moved through a long and dimly lit hallway full of doors. Mitch and the nine went door to door and found nothing except inventions and science experiments covered with dust. When Mitch and the nine reached the last door, the Holy Ghost told Mitch, Don't open that door.

Mitch threw his hand up hand in a fist and the nine stopped in their tracks.

Mitch began to speak Russian., "I know you are in there and have booby-trapped the door. I know you are a scared scientist. We are not here to kill you; we just need a place to stay for the night."

The muffled sound of a man's voice came through the door. "Who are you?"

"My name is Captain Mitch Walker."

"As in James Walker's son?"

Mitch was startled. "You knew my father?"

"I know him."

"He died when I was a child."

The voice moved closer. "What are you talking about? I just saw him last month."

Mitch shook his head. "That's not possible."

"Give us a second and we will open the door."

Mitch spoke in English to the nine. "Take your helmets off and keep your weapons down. I need one man in that room," Mitch pointed to a room at an angle from the booby-trapped room. "But keep your weapon pointed, just in case."

Moments later, the door cracked open and a clean-shaven, brown-haired man with blue eyes, a long face, and a medium pointed nose peeked out. The man locked eyes with Mitch and said, "You look like your father."

"Thank you," Mitch said. "What do you mean you saw my father a month ago?"

"He-he put us here to hide and continue our research."

"What research?"

"A hidden city in the trees."

Mitch's eyes grew big. "Your secret is safe with us. How many of you are there?"

"There are sixteen of us."

"May we stay the night?"

"As long as you take us with you. We have our own place and a mobile lab."

"I can't guarantee your safety," Mitch said.

"But we can," the man replied.

Mitch thought about it for a minute. "Deal," he said. "By the way, do you have a medic?"

"Yes, why?" The man spotted a trail of blood and switched to English with a polished British accent. "Is anyone else injured?"

The eight looked at him in shock. Mitch felt he recognized that voice. "Come in, all ten of you."

Joseph came out of the room he had been hiding in and they shook hands. The room was empty, but the scientist raised his arm as if grabbing something in the air. There didn't seem to be anything there. "Welcome to the future," he said. A cloaking wall moved and an entire lab appeared. A synthetic crystal was sitting on one of the tables. It seemed to emit a bright white light.

Mitch walked toward it and the man said, "We call it Lumite. It is a non-electric light source as strong as diamonds with a weight of a gram per square foot. It can withstand extreme pressures and can be mass-produced with just the dirt you walked in here with. We are also working on a cloaking device made of millions of pinhead cameras that will hopefully be able to cloak an entire city. When our government heard about it, they wanted our technology. So two men took our prototypes to the government, but after they had found out how it was made, they killed the scientist and came after us. Your father found us and moved us from place to place until we ended up here."

"Can it be used for an individual?"

The scientist snapped his fingers and a man appeared out of nowhere, frightening the nine badly.

"That was amazing," Mitch said. Can you make weapons?"

"No, we defend. We do not attack," the scientist replied.

"Okay," Mitch said. Then he got on the radio. "Leroy."

He heard an echo of his voice.

Mitch turned. "What is that?" he asked.

"We can hear everybody," the scientist replied.

The radio squawked. "Sir," Leroy said.

"Set up camp in the buildings, but not all in one building."

"Yes sir."

"Artillery," Mitch called into the radio.

Artillery responded. "Sir."

"Are you able to move the guns?"

"Yes."

"Move them to the coliseum and rest. Tomorrow, we finish taking the city."

"Ten-four."

Mitch and his fifteen regrouped. Leroy joined them at the hidden lab and Isaac came in from the western front to debrief them of everything that had happened. Mitch ordered everyone to stay put and stay alert.

CHAPTER 10

Kazan. Daybreak.

The hidden lab was dark and warm, not a sound could be heard. Green strip lines ran along a white wall, and Mitch tossed and turned, trying to find sleep.

A nine-foot angel dressed in a white cloak and red armor appeared. Without a word, the angel reached down to touch Mitch. Mitch had become paralyzed the moment the angel appeared. The angel's hand moved closer to Mitch's face and Mitch began to breathe rapidly. He could only move his eyes. Monica appeared and grabbed the angel, her loose hair flowing. The angel struggled frantically to break free of Monica's grip. It screeched. The sound was unpleasant. Monica threw the angel on its head and knocked it out cold, then Monica wrapped golden chains around it. Mitch was released from his paralysis and he sat up quickly. Monica threw the angel through the wall.

"Are you okay?"

"What was that?"

"That was a Hypoxide Reaper. You're blessed I showed up in time. If he had touched you, you'd be dead."

"What is a Hypoxide Reaper?"

"Fallen angels"

"Where did they come from?"

"In Lucifer's time, he was in charge of protecting God's creation. He convinced some highly ranked guardian angels to swarm God's footstool, the earth, and destroy the very thing they were supposed to guard. Lucifer let them play with God's creation, but when God found out, He stripped them of their rank and cast them to the center of the earth with Lucifer. Eventually, the son of perdition convinced Adam to give Lucifer the keys. Lucifer released all of his followers and renamed the guardians Hypoxide Reapers. Then, he promoted them above all principalities, powers, and dominions in high places. They fill the air around living creatures with carbon monoxide out of the palms of their hands, stealing the last breath of any living thing. And they hate the human race most of all of God's creations.

When Jesus died at the cross, he went to the center of the earth and was able to win over all of Lucifer's followers. Then he confronted Lucifer, making Lucifer give up the keys. After that, Lucifer banished all the Hypoxide Reapers from his kingdoms. The Hypoxide Reapers created their own kingdoms and made themselves gods and kings. Now they war against each other and us. They rule the air and kill all without mercy. They can even take the life of angels and cherubims."

"Why doesn't God kill them?"

"First, because death is too easy. That is the purpose of the lake of fire, to make them suffer as they have made all of God's creation suffer out of their jealousy. Two, they have a court date to be judged, and earth, the place they used to guard, is now their prison until that day comes. They will attempt to take as many people with them as possible. The Egyptian gods are Hypoxide Reapers, as are the Roman gods, the Greek gods, and every other god you can think of. Jehovah is the only living God."

Monica reached down and touched Mitch's shoulder on the spot where Mitch had been shot. A glow came out of her hand and when she removed her hand, the bloody injury was completely healed. "This Hypoxide Reaper was the last one in the cities. Rest and finish taking the city tomorrow."

"How many did you lose?"

Monica's face fell. "Two legions."

Mitch swallowed. "I'm sorry," he said.

Monica nodded. "They were some of the best I had, but they knew what they were getting into." Monica began to walk away, but Mitch put a hand on her shoulder and hugged her. Monica hugged him back and Mitch whispered a thank you in her ear. She looked over her shoulder once before she walked through the wall.

Mitch stood and tried to feel his way through the dimly lit lab, peering at all the inventions.

"How are you planning on taking all of this with you?" He asked.

The scientist came up behind him. "We are actually in a mobile room; our team has developed a multi-directional drill. We will drill to the water layer of the earth. From there the lab will travel safely, undetected, using low-frequency sonar that will allow us navigate, but will not set off any tremors or audible sound that can be picked up by any of our adversary's equipment. Our sonar will also help us navigate through the waters.

"Fascinating," Mitch said. "Well if you are coming with us may I know your name?"

"My name is Demsi No Vigavitch, but you can call me Demsi."

Flashback

It was a hot day with no breeze and the Walker house was still just at its foundation. The land was overgrown, and a young Mitch was running through the long grass. There were glimpses of his spiky hair as he blazed a trail through the grass.

James was hammering plywood into the floor, and Sarah was cooking in an old fifth wheel with the two RV doors open. The smell of grass, eastern red cedar, and sweat filled the air.

A red Ford expedition pulled up to a tiny clearing around the Walker's RV and a brown-haired, blue-eyed man stepped out wearing a long-sleeved button-up shirt in green plaid. Sarah walked out of the RV and greeted him. "Hello, pastor."

"Hi Sarah," the man said in a thick, old English accent. "Does your husband need any help?"

"Always, but you know him. He never asks".

Mitch came running out of the long grass, barefoot and in diapers.

The pastor dropped to one knee and asked, "How is this little world changer doing?"

"After your prayers, he's great. Thank you so much for that pastor."

The pastor straightened up. "Anytime Sarah. It's a part of the job. And I've asked you to call me Demsi."

Kazan

Mitch spun to look at the scientist. "Pastor Vigavitch?"

Demsi chuckled. "I have not been called that in years. I thought you would not remember me because you were so young."

"I remember the day you came to help my father lay the floor of our house."

"Yes, that was the last time I saw you and your family. How is your mother?"

Mitch looked down at the ground. "She died defending a man we didn't know."

"I'm so sorry, Mitch."

"Yeah, me too." Tears filled Mitch's eyes. "She died in my arms and there was nothing I could do about it."

The scientist put a hand on Mitch's arm. "I can't even imagine what you're going through right now. It's hard to lose someone, and so much harder when it's a family member. I'm here if you need to talk."

Mitch straightened and cleared his throat. "Thank you Pastor Demsi."

Demsi held up his hand. "Please, it's Demsi."

"Do you have a long-range radio?" Mitch asked.

Demsi gestured. "Right this way."

He led Mitch to a state-of-the-art radio with embossed blue numbers that popped out and away from the body of the radio. It had a knob for changing the frequency.

Mitch adjusted the frequency and began to broadcast. "Headquarters, this is Alpha company do you read?" There were few moments of silence and Mitch asked again. "Headquarters, this is Alpha company, do you read?" There were a few more moments of silence.

"Alpha company, this is HQ. What is your name and code?"

"Captain Mitch Walker Alpha, bravo, one, niner, eight, two, three. Do you copy?"

"Good copy. We thought you were dead."

"Not yet." Mitch said.

"Please debrief."

"We have taken the entire east side of Kazan but had to take cover at five, five, point, seven, niner, one, niner, five, six by four, niner, point, two, zero, one, four, seven, three, due to the weather. We are running low on ammo, and we don't know our casualties yet, but we need reinforcements."

"We cannot send reinforcements right now due to the failed mission in Moscow."

"Moscow was a failure?"

"Affirmative."

"So you're telling me that we are surrounded with no reinforcements. What do you expect us to do?"

"Hold the city until we can send reinforcements."

"Hold the city with what? Three hundred people and empty weapons?"

"We will send a care package."

"I need men with that."

"That's all we can do, take it or leave it. We will drop it at five, five, point, eight, five, three, four, seven, six by four, niner, point, zero, niner, three, four, seven, zero."

"That position is in the middle of the enemy's current base."

"Well, I suggest you clear the LZ."

"Are you out of your mind or trying to get us all killed?" Suddenly, all Mitch could hear was static. "HQ... HQ!" No response. He threw the headset away in anger and rubbed his temples.

"I presume they are not coming?"

Mitch shook his head. "I need fresh air."

He walked out the back door of the secret lab. It led outside. There, he began to cry and pray. The sun broke free from a snow-filled horizon. When he lifted his eyes Mitch saw a glare of light from the northwest. He grabbed a pair of binoculars and saw a terrifying battalion of one hundred and twenty tanks and a sea of men marching toward them. He yelled into the radio. "We are under attack! Defense positions. To the roofs!"

Leroy appeared right next to Mitch, startling him. "What do you want me to do sir?"

Mitch put his hand on his chest. "Are you trying to give me a heart attack?"

Leroy laughed as Mitch took deep breaths.

"Grab a group of men," he ordered. "Check the south. If there's nothing there, come back and join the fight."

Leroy gave an exuberant salute and ran off.

"Isaac," Mitch said into the radio.

"Yes sir?"

"As they attack, take the west side of the city. Find big guns and turn them on the enemy. Then get our care package at five, five, point, eight, five, three, four, seven, six by four, niner, point, zero, niner, three, four, seven, zero. Understood?"

"Yes sir."

Over the radio, Leroy spoke. "Captain, we can't start a fight until we have battle music." Leroy began to play Thunderstruck by AC-DC over loudspeakers. Mitch chuckled, shook his head, and called "Battle stations!"

Leroy growled over the radio; "Yeah…. Thunderstruck."

Mitch was laughing now. "Leroy, get off the radio."

Leroy put on a Mexican accent. "Jess sir."

Mitch shook his head again and took a moment to compose himself. He spoke into the radio; "Artillery, how long do you need to set up?"

Static, then, "Fifteen minutes."

"Make it ten."

"Yes sir," the radio crackled.

"How much ammo do we have?"

"Fifty high explosive shells, twenty armor-piercing, and ten anti-personnel."

Mitch drew his hand down over his face. "That's not enough," he mumbled. He paused for a moment and then said, "Hold your fire until you have a clean shot."

"Yes sir."

To everyone around him, Mitch said, "Hold your fire until you get a clear shot. We don't have much ammo, but we can still rain down lead."

A cheer went up as the Russians began their charge.

Mitch yelled, "Hold!" The troops were antsy but they held.

Leroy made it back and said, "There is no one to our South, but I left five scouts."

Mitch nodded and held his hand up as the Russians opened fire. "Hold!" he said. Bullets and tank rounds flew over their heads. When the enemy was within seventy-five yards, Mitch dropped his hand and yelled, "Fire!"

The troop began to rain lead on the Russians, dropping them like flies.

Mitch spoke into the radio. "Artillery, unleash the beast. Halt the backside of the charge."

Leroy was playing another song on the loudspeakers but it was drowned out by the gunfire from both sides. Minutes began to feel like hours as wave after wave of Russian troops rushed the building. Mitch and his two hundred stood firm, cutting them down one after the other. An hour later, the artillery went silent. "Artillery, what's going on?" he asked.

The radio crackled. "We are out of ammo sir!"

"Fall back and find help."

"I'm sorry sir, but we are not leaving." Mitch could hear that nothing would change that decision.

"Fine, check the south."

"Yes sir."

Mitch turned to Leroy. "We have no more artillery." Bullets were flying overhead. Tank shells were landing all around and deafening explosions came one after another.

Leroy smiled. "That's good. That means more fun for us." Mitch saw a medic sitting against a wall and asked, "Hey, are you okay?"

"I'm just taking a breather," the medic said.

"How many have we lost?" Mitch asked.

"Ten. Forty injured."

"Take that breather."

The gunfire from Mitch's troop began to dwindle for lack of ammo. Everyone knew there were still Russians beyond the tree line. A thick cloud of fear grew over Mitch and his troops as they realized they could be overwhelmed at any time. The Russians soon worked out that their ammo supply was depleted. Encouraged by the American's misfortune, a fresh wave of Russian soldiers surged forward. They quickly closed the gap between themselves and Mitch's two hundred, inching their way closer. The stack of dead Russian bodies and burning tanks slowed the advance. The American troops sat and waited for their demise. They talked amongst themselves about what the rumors said Russians did to their prisoners.

When the Russians had come within twenty-five yards of the Americans, a group of painted and masked men darted out from behind the troop, jumping from roof to roof and between buildings, eerily silent. Each masked man had a weird contraption on his legs that made him move faster, jump higher, and seem taller. The mystery troop met the Russians head to head. The masked men were abnormally fast, and as the Americans looked on, they made light work of the Russians with guns, knives, and swords.

One masked man walked up to Mitch and spoke in a southern American accent. "Good job holding them off. Now the Calvary has arrived." He grabbed Mitch's hand, shook it, turned around, and whooped, then jumped right back into the fray.

Mitch grabbed the radio headset. "Isaac what is your sit rep?"

"We found the heavy guns, but the Russians destroyed them and have retreated. They're heading into Moscow. No resistance in the West, we have the city."

Mitch got on his knees and bowed his head, saying "Thank you, Jesus," over and over again. After a few moments, he turned his head to Leroy and asked, "Who are they?"

"I don't know," Leroy said. "But they have the Russians on the run and I'm not complaining."

Demsi, who no one had noticed on the roof before now, spoke up. "They are called the Shadows. A force formed by a man named Eli. He felt a need to develop a new style of fighting, to help the innocents of war."

"How do you join them?"

"You don't," Demsi replied. "They choose you. The only way you find out about them is through a Shadow."

"Are you a Shadow?" Mitch asked.

"Shadow Pastor Demsi. I am tasked to defend this lab at all costs."

Mitch's eyes widened. "Would you teach me?"

"I cannot," Demsi replied.

"Why not?"

"Because you still have much to learn about being a leader."

"I don't understand…"

"You will soon," Demsi assured him. "Plus, I already have two students."

"Well is there anyone that can teach me?"

"There is one, but he has never taken a student that I know of."

With a sparkle in his eye, Mitch asked, "Where can I find him?"

Demsi looked at him. "You don't."

Mitch's face fell again. "Why?"

"Because he is never in one place."

"How come?"

"Eli has made enemies on both sides because he chooses to do right, no matter whose side he is on."

"Have you ever met him?" Mitch asked.

"I saw him just once, five years ago. When I was in trouble, he showed up and bailed us out of a pickle."

"What happened?"

"Fifty of us, the best of the Shadows, were sent by Eli to hold a small town surrounded by a forest near Tomsk until the United States arrived. We were under the command of Shadow Evangelist Harmon Glaze - one of the originals trained by Eli. Five hundred soldiers, one hundred

Spetsnaz, and fifty quiet tiger tanks attacked out of nowhere. They employed a new technique called the moving ambush, and in a matter of seconds, they were right on top of us. We had no time to react. Then a single man appeared, out of nowhere, and began to jump from tank to tank, immobilizing them as if they were untrained farmers.

As we watched this man, Shadow Harmon said 'That is the great Eli, my teacher.' We fought with Eli for two days until the army finally took Tomsk."

"So you didn't actually meet Eli?"

"Not personally, no."

"Then how do you know he was Eli?" Mitch asked. "He sounds like a myth or a fantasy to me."

"Myth or not, he saved our lives that day. I thank God every day for Eli. He is a fearless leader."

"Can he teach me?"

"If he chooses you."

"How do you reach him?"

"You don't. Praying he finds you is the only way. Then you must pray that he chooses you. To find a myth, you must become a myth."

"That doesn't even make sense," Mitch said

Demsi chuckled. "This battle is going to be a myth one day. I can see the title: 'The Kid Named Mitch Who Took The City In Two Days'. Mark my words."

Mitch smiled. "I did nothing," he said.

Demsi tapped his nose. "That is not the way history will see it." Then he put on a mask, walked into a shadow, and disappeared. Mitch walked in the direction that Demsi had gone, and found that the scientist had truly disappeared. He walked further down and tried to enter the hidden lab but found, to his surprise, that the lab was also gone.

Mitch sat and pondered. He felt a strong need to know more about Eli and the Shadows.

CHAPTER 11

Dearest Nissi,

Our first mission was yesterday. Death was all around, and it was as if hell had been given free rein to unleash its. evil. The night is lit with the lights of burning planes, rockets, flares, and tracer rounds. The snow-covered ground is covered in blood, dismembered bodies, bombs, screaming men, and holes made by enemy shells, but throughout all this chaos all I can think of is the first time I saw you.

You were wearing a blue .dress with white sandals on, and you had twin ponytails with white flowers on the hair ties. You told me they were your favorite hair ties. James Paterson broke them to bully you, but what you didn't know was that day he broke your hair ties, I broke his nose .and got my butt handed to me by his gang. I kept fighting because you needed help and I wanted to be your avenger. I had your back even when you were not there.

The memory of that story and prayers have carried me through this battle, helping me survive. I miss you, I am glad you are not here to see this, but I wish I had you waiting for me. I miss the way your hair flowed in the wind as you ran, and I wish I could see you every day instead of letting the years just pass by without your beautiful smile. Without a chance to see us grow. I do not want to let you go, because that is the day I die. This I truly know.

To be yours would be my greatest honor. To see you standing, not as another man's dead daughter, but with your smile bright. To see you glow all through the night...

Now that this letter is at its end there is one more thing that needs to be said. It's been said over and over, but there is nothing else to say, except this overdue, overused saying that I can honestly admit today. I love you, Nissi. I always have and I always will; more than words can express. I must go but I hope I made you smile. I will come home to you even if I must run a million miles.

Yours truly,
Mitch.

Fort Pierce, Florida. Back in the Café. Just past mid-day.

Taavet is holding an old and delicate looking paper. He stares at it, and declares, "This is one of the only surviving papers found from my search of Sitch."

"If his name is Mitch, why did he changed his name to Sitch?" Basheer asks.

"I will get to that part of the story soon." A dark-skinned child with short, black hair runs into the café. Taavet picks up the little boy, sits him on his lap, and smiles. The little boy gestures with his finger for Taavet to come closer. Taavet leans towards the boy and the boy whispers something in Taavet's ear. Taavet looks upset but speaks in a calm voice. "Thank you, run along."

The boy leaves the café skipping. Taavet looks at the puffy-eyed waitress and nods to call her to the table. When he motions to the letter, the waitress stares at it for some time before she reaches out and lays her hand on it. Slowly, she sits down. She says something in an odd language.

"Tara russ abent." A single tear runs down her cheek.

Taavet leans over, puts his arm around her, and responds in the same odd language. "Tara russ abent mar, nar tara ven tu ba ren vas." (I miss him too, but I need you here right now.) The waitress nods and Taavet leans over to whisper something else in her ear. The waitress nods and walks to the back of the café. Taavet yells after her; "And tell them to stop sending children!"

Basheer is studying Taavet. "What did you say to her?"

"You will know soon enough," Taavet replies.

Basheer clenched his fist. "Any news about my son?"

"We have intel that your son escaped his captors - thanks to my troop - and ran into the forest where he called your headquarters to send reinforcement. Your people are now trying to penetrate our front lines because your son told them he found Sitch. I'm not sure if he thought I was Sitch, but his current location does not match up to my intel on Sitch. In other words, your son just ended our ceasefire with a rumor. My men are now escorting him here."

"And when are you going to finally tell me where Sitch is?"

Taavet scratched his beard. "At the end of my story. Now, may I continue?"

Basheer rolled his eyes and slumped backward in his seat. "Proceed."

"Thank you. Now, where was I? Oh yes."

Kazan, Russia. Afternoon.

The sun hovered just above the ash-covered city. The Russians had been defeated, and sounds of celebration filled the air. Men danced, smashed canteens together, and ate their MRE's like barbarians. They sat at one long makeshift table made from school tables they had found. Mitch distanced himself from his troop, dropped to his knees, looked up at the sky, and cried out loud. "Why God!? How can you allow so much death and destruction? Why must we kill to survive? Why have you given me so much responsibility? I'm just a boy!" He dropped his head to the ground and grabbed a hand full of ash-covered snow. Then he rubbed the mess onto his head and rocked back and forth. "What do I do now?" He sobbed quietly.

"Save your people," Demsi said.

Mitch raised his head slowly and saw Demsi sitting on a pile of rubble a few steps away. Without the red apple in his hand, the scientist would have blended into his surroundings completely. He was wearing a black and white snow camouflage jacket with a matching helmet. The apple went up and down with his hand as he bit and chewed.

Mitch sniffed. "What?"

Demsi swallowed. "Your men need you," he said. Not only your men, but others as well. If you lead your troop right, and for the right reasons, many will follow."

"How do I lead?"

Demsi shrugged. "You pray. Because you know your men better than anyone. Follow whatever the Lord leads you to do."

Mitch sat back on his haunches. "The Lord does not care about me."

"If he didn't care, you'd be dead. Furthermore, he would have not given you the city on your first battle."

"That was not God, that was the Shadows."

"The Shadows were not even supposed to be here, but for some miraculous reason, they came right on time. And don't get me started on the Hypoxid Reaper. Yes, I know about that. I call that something only God could have planned."

Mitch squinted at Demsi. "You know about the—"

"The Hypoxid Reaper? Yes. But I'd never seen one until last night."

"How much did you hear?"

"Enough to know not to get involved. See you around sir."

Demsi did a back roll and vanished behind the rubble. Only his half-eaten apple remained. Mitch jumped up and yelled "Wait!" But Demsi was already gone. Mitch stepped toward the pile of rubble and reached out to touch the apple.

"Sir." Mitch jumped and spun around. Leroy stood at attention behind him.

"Yes?"

"The men are going crazy. They're on some kind of feeding frenzy. I think they might have eaten through half of their ration by now."

Mitch nodded wearily. "I'll take care of it. Thank you."

Leroy threw up a salute and ran away. Mitch turned back to the pile of rubble and saw that the apple had also vanished.

Back inside the building, Isaac spotted Mitch and yelled at the top of his lungs. "ATTENTION!" All the men shot up from their chairs and stood at attention. Mitch walked to the front of the room and glared. "What the hell is going on here?! Whose bright idea was it to eat all of our rations tonight?"

Mitch picked one man and squared up to him. The man shrank back. "We got our orders from Jeremy, sir."

Mitch's nostrils flared and he looked around the room. "Where is Jeremy?"

Jeremy stepped forward and looked right at Mitch. "Here, your grace," he said and bent himself over in an exaggerated bow.

Mitch studied him. "Who told you we could spare rations?"

Jeremy swaggered up to Mitch. They stood toe to toe. "The same guy who put you in charge... Oh, wait... No one did."

Mitch leaned forward. "I have nothing to prove to you. But I will say this just once. Take three steps back and sit down."

"Or else wha–"

Leroy and Isaac grabbed the unsuspecting Jeremy by the arms and lifted him.

"What the hell are you doing?!" Jeremy yelled. "I ORDER you to put me down NOW!" He kicked his feet frantically. Isaac and Leroy ignored his high pitched squeals as Leroy kicked a door open. Then they heaved and ho'ed and tossed the underdressed Jeremy outside into the snow. Jeremy, now furious and covered in dirty snow, sat up and turned to scream at Mitch. "What?! You're not man enough to face me one on one?!" Mitch turned his back on him.

Jeremy quickly made a snowball and hurled it at Mitch's head, but Mitch inclined his head at the last minute. The snowball whizzed past and into an upheld hand. Mitch turned, showed Jeremy the dirty snowball, smirked, dropped it, and walked off.

"You better watch your back!" Jeremy called. "You hear me? You better not fall asleep!"

Inside, Mitch turned to Isaac and Leroy. "Thank you," he said.

"We got your back captain," they said in unison.

"What do you want us to do about him?" Leroy asked.

"Nothing," Mitch said. "He's still useful. What I need you to do now is check what rations we still have."

"Will do sir."

To Isaac, Mitch said, "Separate the men who have eaten all of their rations from the ones who have not. Take down the names of those who did not. Number them and report back to me."

"Yes sir."

Mitch went in search of a quiet place again. "Lord what do you want me to do?" he prayed. I will accept whatever you ask of me. Send me, Lord."

A sound broke Mitch out of his meditation. Radio static. Faint, but loud enough to catch his attention. Mitch looked around but saw nothing. He closed his eyes and sought God again. "Lord. What do you want from me?"

The still voice inside of Mitch spoke. Listen.

"To what?" Mitch asked himself.

Listen.

Mitch went still and listened. The faint sound of radio static hissed through the air again. Mitch strained to hear what direction the sound was coming from. "(crackle) Is there anyone out (crackle) we are surround (crackle) we need immediate help (crackle) are fift (crackle) North-east from Masc— (crackle)."

Then there was nothing but endless static.

Mitch lifted his head. "I understand what I must do."

Hours later, Leroy and Isaac found Mitch and handed in their reports. According to Leroy's report, they had three days' worth of rations left if they rationed the food strictly. Isaac reported five hundred and eighty-two healthy men ready to fight, and two hundred that did not touch their rations.

Mitch nodded and thanked them. "Call the fifteen, and Jeremy."

"Yes sir!" Isaac saluted and walked away, but Leroy stayed behind. Mitch turned and faced the setting sun. He was sitting on a giant piece of concrete that had been blown off a nearby building. Leroy walked over to Mitch, put his hand on his left shoulder, and sat next to him. Mitch nodded his head and patted Leroy's hand.

"Captain, I'm sorry."

"What for?" Mitch asked.

"For giving you so much hell in boot camp. For bullying you and making your life a living hell."

"I forgave you immediately." Mitch looked at Leroy and Leroy looked back. "All is well. You're helping now."

Leroy smiled. "Thank you, captain."

Mitch put his arm around Leroy's side and hugged him. "Plus. I needed a little excitement in my life."

Leroy and Mitch laughed and settled down to watch the sunset. Isaac returned a few hours later with the fifteen. Mitch wanted to meet with the others, so he and Leroy stood. Leroy glanced behind him and saw Jeremy. He immediately went into a defensive position.

"You're a traitor." Jeremy said to Leroy.

They exchanged dirty looks and moved their hands toward their guns.

Mitch stepped between them. "There's no need for this hostility! We can't fight a war on two fronts."

"I'm still wondering who put you in charge," Jeremy spat at Mitch.

"I don't care who did or did not," Leroy hissed. "If it wasn't for Mitch, we'd all be dead. And you know it!"

"Jeremy is right." Mitch turned to face Jeremy. "But what I took upon myself I now give to you. You are in charge of defending the city with the three hundred men you fought with. Now go prepare your men."

Jeremy frowned. "Where are you going?"

"Don't worry about me, just worry about your troop."

"Whatever," Jeremy said. He stalked off and walked out of sight.

Mitch addressed the rest of his men. "The reason I have called all of you together is that I am going against orders. I have planned a rescue mission for a trapped squad about fifty miles north-east of Moscow. If you join me, we will probably be court-martialed and executed. But I can't just sit back and watch our fellow men die because our country is too afraid to send reinforcements. If any of you don't want to go through with this, you can leave now. I won't hold it against you. You are still the greatest men and women I know. Whoever wants to join me can step forward now." All fifteen, including Isaac and Leroy, stepped forward. Mitch smiled. "Isaac. Those two hundred men?"

Isaac smiled. "Yeah?"

"Assemble them. We leave at daybreak."

"Yes sir," Isaac said.

Isaac summoned the two hundred that had not eaten their rations and debriefed them. They were ordered to leave half their rations but to carry extra ammo and weapons. In the morning they were going to save lives. Mitch prepared quickly and decided to get some shut-eye. He found a corner, laid his backpack down, and propped it up to use as a pillow. He woke up in the open-air temple.

Jesus, the Holy Spirit, and Monica were standing around a table talking. As Mitch walked toward the table, the three turned and smiled at him. Monica's long, wavy hair was blowing in the wind, and her face was glowing. "It's nice to see you again," she said.

Mitch smiled back and said, "It's nice to see you too Monica." He gave her a long hug, tugged playfully on her hair, and turned to Jesus. He hugged him like a best friend he hadn't seen in a long time. Then he turned to the Holy Spirit and hugged him like a brother.

"I brought you here to show you the next step," Jesus said. He handed Mitch a piece of paper. "Put that in your pocket and read it when you wake up." Mitch put the paper in his pocket. Monica was making faces at him and smirking. He made faces back.

"It's time to go," Jesus said.

Monica tucked her hair behind her ear. "I'll see you soon," she said. Mitch smiled at her and nodded. "See you soon," he replied. He turned to Jesus; "Jesus, thank you. I love you." To the Holy Spirit he said; "Thank you for your guidance. Please never leave me."

"I'll always be there when you need me," the Spirit said.

Mitch woke up.

Leroy and Isaac were sleeping to his left and right. He looked around him and saw that the fifteen had taken spaces around him as well, and beyond them were the two hundred. Three men stood guard at each door. Mitch got up and began to pray. He knelt, intertwined his fingers, and bowed his head. "Lord. Please help me save at least one person in the morning."

Check your pocket.

Mitch reached into his pocket and found the paper Jesus had given him. He pulled it out and found that it unfolded to reveal a map of Russia with weird, highlighted red and blue dots moving across the surface. He tried to touch them, but they were a part of the paper.

You need to take these locations.

"Okay."

One of the marks on the map was a town fifty-nine miles northeast of Moscow. It was a blue dot surrounded by red dots, and the blue dot was shrinking.

Leroy looked over Mitch's shoulder and whistled softly. "That's trippy."

A startled Mitch grabbed his chest. "MUST you do that?"

Leroy giggled. "No. But not doing it is no fun."

Mitch shook his head and laughed.

Leroy poked him. "Plus. It keeps you on your feet."

Demsi whipped his vanishing blanket off and appeared next to Mitch. "Captain."

Mitch jumped again. "Oh hello, Pastor." Leroy chuckled.

"My men and my guns are yours. I will teach your people how to survive, but nothing more."

Mitch smiled and stretched a hand out to Demsi. "Deal." They shook hands.

CHAPTER 12

Kazan, Russia. Right before daybreak.

Mitch and Leroy woke the troops. They were ready to move out before dawn.

Mitch stood before them. "Take off all your equipment and get on one knee." The men did so. In a loud voice, Mitch began to pray. "In the name of Jesus, we ask for grace and mercy as we go to save our men. Guide us, protect us and keep us on the right path. If we are to pay the ultimate sacrifice, we ask that you take our lives into your hands. We thank you for the honor and the privilege of saving our people. We ask that you help us save at least one person. In Jesus' name. Amen."

"Amen," the troop repeated. Their voices were hushed.

Mitch and his troops put on their gear and traveled fast. Mitch lined up the men; the slowest and most experienced he put at the front of the line, followed by the youngest and the newest members of the group. Tailing the line were the fastest and strongest. Mitch was in the back, making sure everyone was okay. Leroy and Isaac stayed by Mitch's side. Leroy cracked jokes incessantly, and Isaac tried to keep a straight face but a smile crept onto his face every time Leroy said something especially funny.

They marched at a steady pace, and Mitch checked his map every hour. He could still see the blue dot fading, and there was a troubled look on his face. He ignored Leroy and Isaac's bickering.

Mitch suddenly stopped the march and called his fifteen aside. "I need you to go out in two's. Scout around and see if you can acquire some sort of transportation to move us faster."

The fifteen saluted him and ran off. They had been marching for two hours when Mitch heard a familiar hum that began to grow.

Mitch spoke into the radio. "Alpha team is that you?" There was no response.

"Alpha team is that you??" There was no response.

"Take cover!"

The men ran into a nearby tree line on both sides of the snow-covered road. Then they dug into the snow and set up an ambush, waiting anxiously as the hum grew.

"This is exciting," Leroy said.

Mitch looked at Leroy. "There's something seriously wrong with you. Do you think you need professional help?"

"Probably. But I have to settle for you."

Leroy began to laugh. Mitch rolled his eyes and looked down at his sights. As the hum approached, there was the squeaking of air brakes and the crunching of snow under tires. It all suddenly came to a stop. Mitch squeezed the trigger. But right before the hammer dropped, a voice broke the silence. "Mitch!" it screamed.

Mitch did not respond, but released his tension on the trigger.

The voice called out again. "Mitch!"

Mitch stood but Leroy grabbed his arm. Mitch tried to pull away. Leroy shook his head and pointed to himself, then pointed at the road. Mitch hesitated, then nodded. Leroy stood and moved slowly into the road with his rifle down. Mitch tried to get a view of the road but could not. Leroy reached the middle of the road.

"It's Alpha squad," he called to Mitch.

Mitch heard a rustling in the brush behind him and scrambled to his feet. He turned and a masked man was swinging an ax at his head. A single shot rang out. Red mist fell on Mitch's goggles. He wiped the blood off his goggles and discovered a man on the ground with his head half blown off. Leroy rushed to his side.

"Well. That was a close one." He giggled.

Isaac took the mask off and revealed Jeremy. "Well," he said. We don't have to worry about him anymore."

"What about the troops in the city?" Mitch asked.

"What about them?"

"You're going to kind of hate me but..."

"Hell no. You are not sending me back to that hell hole."

"I just need you to head back and set a new captain."

Isaac rolled his eyes. "Fine. But if I'd been the one who shot this idiot, you'd be sending Leroy."

Mitch nodded. Then shook his head. "No. I just see you as a capable leader. Better than this psycho." He pointed at Leroy.

Leroy smiled and nodded. But he soon realized what he'd heard and frowned. "Hey!" Then he paused and shrugged. "Yeah, you're probably right."

They all laughed.

"Okay," Isaac said, still laughing.

They walked to see the transports. There were fourteen snow camouflage Cougar MRAP personal trucks and one Humvee.

Mitch approached the Humvee. "Pick five men and take the Humvee. Meet me at Remmash," he said to Isaac.

"Ten-four," Isaac replied.

Mitch and Leroy loaded the trucks and tried to fit two hundred men into fourteen Cougar MRAP trucks. Each truck could only carry twelve. Leroy realized all the men were not going to fit inside the trucks. "Why don't we have the tail end of the line hang off the sides and sit on the roof?" he suggested.

"Are you crazy?" Mitch asked.

Leroy puffed his chest out. "We've already established that. But really. We're not all going to fit into those trucks."

Mitch thought for a moment. "Alright, but the men outside will need extra jackets. It's going to get cold."

"Agreed."

He shook Mitch's hand, did a weird bow, and started barking out orders.

"Alright! Everyone in the Cougar take your top jacket off and hand it to the people outside!"

Within twenty minutes they were all loaded and ready to go. Mitch and Leroy were on the lead truck. Mitch hung from the driver's door and Leroy hung off the passenger. Mitch gave directions as Leroy sang travel songs at the top of his voice.

The driver, a boy named Scott, turned to Mitch and asked; "Is he trying to get us all killed?"

Mitch chuckled. "Most likely."

Scott shook his head. "This is going to be one hell of a fight."

They drew close to Remmash, and Mitch suddenly yelled "Stop!" Scott stomped on the brakes and the boys on the outside flew off and into the snow.

Mitch threw his head back and laughed. "I'm sorry," he wiped tears. "I had to."

Scott glared. "Are you trying to give me a heart attack?"

Mitch composed himself. "I know you're one of the fifteen," he said. "But I'm leaving you in charge to set an ambush in the tree line we just passed."

"What about you?" Scott asked.

"I and the fourteen will flank the enemy and create a hole for the trapped men to retreat through. The enemy will funnel themselves trying to give chase. Then we will fall back and leave you to unleash hell."

"Yes sir." Scott saluted. "I hope this works," he said under his breath.

"Me too," Mitch said. They looked at each other and smiled.

The men on the outside dismounted and ran full force at the enemy, breaking their front lines and making way for a thousand men to escape to the tree line a mile away. Mitch's plan worked perfectly. As the freed men escaped to the tree line down in the south, the enemy line on the north pushed forward. The east and the west began to push down south also, but those in the south tried to circle back. The pushing troops became a funnel. They forgot to spread out and ran headlong into the ambush in the trees. That day, Mitch's two hundred killed seven thousand men and injured ten thousand. Mitch's casualties were almost nonexistent. Mitch did not lose a single man in that battle. His strategy saved one thousand three hundred and seventy men and helped take back the city for good. His team helped set up a hospital before they moved on, heading for another fading blue dot two hundred and fifty-four miles east.

Isaac's voice came in over the radio. "Captain."

"Mitch. Go ahead."

"The big wigs found out what you're doing. They're looking for you and they want me to search for you. What do you want me to do?"

"Search for me."

"But I know where you are."

"Then get near me, but just miss me. Plus, you can be my inside man."

"Ten-four."

"Make it convincing," Mitch said.

"Will do." Isaac signed off.

As Mitch left with his two hundred, he caught a glimpse of a shadowy figure in the trees. As soon as he saw it, it disappeared. He stopped the march and ordered the men to pull over. They were going to build a camp in the trees.

Mitch tied his paracord as high as he could between two trees ten feet apart and tied a hammock just underneath it. He threw his poncho over the hammock and tied the corners of the poncho to four big rocks, creating a makeshift tent. Then he built a fire just outside the makeshift tent and lay inside his hammock with his feet toward the fire. The men set up their tents around him.

They had all settled down to rest when the screeching of tank tracks and the breaking of trees sent everyone scrambling for weapons and any kind of cover. The creaking and breaking stopped and they heard a woman's voice in the distance speaking a language no one could understand. Mitch looked at Leroy and Leroy got the message. He gestured and the fifteen began to creep forward. Leroy, ahead of the rest, came back through the trees grinning, with his arm over a woman's shoulder. She was five feet and five inches tall, with Indian features. She held a mask in one hand and a rifle with a white cloth tied to its barrel. The gun rested on her shoulder and she was clutching her rifle strap.

Leroy's grin was even bigger up close. "She wants an audience with you." He took his arm off her shoulder.

"Alright," Mitch said. He glanced behind him, slightly nervous. "What would you like to talk about?"

The woman glanced at Mitch then looked at Leroy. Then she glanced back at Mitch. Mitch got the message. He tipped his head at Leroy and Leroy began to walk away, backward. He had a ridiculous look on his face. When he was outside the woman's line of sight, he began to make dry humping motions. Mitch kept a straight face.

"Let's talk." He said to the woman. She approached him and they began to walk.

"My name is Isi."

"It's nice to meet you Isi, I'm Mitch." Mitch put his hands behind his back.

"I know who you are," Isi said. "You have become a kind of hero. A legend like Robin Hood. Or Zorro."

Mitch lowered his head. "Thank you, but I'm just trying to do what's right."

"I'm here to help," she said.

Mitch turned to look at her.

"I brought two hundred and fifty men, ten medics, three tanks, and twenty-five Cougars. Two of them are filled to the top with food and ammo."

Mitch let out a low whistle. "That's impressive. Where did you get all that?"

"Most of the food is from the enemy's stockpile. The ammo is from airdrops. We had more ammo than we knew to do with."

"How did you get so many Cougars?"

"We had one hundred and seventy-five working Cougars from our attack. We were twenty-five hundred strong with two hundred and fifty Cougars when we hit the city. The rest is history."

"Thank you," Mitch said. "Your help is appreciated. Welcome to the Freedom Battalion."

Mitch went from city to city, saving men, women, and citizens for two years. Always changing his strategies to conquer besieged cities; halting the Russian's plans to repel the Americans, and thinking defensively. In every city, his troop grew bigger. Isaac always seemed one step behind. They got into occasional scuffles. There were never any casualties on either side. The Shadows never interfered with the growing legend. Mitch never lost hope in Nissi. He wrote to her constantly and poured out his feelings in every letter;

... I don't care about the fame or the stories, all I care about is coming home to find you again and getting to know you. I just want a simple life. A piece of land with a house we build. Four children running in the yard with our dog. Children that will watch us grow old together in peace. That's all I ever wanted. Not this...

He continued to search for Eli as he saved cities, hoping that he would find him one day. Demsi began to train Mitch's men, however, and he took a special interest in Leroy. Demsi would not teach Mitch. He would not allow Leroy to teach him either and continued to insist that Mitch's time of training was coming soon.

Leroy began a movement called the 'sub-Zealot'. Scott became his second-in-command. They took the teachings of the Zealots but did not follow them to the tee. A sub-Zealot could talk, be around the other troops, and had no special living quarters or equipment. Sub-Zealot volunteers were the original two hundred.

Leroy would sit with Mitch once a week and talk about how to improve the troops living conditions, and Leroy soon suggested having their HQ near a city they had rescued. He had big plans.

"Instead of setting up HQ in a school building or something, we could build something. We could have a recreational area or even a movie theater! We could hide everything in the trees with cloaking blankets, or even invent something else to help hide it all in plain sight."

Mitch listened but continued to decline. "We don't have time or the technology to do stuff like this."

"Then let's find some brilliant people to help out!"

Mitch would chuckle. "Okay," he'd say. "You're now my head researcher. Go find some brilliant minds. Do whatever you have to."

"Thank you," Leroy would say.

Mitch would shake his head and continue to work.

Leroy asked Demi for help. Soon, Demsi and Leroy were heading out to track down leads in the most dangerous places. Their leads led them to the deepest, most heavily fortified locations in Russia to free scientists that had been accused of working with the Americans. As Leroy freed them, he recruited those who wanted to join the RSR (Russian Science Research). Leroy called it Humanitarian Rescue (HR).

Leroy stayed behind in each city to be sure of the citizens' safety, and to further his research. He kept his work and progress from Mitch, hoping to reveal things to him sometime in the future when everything would be perfect. One night, during a fierce fight, Leroy was struck in the center of his bulletproof vest. He was knocked to the ground and the enemy rushed forward to swarm him. Mitch held the enemy at bay with an M-60 E7 light machine gun as he dragged Leroy to safety. That night, Leroy spoke seriously.

"Stateside, I was always known as the leader. The brave one. The strong one. Always unwilling to step into position but still forced to play the part. Never able to be me. So I finally decided to step into that role when the trucks came for me and my friends. I was terrified, but I couldn't show it. Then you came in and took the attention away from me. I didn't know how to react, because for the first time in my life I had the choice of being me. But I'd been playing the serious role for so long, I'd lost myself. He looked Mitch in the eye. "Until you believed in me. You saved me again today and I owe you everything."

"You owe me nothing," Mitch said. "I owe YOU so much for everything you have done for me."

"I've done nothing but give you hell."

You challenged me and made me who I am today. You are more than my second in command. You're my best friend."

"My friend. My captain." Leroy tapped his chest with the closed fist of his right hand. Mitch reached over, grabbed the back of Leroy's head, and touched foreheads with him.

In two years, Mitch acquired ten thousand men and women, one hundred tanks, and countless Cougars to help fight. He divided the troops into groups of twenty-five hundred troop companies, setting captains over them and sending them on freedom missions. Isi and her twenty-five hundred became Mitch's back up in case he got into trouble; which only happened the one time when the Russians set up a counter-ambush. Then, Isi arrived at the nick of time, scattering the Russians with a counter-attack. Isi saved Mitch's life that day and he never forgot it.

CHAPTER 13

Summer, Saratov. Russia at sunrise.

Another bitter winter had just released Russia from its grip. Mitch was now sixteen years old with a clean-cut, dark brown goatee and short hair. At some point, he had hit a growth spurt and was now six feet and one inch tall. They had just helped take Saratov.

Amid the city's rubble, Mitch was astounded to see a one-story whitewashed church with a brownish-gray roof and three rows of many small and beautiful arches. The church overlooked the area with a bell tower that sported a few arches of its own, and a steep-sloped roof led to a golden cupola with a golden cross on top. There were three additional arches surrounded by small, onion-like domes. The multi-colored domes made the church look like a birthday cake.

The church sat there, seemingly untouched by the chaos around it. He stood before the church, fell to his knees, and began to pray quietly. Leroy dropped to one knee beside him and put a hand on his shoulder. Then he began to pray as well. A few moments went by. Mitch opened his eyes and saw Monica.

"Hello, Monica."

"Hey, Mitch."

"What's up?"

"We are mobilizing angels for your attack on the next city."

"Where's the city?" he asked.

"Check your map."

Mitch opened his map and saw a multitude of red dots moving quickly to a city called Voronezh. He turned pale and Leroy noticed.

He sat down next to Mitch and stretched one leg out. "Hi Monica," he said.

"Hi Roy," she said, and then she turned to Mitch and asked, "What's wrong?"

Mitch turned the map to her. Then he handed the map to Leroy. Leroy saw the mass of red dots bearing down on Voronezh.

"What do you suggest?" Mitch asked.

"We've taken on more, but this one seems fishy."

"What do you mean?" Mitch asked.

"Something just doesn't feel right. Maybe we should sit this one out."

Mitch studied him. "All these years, I've never once seen you back down from a fight."

"I know," he scratched his chin. "But this one doesn't feel right."

"Okay. If you're so concerned, I'll get group two to cover our backs and we'll attack from the north. Group three will hit from the east and I'll have group four cover them."

"Mitch," Leroy said. "You're not hearing me. I don't think we should get involved in this one. Let's hit this other red dot in Lipetsk."

"What are you afraid of? You just said we'd fought tougher battles."

Leroy shook his head. "This is a really bad idea."

"Our duty is to save as many as we can," Mitch said in a tight voice.

"No," Leroy said. "Our duty is to save at least one. And it's definitely not to get our men killed."

Mitch squinted at Leroy. "Is there something you're not telling me?" he asked.

"I've heard rumors that the Spetnaz are nearby."

"All the more reason why we should help them," he tapped the map, "instead of Lipetsk."

"Mitch…"

"Leroy! We are going to Voronezh. End of discussion."

Leroy tapped his chest with a fist and bowed his head. "My captain."

Mitch turned to walk away. Monica reached out from behind him and put her hand on his shoulder. She squeezed. Before she could get a word out, Mitch said, "Divert your troops to Voronezh." Then he yanked his shoulder away and kept walking.

"I can't." Monica said quietly.

Mitch stopped and turned. "Then we are on our own. So much for a guardian angel."

He turned and walked to the front of the tired troops. He climbed a Cougar and announced, "I know you are tired, but there is a trapped troop three hundred plus miles away from here. It may be our biggest challenge yet, but I believe we can free these men. Who's with me?"

All the men saluted him, but Mitch spotted Leroy in the crowd shaking his head. He jumped off the cougar and began to make his way toward him. As the men boarded the Cougars, they passed Mitch and each one tapped Mitch's shoulder saying "My captain." Mitch nodded and touched shoulders, but kept moving toward Leroy.

When he reached him, he grabbed his shoulder and apologized. "I'm sorry. But I can't just sit here and let them die."

"I didn't say let them die, I said let them handle it."

"They will die," Mitch said. "And you know it."

Leroy sighed. "I will follow you," He said. "But can you do me one favor?"

"Sure. Anything."

Leroy slipped a piece of paper to Mitch. "When you find Eli, give this to him."

"Ha-ha, very funny. Don't start acting like we're going to die, we're going to be alright."

Leroy wiped some tears from his eyes and chuckled. "Right," he said with some seriousness. "Let's go have some fun."

"That's the spirit," Mitch said. "But not the attitude."

Leroy smiled and walked over to the trucks without another word. He mounted the lead Cougar. Mitch was close behind.

Mitch pulled out the map, stared at it, and then folded it up and put it back in his coat pocket. He didn't realize the pocket had a tear. The map slipped out unnoticed and fell to the dirt. Mitch got into the Cougar. Mitch spent some time on the radio trying to ready all the leaders. Everything went silent after an hour.

"So you know Monica?" Mitch asked Leroy.

"Yes. We've met."

"Where?" Mitch asked.

"After the rescue of Ramdas in Surgut, Monica saved me from an Expiry."

"What is that?"

"It's a servant of a Hypoxide Reaper; a shape-shifting demon that likes to hide as witch doctors and medicine men. They hex and torment you with just one touch, and if they touch you, you become a target for Hypoxide Reapers."

"Wow, that's awesome," Mitch said with big eyes.

"Look who's the crazy one now."

Mitch chuckled. "Maybe I've been hanging around you for too long."

When he estimated that they had drawn up close to Voronezh, Mitch asked through the radio; "Are all of you in position?"

"In position."

"Execute."

They infiltrated from the east side of the city. Group three hit from the north. Mitch ordered the backup soldiers to siege the south and west but to not advance into the city. Group one and group three waded into heavy fighting and Mitch managed to get the Russians to retreat within three hours. They took the city, and the trapped Russians began to surrender.

"I told you it would be easy," Mitch said to Leroy.

"I would not celebrate too early," Leroy warned.

"What do you mean? We've taken the city."

"Yeah, but it was extremely easy. Too easy."

Mitch was upset now. "Why can't you just be happy we beat your unbeatable Spetsnaz?"

Leroy shook his head and walked away. "I thought you were better than your pride," he said under his breath. Mitch heard him and hung his head. He sat down on a pile of rubble and took off his helmet and mask. Then he began to cry and pray.

Scott ran up to Mitch. "Captain!"

"Scott. What's going on?"

"We've lost communication with groups two and four."

"Send scouts," Mitch said.

"We have."

Mitch waited. "Well? Spit it out."

"They've not yet returned."

"Rally the troops and prepare an attack," Mitch said.

"Done."

"Well then. Move out."

Mitch and his group rushed to check on the others. They found dead bodies. At the top of a pile of bodies, Isi was hunched over on her knees and blood was pouring out of her mask.

"Scott. Prepare a retreat to the north." Mitch said.

"Captain." Leroy's tone was strange.

Mitch turned and saw that Leroy was holding up a man that was barely alive. He was mumbling nonsense - "They came in the night of day. No one sees their face. No one hears their breath. They're like a wind in a storm."

Mitch dropped to his knees in front of the man. "Hey. What happened?"

The man continued to mumble incoherently. "They're coming. They're coming. There's no hiding."

Mitch peered into the man's face. "Can you hear me?" he asked.

"We're all dead," the man groaned. "There's nothing we can do, hehe. I see one. I see one in the blood."

"Someone find a medic!" Mitch called out. Disturbed by the survivor's odd behavior, he ordered his men to move out. They moved cautiously through the city and stopped when they reached the northern border. Mitch told them to move into the forest and set up an ambush quickly.

He sent a group of men back into the city with the prisoners. They would be locked in a building until the fight was over. The forest was quiet. The sun dropped behind the trees and all of a sudden there was no noise and no movement. Leroy snuck to Mitch's side and brushed his arm. Mitch swung the point of his gun at Leroy. Leroy grabbed Mitch's trigger finger before he could put pressure on it. Leroy made a shushing gesture and Mitch released the trigger. He grabbed his chest and groaned. "Why must you constantly do that?"

"Because you make it too easy."

"Leroy. I'm scared."

"I know, but don't show it," Leroy replied.

"Where were you?" Mitch asked.

"I was scouting but I couldn't find anything."

"Do you think it was the Spetsnaz?"

"Maybe. Or maybe it was an Und Das."

Mitch rolled his eyes at him. "Now I know you're making things up."

Leroy cleared his throat. "An Und Das is an angel that God created and chained up until the end time, when the creature will be released to take many lives each day. They're much worse than Hypoxide Reapers and even Lucifer. If an Und Das chooses you, just his presence makes your blood start to boil, and your blood cells begin to multiply so rapidly that they may become too much and cause you to explode. I don't know who released him, but I know it is not his time."

"How do you know so much?" Mitch asked.

"One of the lessons in becoming a Shadow Pastor is demonology."

"Okay, well. How do we put the demon back wherever it came from?"

"God sends an angel like Michael, but Michael is dealing with the Kings of Predemon in the southern mountains."

"Right. And Santa is a polar bear."

"Believe me or not, the Und Das didn't kill all the men. It'll be back."

"Leroy is right," Monica said over his shoulder.

Mitch jumped and grabbed his chest. "If the Spetnaz doesn't get me, I think I'll lose my life trying to deal with you guys."

Monica and Leroy chuckle. "The Und Das is not alone; neither did he kill the five thousand."

"How many did he kill?" Mitch asked.

"One thousand."

"What happened to the rest?

"The Spetsnaz."

"That's impossible. I cleared the area."

Shots rang out. Men began to yell from every direction and they heard the sound of grenades falling. Mitch looked around but saw nothing. Mitch's men stood back to back and began to rotate. They glimpsed shadows in the trees. Mitch aimed and struck a figure. It fell.

Mitch and Leroy rushed to the body but found nothing when they got there. Another sound joined the cacophony. It seemed things were dropping from trees. They soon realized the things were men when they heard several footfalls rapidly approaching. They unloaded their magazines.

"Duck!" Leroy yelled.

Mitch quickly threw himself onto the dirt and Leroy swung at the air with a pair of Damascus curved swords. Mitch heard a gurgling sound in front of him and a man flickered into view. There was a giant slash on his face and throat. Mitch jumped back toward a tree and watched Leroy fight an extremely faded silhouette. Leroy was soon fighting with his eyes closed, taking men out as fast as they could approach. They had been ambushed. Mitch looked around and saw none of his men. Figures were fighting all around. Far off, the trees began to sway and creak and a frightening noise grew louder. It sounded like something massive was running toward them.

The creature broke through the trees and Mitch saw that it was a ten-foot-tall angel in medieval style armor. Red trimming outlined all of its armor and it was looking straight at Mitch. As the angel touched men, they exploded in their armor. When the Und Das was within ten feet of Mitch, Monica attacked it. She landed in a beam of light with two Hypoxide Reapers. As they landed, the Und Das grabbed one of the Hypoxide Reapers. The other Hypoxide Reaper stood and rushed the Und Das, trying to thrust his claymore into the Und Das' side. But the Und Das countered and thrust his swirled dagger into the Reaper. Then it picked up the Reaper, thrust its dagger into the Reaper's other side, and drove the dagger into the Reaper's head.

Monica told Mitch to run. Mitch took off. The Und Das looked at Mitch and attempted to chase Mitch, but Monica hit the Und Das' leg and made it lose its footing. It fell to the ground. The Und Das, now furious, turned its attention to Monica. A man six feet and seven inches tall landed next to Mitch and kicked him into a tree. He was wearing black and white spotted armor, a black mask with a vampire mouth and red eyes painted on it.

The man spoke to the Und Das. "Sho bo nee res cor has" (I order you to kill them.)

The Und Das looked at the man, nodded and smiled. "Hes ferb na ren" (With pleasure my master.)

The Und Das grabbed Monica and began to pound her into the ground. Mitch sat where he had fallen, not knowing what to do. A man rushed toward Mitch and Leroy tackled him. They fell to the ground. Mitch saw two blades protruding out of Leroy's back and groaned. The man pushed Leroy's body to the side and pulled his blades out. Then he turned his attention to Mitch. At that point, three men appeared out of nowhere. They wore black camouflage and had weird paintings on their masks. The Spetsnaz looked at the three Shadows. Two of the three were holding spears, but the Spetsnaz dodged their thrusts, then made quick work of the Shadows, slashing one and stabbing the other.

"Finally, Eli. I've been waiting to kill you," the Spetsnaz grinned.

The one he had called Eli had his head down. He looked up, and without a word, took off from the earth with the springs that were attached to him. He hit the Spetsnaz in the chest so hard and fast, the man could not react. He was sent flying. Eli hit him again, and the Spetsnaz tried to counter Mitch's punches without success.

As Eli fought, Mitch looked to Monica and saw her getting pounded. Just then, another angel in white armor and a silver helmet appeared and hit the Und Das. The punch sent the Und Das hurtling through the forest. The Und Das reappeared and seemed surprised to have been caught off guard. Monica jumped on its back and stuck her swords in. The Und Das made an unsettling sound. A hundred fallen angels landed in a black cloud. They were cloaked in black mist, with red and silver talon-like claws.

The angel close to Mitch blew a shofar-looking horn. Angels clothed in white and silver armor landed in beams of light. The Und Das pulled Monica off its back and threw her. It ordered its angels to attack. The white angels attacked at the same time. Mitch watched all of this unfold and saw six white angels surround Monica, who was badly wounded. He turned his attention back to Eli and the first Und Das. They were exchanging blows. The man pulled out a handgun, and Eli quickly disarmed it by grabbing and yanking the slide of the gun so powerfully, it broke the slide right off. The sound of gunfire and explosions encompassed Mitch. He could hear his men dying, but he did not know what to do. He turned his attention to Leroy.

Mitch ran to Leroy, slid down next to him, and took off his mask and helmet. He leaned Leroy back and stretched out his legs, then took off his helmet.

"Looks like I was not f... fast enough this t... time."

Mitch was crying. "Leroy. Don't you leave me."

"I b...b... believe I don't h–" He was choking on his own blood. He coughed and blood bubbled up. "...have a choice."

"Yes, you do." Tears splattered on Leroy's face.

Leroy reached up, grabbed Mitch by the back of his neck, and pulled Mitch's forehead down to his own. Then he said "Re Clande," (My captain) and began to breathe rapidly.

Mitch sobbed and rocked Leroy. "Don't you dare leave me... Don't you dare."

Leroy made a gargling noise and Mitch held him tight. Then he began to sing an old hymn:

Gardens of grass, flow out like a meadow.
Stone hills of the past, stand out from the echoes.
The sun is blind, through rains of tears.
Until my children come home.
Till fear is gone, and sun does shine, I will pray day to day.
Water carry my drops of sadness, until my children come home.
Now sleep in peace. God's hands will be, where I will wait for you.
Rest in the place where angels play, until my children come home."

Leroy went limp, and Mitch cried bitterly. Snot and tears ran down his dirt-covered face.

"Go with God," Mitch managed to say. "Goodbye, my brother."

Mitch lay Leroy's head down and shut his eyes. He saw a spear close by that belonged to a fallen Shadow. He grabbed it and spotted the man who had killed Leroy, not too far away. Mitch charged at him, spear in hand. At the last minute, the Spetsnaz grabbed the spear and backhanded Mitch. Everything went black.

CHAPTER 14

Fort Pierce, Florida.

"A fully armored Hispanic man with jet black hair barges into the café shouting. "Ta shadaban han dedoos; ten sin ra ba a sen fends. Sho be na be?" The invasion has begun; they will be here in six hours. What do we do?

"Tev tem via nar shanor ta rell." Let them come but prepare the wall. Taavet looks at Basheer and says, "Looks like you are now prisoners of war. Please make it easy on yourselves. Relinquish your weapons and gear, or there will be bloodshed."

A man jumps out of his seat and draws a gun. "Bod droser cor ne borba." We should kill him now.

"Re bon tob cono?" What would that solve? Taavet asks. The man walks toward Taavet with his gun still pointed at the old man's head. "I would not do that if I were you," Taavet warns.

"And what are you going to..."

Taavet, so fast he's barely seen, snatches the gun from the man's hand and holds it to the soldier's head.

"You do not know the powers you're messing with son."

Taavet releases the magazine and lets it hit the floor. He unchambers the round then pulls the top off the gun and hands it back to the man.

The furious man drops the dismantled gun and reaches for a second handgun. Taavet grabs a knife on the diner's table. The man takes aim and shoots.

Taavet throws the knife and the blade deflects the bullet. The knife goes on to bury itself in the man's eyeball. More men make attempts to stand and Taavet sighs in frustration.

Basheer raises a hand. "Stop. Sit." His men freeze. "Fools. Did you forget something?"

The men look around and amongst themselves, confused. Basheer points at the Zealot, who is now pointing his weapons at the men. "Give them your weapons," Basheer says. "We will fight another day."

Taavet grunts. "Wise choice. I am too old for this constant fighting."

"How can you speak Alafindra?" Basheer asks.

"I used to be you," Taavet says.

"What does that mean?" Basheer asks.

"Wait till the end of the story and you will find out."

"Fine. But can I send a man to stop the invasion?"

Taavet looks at Basheer. "So it is an invasion."

Basheer looks around frantically as he confesses. "Yes. It is. But to find Sitch."

"Basheer, I know you're not telling the truth. What are your targets?"

"Sitch is the target."

"And where is he?"

"I don't know."

"You're lying Basheer."

"I don't know!"

"I will ask one last time. For the sake of your men. I hope you answer truthfully. What are your targets?"

"My men are expendable. They will die and be with Allah."

"Not if they are killed by women. Isn't that so? Are you going to rob your men of their destinies with Allah?"

"They will be remembered as martyrs and heroes. Kill us, and more will come."

Taavet shakes his head. "Tran ta zarnor na serno ta ve, findas tem renu na ver ta sentens." Call the Zealots and separate the men. Interrogate them until we know the locations.

The Zealot nods and steps out for a moment. Basheer asks, "What is that language?"

"It's called Arcadic. A language from eastern Eden located in the second heaven and where the earth resides."

Basheer looks confused.

"It is an angelic tongue that can only be understood and spoken if the gift is given to you by someone who has it. Or by an angel of God.

Basheer, still confused, responds, "Okay."

Taavet chuckles. "I knew I would confuse you."

A group of Zealots enter the building and pour out from the back room. They surround the ISA troops with weapons drawn. The ISA troops try to look unfazed, but they tremble.

"Ask your troops to follow the Zealots and do exactly as they ask. Be aware they do not speak. And please don't shoot at them, because it will just piss them off and will most likely kill everyone."

Basheer turns to his second in command. "Did you hear that?" The man nods. "Relay the message." The man nods again.

"By the way, you can send one man to try to stop the invasion, but they will not succeed in doing so."

"How do you know?"

"Because when the ISA makes up their mind, there is no stopping what you like to call progress. Now send your man."

Taavet calls the waitress over and whispers something in her ear. The waitress nods and runs off. Basheer gives a letter to a young man and sends him off. He stands up.

"And where are you going?" Taavet asks.

"With my men," Basheer says.

"Not until I have finished our story. Please take a seat." Basheer takes a seat.

Taavet waits until everyone has left. Only Taavet, Basheer, and the Zealot remain in the room. "Would you like something to drink?" Taavet asks.

"You know there would be no need for an invasion if you just told me Sitch's location."

"Waitress," Taavet called. "Can we have three..." He corrects himself after seeing Basheer's face. "...Two sweet teas. One for me and one for Ben please."

"Coming up."

"How about something to eat? You must be starved."

Basheer snaps. "Are you mad? You know we will destroy everything you hold dear, starting with your wife."

Taavet laughs hysterically. "So you know my wife? Well, I would like to know her too."

"You are mad," Basheer says quietly.

"Maybe a little, but at least I don't have crap coming out of my mouth."

"Just tell me."

"The ISA has been planning this for years and has simply waited for an excuse to..." Taavet doing air quotes "...justify their attack and try to win over the people you oppress."

"That's not true."

"Who's the mad one now?" Taavet laughs.

"They are bringing peace to the world."

"By being the source of a war?"

"We would not have this war if it were not for Sitch."

"This war was started a long time before Sitch."

"You are an infection to this world," Basheer says.

"Let's say that is true, why then do you kill your own people?"

"There is only one God, and Mohamed is his prophet."

"That was what the Zuni believed but you killed them also."

"They were not truly devoted to Allah like us."

"But they believed."

"You are blinded by your false God."

"Am I?"

"You are so full of hot air; talking about love, compassion, and forgiveness. But you are always the first to cast the stone."

"A Christian saying, but it is true. Some of us—"

"All of you."

"Some of us," Taavet says, "cast the first stone. But those who do, do not know my God."

"Allah gives us power over our enemies."

"And my God gives me the power to love mine.

"A fool loves his enemies. A warrior kills them."

"A soldier kills his enemies, but a true warrior knows when to let live."

Basheer sneered. "You say you love God, but you will not die for him."

"Dying for a cause or a god is easy. Living for one is hard. That is why my God calls it a living sacrifice in Romans twelve verse one of my Bible."

Basheer looked at Taavet and shook his head. "How the mighty have fallen. A man who does not value life is more dangerous than one who fears death."

"Don't underestimate a man fighting for a cause, family, and home. Especially all at the same time."

"You will die like a dog."

Taavet grinned. "I would not speak too loud seeing as you had your butt handed to you by an old fart."

Basheer sits hunched in his seat, silently fuming, then suddenly asks, "What happened next?"

Taavet looks puzzled. "Next in what?"

"In the story you haven't shut up about."

"I will continue after lunch." Basheer rolls his eyes.

"Waitress."

She appears. "Where's the water please?"

"We would also like to have…"

"Three."

"Three burgers please."

"And a coke," Basheer adds.

"And a coke please."

The waitress smiles and flicks her hair. "Coming right up." She walks away. Taavet smiles and shakes his head.

"Is that your daughter?"

"You could say that, but she can hold her own."

"How did you find her?" Basheer asked.

"Why are you so interested?"

"You know when we come, she will disappear."

Taavet turns to the Zealot. "Ben, shanor ta yenest taran, ten nir vian ri ta aqueen." Prepare the heavy ocean, they are coming by the water.

Zealot Ben stands up, hits his chest, does a bow, and walks off.

The waitress, coming out with the coke, sees Ben walking to the back. "Where's Ben going?" she asks.

"Tu ri teni ma re yaban a or fends. Ver tu ri neut solen, ni tara sin miar tu pran" You are going to be taken in a few hours. Know you are never alone, and I will see you soon.

The waitress smiles. "Tara mes cla."

Taavet chuckles and shakes his head. "Ben dros." Don't smile.

The waitress struggled to hold herself together but bursts out laughing. Taave bursts out laughing too, and Basheer becomes upset. "Can I get in on the joke?" He asks sarcastically.

"I was sharing a memory of when I was getting to know her. She grabbed a spoon and tried to stab me."

"Right," Basheer says in a droll voice. He turns to the waitress. "How long until the food is ready?"

A ring is heard, and the waitress says, "Now!" then skips away like a happy little girl.

She returns with the burgers in a few minutes. Basheer grabs a burger as soon as it hits the table but as he is about to take a bite, he notices Taavet folding his hands together. Basheer makes a face and takes a bite, as if defying Taavet's gesture.

"Father," Taavet begins. "Thank you for this food. Thank you for a successful day today. We ask that you bless this food and sanctify it. That it may fill us as we prepare to save a life. In Jesus' name. Amen."

Basheer rolls his eyes and shakes his head. Taavet and Basheer eat in silence. After they have eaten, Taavet calls the waitress and holds her hands. "Thank you so much for the food. it was delicious." Then he hands the plates to her.

She smiles and grabs the plates. "No. Thank you for eating." Then she walks into the kitchen.

Taavet shakes his head and looks at Basheer. "Let's continue our story."

The air was thin and it smelled wet. Mitch was standing in a dark place with no light.

"Leroy? Monica? Where are you??"

He heard an echo of his voice, as if he was standing in a cave. He ran to the left, and then to the right, trying to find a way out. When he had exhausted himself, he curled up into a ball, stuck his head between his knees, and began to sob. "I don't know what to do," he mumbled. "I don't know what to do…" After a few minutes, he put his head on his knees and opened his puffy eyes. He saw a light.

Mitch thought to himself, "I know I'm not supposed to go into the light, so I will stay here." But the light grew in intensity and was soon so bright that Mitch was forced to hide his face between his knees to cope with the blinding glow. As it grew, it seemed to make a sound. It all blinked off as fast as it appeared. Suddenly Mitch was plunged back into darkness and silence.

When he heard the crackling of a fire, he peeked around his knees and saw a man sitting with his back to Mitch, poking a fire. Mitch tried to make out who it was but felt a piercing pain in his head. He clutched his head and groaned.

"Welcome back to the land of the living," he said. Before you ask, yes, the battle did happen. No, there were no survivors, and we gave Leroy a proper burial."

Mitch rubbed the back of his head. His eyes started to fill with tears. "Can I visit him?"

"Only Shadows are allowed."

"I can't be a Shadow until I find Eli."

"Maybe Eli is a myth. Your actions and decisions in your last battle have shown me that you are not ready."

With hot tears streaming down his face, Mitch blurted, "I know I'm not ready and I know no matter what I say, it will never change your mind. But if I have to spend ten thousand years looking for a myth just to see my friend again, I will do it for all eternity."

"And what would you do if you found him?"

"I would humble myself and follow him till I am ready."

"The only one you should follow is Jesus, but I understand where you are coming from. You have grown since the first time I saw you at the battle of Kazan." Mitch looked puzzled and looked around.

The man continued to speak. "You are a great leader and you have a good heart, but you lack discipline and proper training, and you do not listen to instructions. That is what got your men killed."

Mitch spotted a helmet sitting next to the man. It was camouflaged, with a slightly tinted non-reflective lens, and a black accent from the bridge of the nose to the top of the lens. The mouth plate was solid and narrow, but the biggest defining feature was the slash on the nose of the helmet.

"You're the man that saved me in Kazan."

The man stopped poking the fire. "Very perceptive."

"You're also the man called Eli."

"That's right."

"Are you Eli?"

"I am known as Eli the myth, but I'm just a man trying to make a difference."

"I found you," Mitch said, incredulous.

"Technically," Eli replied. "I found you."

Mitch got on his knees and bowed. "Master Eli. Please make me your student."

Eli reached down, grabbed Mitch, and pulled him up. "Don't bow. I'm nothing special, just an old man wanting to go home. And no, you are not ready."

"Who truly is ready to step into this?"

Eli did not answer.

Mitch continued. "God led me here for a reason. I don't know what the reason is, but I'm willing to go the distance."

"Your father was a close friend of mine when we were in prison. He taught me that there are more important things to do than play this game of war. We all have a choice, to either give in to fear and allow it make us irrational or accept it and move on. You are not ready. Your mind is full of revenge, and your heart full of sorrow. If I take you now, you will learn our ways for the wrong reasons."

"How can you tell the outcome of something that has not happened yet?"

"Because I see the future."

"Are you a psychic?"

"A prophet. And that is why you are not ready."

"Do you know Monica?"

"I do, but she is in bad shape. That Und Das almost killed her."

"Do you know the origins of the Und Das?"

"The Und Das is a destroyer said to be much worse than Lucifer. It was designed by God to kill a certain amount of lives a day both physically and spiritually. It is almost unstoppable. The only one who has faced off with an Und Das solo and survived binding it without a lot of injuries is Michael the archangel. After binding it, Michael hid it in a deep and secret cave guarded by angels with swords of fire. I don't know how the Russians got past the angels and freed the Und Das. Michael saved Monica just in time, but the Und Das escaped and the angels can't get to it."

"What happened to the big man you were fighting that killed Leroy?"

"He escaped as well, but not unscathed."

"So he is still alive."

"Yes, but he will be caught."

Mitch's expression went from sadness to hatred. "How did he escape?"

Eli turned. He was six feet tall, with a full beard and a fresh cut across his nose line that was still clotting with blood. His left eye was gray and his right eye was brown. The gray eye made him look blind. His white hair was longish, and his face had a long, round chin with a scar on the left side.

"I saved your butt," Eli said. "You must know when to end a life and when to save it."

"You should have let me go," Mitch said.

"I wanted to," Eli said. "But you are a part of a bigger plan."

"And what plan is that?" Mitch asked.

"You will find out soon. Until then, try to keep up."

Eli stood and stepped into a shadow. Mitch jumped up and tried to rush him. He tried to grab Eli's uniform, but Eli just managed to elude his grasp. Mitch heard Eli's voice, airy and distorted, coming from every direction at once. "You are fast," he said. "But not fast enough. Pre lesson: Stop using the five liars and start using the elders."

Thoroughly confused now, Mitch called out. "What are you talking about?"

"React not with your eye but with your heart."

Something shot out of the darkness and hit Mitch in the head. Mitch dropped to his butt and grabbed his head. "What the hell…?"

"You want to prove you are ready… Catch the stone…"

"How can I catch something I can't see?" He yelled.

"Stop trusting the five liars…"

"Yeah, yeah. And trust my heart."

Mitch stood and another stone flew at him from behind. It hit him in the back of the head and dropped him to his knees. Mitch grabbed the back of his head, cringing and crying. When another stone hit Mitch on his shoulder, he curled up into the fetal position. A flurry of rocks rained down on him. Mitch hunkered down, flinching at every hit.

Eli walked back into the light and the attack stopped. "You see. You're not ready yet," he said.

CHAPTER 15

Location: Unknown.

"You're not ready," Eli repeated.

Eli walked past Mitch and toward his helmet. When Eli turned around, Mitch was gone.

Eli nodded. "Not bad."

When a stone flew out of the darkness at Eli's head, Eli bent and the stone whizzed harmlessly past.

"You have some skill," Eli conceded.

When a second stone flew toward Eli's back, Eli turned, deflected the stone with a staff, and sent it back into the shadows. It hit Mitch, who tripped and slid across the rocky floor. When he came to a halt, Eli walked over to him and put a hand out to help him up.

"How did you do that?" Mitch asked.

Eli walked towards an opening Mitch had not seen before. Cold air was rushing in. It was night-time.

"You have potential," Eli said. "But you need time to grieve. Take ten days off and meet me back here."

"I'm ready now," Mitch said.

Eli put his mask back on. "Ten days," he insisted. Then thin rods sprouted out of Eli's calves like leaves. The rods lifted his two feet. Eli bounced a little, then jumped out of the cave. Mitch ran to see if he could follow and saw that they were in a cave within the side of a canyon.

Mitch thought to himself, "I can stay here and mope for ten days or I can try to follow Eli."

Feeling like he didn't have a moment to lose, Mitch jumped out of the cave and fell about twenty feet before he hit ice-cold water. He thrashed around for a few moments, like a fish on a hook. Then he stopped for a moment and looked around him. Eli was crouched on the bank of the pool, looking at him. He reached down to help Mitch out of the water. "You really want to learn, huh?"

Mitch, shivering, reached up and grabbed Eli's hand. "M-more t-than a-anything."

Eli pulled him out of the water.

"P-please, I don't have anything else." Mitch's voice and body shook as he struggled to hold back his emotions. "First I lose my dad, then my mom, and now my friend. Why would God do this?"

"Your mother is dead?" Mitch nodded and Eli turned away. "How did she die?"

"What is it to you?" Mitch asked.

"I would like to know, to honor your father."

"She was killed trying to protect her terrified son." Mitch sat down and began to cry. "I couldn't do anything. And in the end, she died in my arms. For what?" He sniffed.

Eli's voice was firm but kind. "I'm not going to justify the reason God took your mother, and I am not going to tell you everything is going to be alright. The past is gone, and the future is not guaranteed, but all you can do now is move on. If not, you may be the next to die."

"Maybe that's what I was made for," Mitch mumbled.

"We were all made for that," Eli said. "All of us will die someday. But we can die in many ways: old, young, cowardly, or brave. Your death does not define you. What you do with your life does." Eli turned. Mitch was watching him. "Do you think you can keep up?" Eli asked.

"I'm willing to try," Mitch replied.

"Then wipe your tears and let's get moving."

Mitch shot to his feet and Eli took off into a dense forest. Mitch struggled to keep up with him, but he kept hitting every low hanging branch and tripping over vines. Somehow he kept Eli in view until he saw that Eli was fading. Eli vanished.

Mitch stopped. "Eli!" He screamed.

All he heard was the echo of his voice reverberating in the distance. "Eli!!"

He heard a whisper. It sounded like Eli. "Don't trust your eyes… Don't trust your instincts. Trust your heart… What do you hear?"

Mitch listened. "I hear nothing," he said softly.

The whisper came again. "Use your other set of ears."

"What?" Mitch said.

"Take a deep breath," Eli whispered. "And let go of all your fear, anger, pain, and joy…"

Mitch closed his eyes, took a deep breath, and released it.

"Search your heart…"

Mitch was still.

"Now what do you hear?"

"I-I hear bats flapping through a cave…" Mitch began. "I hear echoes of water droplets splashing into a puddle." Mitch paused for a moment. "I hear breathing. I hear you breathing."

"Good. Now find me… With your heart."

Mitch waited a moment and then turned around and looked into a shadowy corner. He pointed. "There."

Eli stepped out of the shadow and into the dim light of the moon, wearing his mask. "Good," he said. "Good. Now, where are we?"

"I have no idea," Mitch replied.

"Piece it together," Eli said.

"I lost track after I ran into the forest."

"Think, boy. Use your head, not your heart."

Mitch closed his eyes and went into a trance-like state. Eli smacked Mitch in the back of the head to snap him out of it.

Mitch rubbed his head and sulked. "What was that for?"

"We don't have time for that. Where are we?"

"I don't know," Mitch replied.

Eli got into Mitch's face. "Tell me, boy!"

Mitch cowered a little. "A cave?" he whimpered.

Eli backed off. "That is correct."

Mitch gawked. "But how is that possible?" he asked. "There are trees, and there's the moon right there."

"But where's the moon?" Eli asked slyly.

Mitch looked around, puzzled for the umpteenth time. "I don't see it."

"That is Lumite. Made by Pastor Demsi's research group."

"Yes I've seen it, but where is it now?" Mitch asked.

"Behind the veil," Eli replied.

"A cloaked veil?"

"Exactly," Eli said. "I have to patrol. Ten days." Eli walked off into the shadows and vanished. Mitch rushed forward, trying to grab a hold of Eli, but he slammed into a cave wall instead.

Mitch turned, leaned against the rigged wall, and slid down until he was sitting. "What am I supposed to do now?" he mumbled.

Mourn the loss of your mom, Leroy, and your freedom.

"I don't want to mourn," Mitch said.

If you don't mourn, it'll get worse.

"What will get worse?" Mitch asked.

Your mind. And eventually, your physical body.

"How do you figure?" Mitch asked.

If you don't mourn, you'll be alright for a few days, weeks, months, or even years. But it'll get worse on the inside, and one day it'll all come pouring out.

Mitch sighed. "I doubt that. I've done well so far."

Exactly. 'Well.' And look what happened.

"That's harsh."

Well, you're being a hard head and a know-it-all.

Mitch scowled. "No, I'm not."

Open your eyes and grow up in your mind. You're not as high as you think you are.

"I don't have to listen to you."

True. But if you did, Leroy might still be alive.

Mitch jumped to his feet and began to pace. "That's not fair! That's a low blow!"

And you wouldn't have lost your whole army in one mission.

Mitch clenched his fists. "I'm warning you!"

How would your mother feel?

"That's enough!" Mitch yelled. He grabbed his head and pressed as if trying to squeeze the Holy Spirit out. Then he grabbed a rock, flung it at the darkest corner of the cave, and began to cry hysterically.

We need to accept what has happened, learn to deal with it, and move on. It'll be a long, hard process, but it will be worth it.

Mitch sniffed and wiped at his face. "How would you even know how I feel? You are an eternal being, you never have to worry about dying, hunger, sadness… Nothing!"

Half of what you said is true. I am an eternal being, and I do not have to worry about dying. But I do hunger. Not for food but for you. I am you. You beat me, hate me at times, try to kill me, I feel your sadness and that makes me sad, I feel your anger, your joy, your fear, your disappointment. I am here through it all.

"I cannot move on," Mitch said.

Moving on does not make you a failure, it makes you free. Letting go does not mean forgetting, but it gives room for healing. You never forget, never, but the wound needs to heal so you can continue helping. Your heart has a wound that takes time to heal and it will always leave a scar, but the scar will not hurt.

Mitch began to cry again.

God gave us the process of grieving to heal that portion in us, but it takes time for us to heal. I am with you and always will be. Let's do this together and leave the rest to God.

Mitch sniffed. "Okay. Where do we start?"

Don't hide away your pain. Accept what is happening and what has happened. Cry if you need to. Get mad. But in all of this, find what makes you happy and hold on to that for dear life. So. What makes you happy?

Mitch leaned his head back against the cave wall and closed his eyes. "One day I will find Nissi and marry her," he said.

Okay. Hold on to that and build from it. What else?

Mitch thought for a moment. "Helping people."

Now, how can you help someone if you need help? How can you heal someone if you're sick?

"I am not sick," Mitch said.

You are, psychologically.

Mitch shook his head. "How did you come up with that?"

You can pacify your feelings, and you can hide your pain, but they'll always be there. The only way forward is to face your pain, face your feelings, and deal with them.

"I don't want to feel. And I don't want to hurt. I just want to help people and go home."

There's nothing wrong with that... This was a new voice. Familiar, but new.

Don't listen to that voice, The Holy Spirit warned.

Mitch was already shaking his head. "No, there's nothing wrong with that at all."

You're alright, Mitch. You can do this. Start training.

The Holy Spirit's voice was fainter now.

You CAN do this, but you have to do it the right way!

What does that old ghost know? He's from biblical times. He doesn't understand that things are different now.

Mitch nodded. "You're right."

The small, still voice of the Holy Spirit was very small now.

He will lead you to...

Mitch heard nothing more.

The other voice filled Mitch's head.

The Bible says you should love your enemies. You can't kill them if you love them.

"That's true," Mitch said.

If you can't kill them, how else can you avenge the people you love?

Mitch sighed.

Eli won't know if you mourned or not. All you need to do is pretend you did.

"But the Bible…" Mitch began.

The Bible is an old book full of fairytales and stories of old people. Who needs an all-knowing God that only helps when it's convenient?

Mitch shook his head. "The Bible may be old, but it tells you the right way to live your life."

Yeah. Behind invisible bars. You are forced to live your life, to think, to feel a certain way. But you can be completely free. Free to do what you want and what needs to be done. Free to enjoy life without worry, without regret, and without pain.

Tears filled Mitch's eyes. "That's all I want."

Then grab your feelings and use them as fuel! Use your wrath. Vent your pain on your enemies. They are the reason everyone around you is dying… But don't let anyone know, lest they try to take your power and freedom from you.

"Who are you?" Mitch asked.

I go by many names. But at the end of it all, I am you.

"I don't understand…"

The voice swelled in Mitch's head.

I am the one God cannot conquer! I am in every single person. I bring hope where there is none.

"I still don't understand."

I'm your brain, stupid. I am the one who reveals logic and reality. I make the decisions no one else wants to make. You stick with me, kid. I'll get you home.

"How can you be so sure about things?"

Because I brought you this far. Those delusional visions you think you saw of Jesus? The voice sneered as it spoke the name. **None of them were real. Plus. What does the old book say? Doesn't it say that no man shall see God unless he dies?** The voice chuckled. **I am the one who showed you those visions. It is impossible to go to heaven without dying. And you're not dead yet, kid.**

"You're right… I'm not."

I know these things because I am logic. I am the one who can make your wildest dreams a reality. It was I who revealed

gravity to Newton and electricity to Benjamin Franklin – who was not the first to discover it by the way. He stole it from the Chinese. But whose name went down in history? The voice laughed deeply. It's time to wake up child. **It's time to live. Death is your life and you're nothing but a blip in the books. No one is going to remember your name, what you did, or how you lived your life. You are nothing. And you know it.**

Mitch bristled at the thought of everything he had sacrificed. "Then what's the point of fighting? If none of it means anything anyway?"

You fight to survive. You fight because you have to. You fight for what you want, and not for the sake of another man's war. All this war is about is seeing who's more powerful. Why would you want to die for something as stupid as that?

Mitch thought of his men. He thought of David and his mother, and his friend Leroy.

"Okay," he said. I'm in."

CHAPTER 16

Dearest Nissi,

I finally found Eli, and he's much bigger than I could have ever imagined; just as amazing as I thought he would be, and so familiar. I remember his voice from somewhere, but I can't place when. I wish you could meet him. He reminds me of my dad, or the person I think my dad was. I barely remember anymore.

Eli met my dad in person; he said they were cellmates in prison. I have so many questions to ask him, but I don't think he'll tell me anything more. On the bright side, I begin my training tomorrow. It should help me take my mind off of all these feelings and pain. I've lost so much since I left home. You're the only thing I can still hold on to. Seeing your smile, just once, would make all this loss and bloodshed worth it.

I remember when we were children and you used to pick on me. I chased you around the church like a lost puppy. I never knew how to talk to you, so I tried to show you how I felt by my insignificant accomplishments. I defended you long after you were gone, and no one could speak wrong of you, even after you left.

I don't know where I am now. All I know is I'm in a massive cave that has a river running through it. I cannot find a way out of it, but I will. One day. But I'm not just talking about this physical cave I'm in right now. I'm talking about this dark place I'm in emotionally as well. Sometimes I feel like you're the one who holds the key to my freedom. You alone will free the love I've locked away deep inside of myself. I may be a fool; I may be delusional, a dreamer, a hopeless romantic. All I know is you will always be in my heart. I'm no good at poetry Nissi, but you make me feel like a poet.

I'm not in a hurry. I want to dance until the night is gone, without a worry for the past, present, or future. Until the sun rises and shines on. I will not stop thinking about you until I find your face under a sun-filled sky. You shine brighter than my darkest hour. You are the light that keeps me going. My hope, in this tunnel that has no end. When I find you, I will know I have come to my resting place.

Yours truly,
Mitch.

Unknown Location.

Ten days went by. Mitch explored the cave and could not find a way out. He felt the walls of the cave and observed that they were smooth as if made of a kind of marble that looked like stone.

"Where am I?" he asked his new friend.

I don't know. This place looks like a cave, but the walls are manmade. It's made to seem like a cave. But it appears to be made of some kind of marble, and there's a river flowing through the middle. There's also the matter of these trees.

Mitch went up to the trees to investigate. He felt one of the trees, and it seemed real, but these trees were strange. Over the past ten days, they had transitioned from being full of green leaves to bare – as though the days were changing seasons. He had walked through the trees and found no leaves or branches on the ground. There was also no snow in the odd places where snow was 'falling'. Mitch had looked up and found that the roof was obscured by a thick, cloud-like fog.

"This is a strange place," he said.

"This is the training ground," came Eli's voice.

His sudden appearance startled Mitch.

"It's one of our underground training centers."

"Oh. Well, that makes sense," Mitch said. He touched the walls. "How is this possible?"

"Pastor Demsi's work. It's a chemical reaction called marbling. It starts with massive inflatable templates. An incision is made in the outer layer of the template, and the water seeps into the template; mixing with the inner layer of the mold to create instant marble-like walls.

"How can we breathe down here?" Mitch asked.

"The river running through the center of the training hub goes through a series of hydro-generators. Oxygen is pumped in from the surface and recycled. That's why we can build a fire in here and not get smoked out."

Mitch nodded. "It's unbelievable."

"How do you feel?" Eli asked.

"I feel good." Mitch grinned. "I think I'm ready for training."

Eli studied Mitch with his clouded eye. "Are you sure?" he asked.

"Of course," Mitch replied.

"Run to the end of the river and back as fast as you can."

"Okay." Mitch took off like a firecracker.

When he reached the end of the river, he looked back and saw Eli sitting on a ledge of rock. He slowed down when he reached a wall.

"Don't slow down," Eli called. "Move it."

Mitch touched the wall in front of him and ran back. When he reached Eli, he was winded. "Do it again," Eli instructed.

Mitch took off a little slower this time. Every time he came back to Eli, Eli would send him off again.

Mitch ran until he couldn't anymore. He had only run back and forth five times.

After the fifth run, he stopped and bent over. "Stop. I can't. No more."

Eli stood. "One. Use proper English. And two. If that's all you have, we have a problem."

Mitch was gasping for air. "Why is that?" he managed to ask.

Eli turned his back on Mitch. "No more questions," he said. "Just do as I say."

"Why?" Mitch asked.

"Walk with me," Eli said.

Mitch dragged himself after Eli. Eli did not say a word until they came to a stop. Mitch was still gasping for air.

Eli pointed at a wall and said, "Climb that."

"Are you crazy?" Mitch asked.

Eli pointed at the wall and didn't say a word.

"Do I at least get safety equipment?" Mitch asked.

Eli kept pointing.

"Okay," Mitch said. "But I don't think I'm going to make it very far."

"Then we're done for today."

"That's it?" Mitch asked.

Eli walked away without a word.

Mitch followed Eli, "Hello? And my training? Why so short? Eli?"

Eli just kept walking. They arrived at the spot Mitch had found himself in when he first woke up. Eli pointed at a sleeping bag on a cot near the fire.

"Sleep," he ordered.

Mitch stared at him. "That's it?"

"Would you like a bedtime story?" Eli asked.

Mitch got into the sleeping bag reluctantly. The fire crackled. A few minutes later, Mitch asked, "How well did you know my father?"

"He gave his life for me," Eli replied. "He taught me everything I know. In time I will tell you more. But now you must sleep."

Every day for one week Eli asked Mitch for the same thing. Mitch would sprint five times and wear himself out, then Eli would take him to the wall. Mitch would try to climb it, but never got far before he gave up. Finally, Eli said something new to Mitch.

"You are failing because you have already failed in your mind. You have put a limit on your ability, and you do not believe that you can surpass this limit. This is why you cannot succeed."

"You're asking me to do an impossible task!" Mitch argued.

"It is only impossible to you. You have convinced yourself you cannot, so you do not."

Mitch clenched his fists. "It is not possible."

"Then why are you here?" Eli asked. "To learn to fight? To be the best? You know how to fight, and you were the best."

Mitch was still gasping for air from the effort.

"You can be the best, but there will always be someone better than you. Because when you're the best, someone will train harder to be better. War is not a competition, nor is it a game. All of war is nothing but a struggle for power and dominance. If you want to join that game, keep going down the path you are walking on now. But if you want to make a difference, wake up and stop listening to your noggin. Because your brain will always limit you."

Mitch looked up at Eli and shook his head. Disappointment was etched on Eli's face. "Then this is your last lesson," he said.

Eli pointed at a small vine-like rope in the center of the cave and said, "That's your way out." Then he turned and walked away.

Mitch stood there for a few minutes, hunched over and panting. After a few moments, he straightened up and began to run toward the vine. Eli saw him running and shook his head.

A few hours went by. Eli sat quietly in front of the fire. Suddenly, something clattered to the ground beside him. He looked up and saw Mitch, then looked down and saw a pair of spring stilts from the cave at the top of the wall Eli had asked him to climb. Mitch was severely out of breath.

Eli turned back to the fire. "Am I supposed to be impressed?" he asked.

Mitch fell flat on his back and gasped for air like a fish out of water.

"I hear that you've pushed past your limit. And now, you expect me to teach you, right?"

Mitch sat up and looked at Eli. Eli turned to face Mitch.

"You had your chance to prove yourself and you failed. I will not teach you anything else. The most I can do is let you have these stilts that you think you deserve, because being a Shadow means more than you can imagine. It means giving your all without compromise. Without thought. It means doing what needs to be done when it needs to be done. It has nothing to do with strength, or power, or skill. It's about heart. But you lost yours somewhere in the mountains, while you were on your high horse. I will not pet your ego. Keep what you have and leave the real work for the ones who want to do it."

Mitch opened his mouth. "I want to—"

Eli cut him off. "Don't come to me with that bull. If you truly wanted to be here, you would have climbed without questions. You lack trust. To earn trust, you must first give it. But you don't even trust yourself."

"You know what?" Mitch replied. "It's true. I don't trust myself, I don't trust you, and I don't trust anyone else."

"And that's why you fail. If you can't trust the person next to you, two things will happen: one, the man will ditch you and leave you to fight alone, or two, you will kill or get each other killed."

Mitch dropped his head in shame.

"Stay here, go away, I don't care. But we're done." Eli grabbed his helmet, put it on, and then jumped out of the cave.

It's a bright, sunny day, and a little boy is crying with his back to a palm tree. Three older boys walk up to the little boy and start to make fun of him, but another boy walks up behind them and says, "Leave him alone."

The three boys turn to the boy behind them and the fattest speaks. "Oh yeah?" he sneers. "What are you going to do about it?"

The boy smiles. "Come here and find out."

The three big boys charge and the boy rushes into them headlong. At the last minute, he jumps and kicks the fat boy in the face. The fat boy falls to the ground, but the other two are still standing, and they both punch the smaller boy at the same time. The boy hits the ground and quickly tries to get up, but one of the big boys throws himself on top of him and pins him down. He begins to beat the boy's face with his fist, and the other big boy kicks the smaller boy in the side of the head. The fat boy rolls over and spits out blood from a broken nose. "You're stupid," he says to the smaller boy. "Three always wins." The other two leave the boy alone, and one of them gives the boy one last kick in the side.

He groans in pain. "You may have won today," he mumbles. "But your muscle is gone."

One of the skinny boys says, "I'm the muscle.". The smaller boy with the beat-up face starts to laugh.

The skinny two are about to jump on top of the little boy again when Sarah shows up. They freak out and run, leaving the fat boy behind, but not before delivering one last kick to the smaller boy's head.

"What were you thinking? You were outnumbered." Sarah says to the little boy, and she reaches down to help him up.

The boy sniffs and groans. "My friend needed help," he says. Then he grins. "I took one down with me though."

"Well I'm taking you to the hospital," Sarah says.

The boy points at the big bully. "Don't forget fatty."

Sarah peers at the fat boy. "He'll be okay."

"We should at least call for help."

"Help is coming," Sarah says. She stands and stretches out a hand.

"Now let's go to the hospital."

"Okay," the boy says.

Sarah turns to the other boy, who is still crying close to the tree. "Come on sweetheart. Stop crying. Let's take your brother to the hospital."

Training ground, Russia.

Do you remember who the little boy was?

"Yes," Mitch said. "I have the faded scar to prove it."

What exactly happened to that boy?

"He's still here."

The voice turned into a snarl. If he was still here, you wouldn't be giving up right now. Then it went back to normal. You know what, just give up. You gave your best and Eli gave up on you. So you should give up on him.

Mitch was quiet for a moment. "Voice, shut up," he said out loud. "God, don't say a word. And you devils hold your peace." He began to pace. "What was the real reason I wanted to find Eli? It wasn't because I wanted to be the best… I just wanted to learn more about my dad and how he died."

With that thought, Mitch put the spring stilts on and tried to stand. He staggered around like a newborn stag for a few minutes and even fell a few times. But he soon found balance. When he tried to take a step, however, he fell flat on his face. Bruised and annoyed, he considered giving up on the stupid stilts, but he stood instead and tried again.

It took him some time, but he finally learned how to walk. Then he attempted to jog. After a bit of stumbling, he eventually got the movements right. He did not attempt to run. He spent some time getting comfortable with the stilts then jogged to the vine and walked around it. Then he reached out and grabbed it. The ground rumbled and the vine began to hum. Before Mitch realized it, he was several feet off the ground on a dirt-covered metal platform.

Halfway up, he saw a second platform approaching, coming straight down at him. As he looked, the second platform split apart about eight feet above him, and as it descended, his platform also split. The two intersected, and Mitch's platform continued to go up while the other continued to go down. His platform hurtled toward a solid concrete roof, but as they got closer the roof split open and created just enough room for Mitch and his platform to pass through. Once through, the platform stopped and formed a part of the ground they had just arrived on. The only thing now marking the spot he had just come through was a vine in a forest full of vines. Mitch dropped to one knee and examined the ground. Just ahead of him was a pair of deep impressions in the ground. Mitch concluded that a Shadow must have jumped from that spot. He looked up and saw a slightly stripped vine that looked like it had been grabbed and used to swing to a nearby tree.

Mitch followed the subtle trail, assuming that it was made by Eli. Suddenly, there were no longer any visible tracks. As he turned around looking for clues, he spotted something written on a tree. The words were difficult to make out, and they made no sense that Mitch could see, but he read them out loud anyway.

"Aben fas fandro ma entru neb fornet ta shotono ne ta edren." He who wants to enter must speak the language of the Eden.

As Mitch spoke the last syllable, the ground opened up next to a tree. He peeked into the hole and discovered a tunnel. After a second's hesitation, he jumped into the hole. The entrance closed behind him and plunged him into darkness. He looked around but could see nothing. Then a familiar voice echoed through the tunnel.

"Welcome to the world of shadows," it said.

The voice was not Eli's. It got louder, as if approaching him, but Mitch could not pinpoint what direction the voice was coming from.

"It's been a while," the voice said. "I'm sorry about Leroy."

"How do you know about Leroy?" Mitch asked the darkness.

The voice was now right beside Mitch's ear. "I trained him," it said.

Mitch whipped around and discovered the silhouette of a man holding a staff. Attached to the top of the staff was a Lumite crystal. The light emitting from the crystal was almost blinding.

As Mitch raised his hands to shield his eyes, the man reached for his shoulder.

"Who are you?" Mitch asked.

"Demsi," the silhouette replied. "Don't tell me you already forgot about me."

"Demsi!" Mitch gasped. "It's so good to see you again!" Mitch hugged Demsi.

"It is good to see you too. Leroy was the best man I ever trained."

A lump formed in Mitch's throat. "He was a great friend."

"Leroy is in the light of heroes where he is honored with the other fallen Shadows."

Mitch searched Demsi's face for answers. "Why didn't I listen to him?"

Demsi put a hand on Mitch's shoulder. "What happened, happened. We must learn from our mistakes and move forward. Let the past be a guide for the future. Don't stay in the past lest you are left behind."

Another voice, female and familiar, floated through the tunnel. "Listen to his wisdom Mitch."

Mitch spun toward the direction of the voice. "Monica!" he exclaimed.

Monica stepped into the light. She was wearing a white robe and a gold belt. "It's nice to see you again, Mitch."

Mitch blinked back tears. "I'm so sorry I put us all in this situation."

Monica smiled. "All is well. I will follow you to hell and back. Just try not to get me killed next time." She giggled.

"So you remember Monica, but not me," Demsi said with a sly tone in his voice.

Mitch smiled but then his expression turned serious and he whispered under his breath; "Monica is not real. She's a hallucination. Monica is my longing for Nissi. She is a hallucination. Monica is my longing for Nissi."

Monica's smile was sad now. "You may not believe I am real anymore, but I will keep protecting you," she said.

"It's a shame you're holding on to revenge instead of moving on," Demsi said.

Mitch was angry. "Hell yeah, I am holding on to revenge! I will find justice for Leroy."

Demsi shook his head sadly. "Then he would have died for nothing."

"He died for my stupidity," Mitch said.

He closed his eyes as if reliving the terrible battle. "I could have prevented his death if I had just listened to him. How come the map showed me that dot if God didn't want me to go?"

"The map was influenced by your desire for power," Demsi explained. "It was a test, and well, you know how it went. By the way, your Arcadic is flawless."

"What are you talking about?" Mitch asked.

Demsi laughed and began to walk down a tunnel. After a few steps, he turned. "Are you coming?" he asked Mitch.

Mitch moved forward and stumbled a little because of the stilts, then he followed Demsi into the dark.

CHAPTER 17

Fort Pierce, FL.

Basheer slams a fist down on the table. "Why the hell are you telling me all this crap?"

"To show you why men follow Sitch," Taavet replies.

"We can prevent so much bloodshed if you just tell me where he is!" Basheer cries.

Taavet eyes him shrewdly. "Yeah. Then we can all hug and kiss and be at peace. You know, we didn't start this fight. But we will finish it."

Basheer leans forward. "We will wipe you from the face of the earth."

"You may win a battle today, and I may win a battle tomorrow. But when can we truly say we have found peace?" Taavet asks.

"When the war is over," Basheer replies.

"I beg to differ," Taavet replies. "War will never end. We humans look at it as some kind of game."

"No, we don't."

"A fool may seem wise if he just keeps his mouth shut," Taavet says.

Basheer bristles. "Are you calling me a fool?" he asks.

"It's all a matter of perception. If the shoe fits..." the old man replies. "Now, shut up and listen."

"I don't have to sit here and listen to an old bag of hot air babble on about shadows and delusions. The Shadow is dead, the one you should fear is the Ghost." Basheer moves angrily out of his seat, but before he is fully out of his seat, a knife flies out of a shadowy corner of the café. It passes inches from Basheer's body and pins his sleeve to the table. Stunned, Basheer looks at the knife. The blade is made from a weird material that shimmers like a rainbow in the light and vanishes completely when looked at from certain angles.

A masked person steps out of the shadows. He's wearing a black helmet with a beaded metal faceplate and big eye lens. One white stripe extends from the ear to the jawline and ends almost in the middle of the chin. The masked person sits and takes off his helmet. It's a woman.

Taavet grins. "Hey baby," he says. "It's been a while."

The woman looks to be in her early 40's. She has short salt and pepper hair and her well-proportioned body is evident through her clothes. She has a round face and a jaw that sticks out a little. A scar on her face runs in the same direction and length as the white stripe on her helmet.

"It has," she says to Taavet. Basheer moves to pull out the knife from his sleeve but stops when the woman says sharply, "Don't touch that blade."

"Babe," Taavet coos. "Play nice."

"You know I hate people touching my knives," she says.

"Well then grab it."

Basheer has been looking from Taavet to the woman. Exasperated, he turns to Taavet. "Who is this?" he asks.

Taavet shrugs and Basheer turns to the woman but she's already gone. So is the knife.

"You'll find out soon enough," is Taavet's response.

Basheer examines his sleeve and looks warily around the room. "What does that mean?" he asks.

Ignoring Basheer, Taavet resumes his story.

Unknown location, Russia.

Ahead of them, beyond the glow of the Lumite crystal's light, the tunnel was pitch black. Mitch felt like he was walking into a black hole.

Demsi walked at a steady pace.

"Where are we?" Mitch asked.

"The world of shadows. Impossible to enter unless you know how to speak Arcadic."

"I don't understand," Mitch whined. "What is Arcadic?"

"Arcadic," Demsi explained, "is a heavenly language that was first spoken in the East of Eden. Have you ever heard people babbling sounds that kind of seem like words in church?"

"No," Mitch said.

Demsi froze and turned to face Mitch with a puzzled look on his face. After a moment, understanding dawned on his face. "Oh. You're a poly," he said.

"A what?"

"A poly," Demsi repeated. He saw the frustration on Mitch's face and chuckled. He turned and continued walking. "People like you are known as polyglots; you can speak several languages. So you can speak Arcadic, but can you read it?"

"I don't even know what you're talking about," Mitch said.

Demsi turned and handed Mitch a paper, then asked Mitch; "Can you read this?"

Mitch looked at the paper but all he could see were symbols and hieroglyphics. As Mitch opened his mouth to say something to Demsi, he began to speak. "Ta shotono ne insina urnesi a va shan serd insina osh ta vianne ta yerdon." The language of angels revealed in man shall lead angels for the coming of the kingdom.

"That's impressive," Demsi said.

Mitch said, "I don't know where that came from because all I can see here are symbols and glyphs."

"So you're an orac as well."

"Now I know you're making things up," Mitch said.

"I wish I was," Demsi said.

At that precise moment, Mitch and Demsi passed beside an opening that revealed a command center. A low growl-like sound was coming through a speaker in a strange pattern that seemed oddly familiar. It sounded like Morse Code. Mitch listened and thought he heard; "Spetsnaz located at sector." but he could not understand the rest. A dot appeared on a map that was being projected onto a wall.

"Oracs are ones who have no prior knowledge or understanding of Arcadic literature yet speak and read it perfectly. There are many, so don't get a big head."

"Where are you taking me?" Mitch asked.

"You will see soon," Demsi said.

A door cracked open, letting out a bright white light. As the door opened wider the light became more intense, causing Mitch to stop in his tracks and cover his eyes. He dropped to one knee. When the intensity of the light had subsided, Mitch went into the room to investigate. Silver owls were sitting on bronze branches lined up in rows. On the chest of each owl was a name. Mitch walked slowly past each owl until he saw one with the name 'Leroy'. He stopped, dropped to his knees, and put his palm against the pedestal.

"What is this place?" he asked bitterly.

"This is the hall of light," Eli said. Mitch turned sharply at the sound of his voice and saw him standing in a corner of the room. "We fight in the shadows our whole lives only to be buried in dark boxes. Even though our bodies are temporary and the person is no longer in it when he dies, we cremate the bodies of fallen heroes and set them in these owls so they can sit in the light for the rest of their days."

"Why show me this place?" Mitch asked.

"To show you all the people who believed in doing right, and for closure."

"Thank you," Mitch said.

"Demsi convinced me to continue training you. I don't expect you to obey without questions, I just expect you to listen. Because the crappy training you've been given is not going to cut it," Eli said.

"Yes sir."

"You will not be a mindless soldier. I will teach you to think for yourself and listen to that still small voice you no longer believe in."

"Yes sir. Thank you for–"

Eli cut him off. "Next lesson, your stilts are your life. Learn them and love them because they will become a part of you."

"I understand," Mitch began, "But when…"

"I cannot fill what is already filled," Eli said.

"I don't have a full cup," Mitch said.

"You are right," Eli said. "You do not have a cup; you have a truck."

Mitch's head snapped up and he gave Eli a dirty look.

"Get rid of the truck, but don't forget it. Fill your mind with the things you are taught, but continue to keep an open mind." Eli knelt and put his arm around Mitch. "You have the potential to do great things, Demsi saw it," Eli pointed at Leroy's owl, "Leroy saw it, and I can see it. You just need to get your mind right." Mitch rolled his eyes.

"You know what?" Eli said, "Close your eyes."

"Why?" Mitch asked.

"Close your eyes."

"Fine," Mitch said. And he closed his eyes.

"What do you see?" Eli asked.

"The back of my eyelids."

"That's very funny. Empty your mind and think of nothing. Now tell me, what do you see?"

"Nothing," Mitch said.

"You don't see what you don't believe. Now clear your mind and look harder. Tell me what you see."

Mitch took a deep breath. "I am in a room. Half of it is dark and the other half is light. I'm standing in the middle."

"Which side calls to you?"

"Both. But the louder voice is in the light."

"Why?" Eli asked.

"Because I can see…" Mitch said.

"Everyone fights for the light, but no one wanders into the dark because we say it's evil. You can choose to walk in the knowledge of everyone before you or you can move into the unknown and lead the way. You may stumble and fall but a true leader keeps going and never looks back."

"But isn't God light?" Mitch asked.

"According to what you have begun to believe, there is no God. But

God works greater miracles in the unknown than in the known."

"Why?" Mitch asked.

"So you can depend on him, and not your understanding. If you do it because you know, who gets the glory?"

"God," Mitch said.

"Tell that to the world and they will laugh at you. The glory goes to your pride because you did it without help. Now if you did something that seemed impossible, people call it luck. But if you do it constantly, we know that it's God."

A few moments of silence passed and Mitch heard a deep, dark voice. "Open your eyes," the voice said.

Mitch opened his eyes and found himself in pitch-black darkness. It was darker than the tunnel they had walked through. Yet when he lifted his arms to look at himself, he could see himself.

The dark voice came from every direction. "Welcome to the dark hole," it said. "Here you will be taught how to truly open your eyes."

"What?" Mitch asked.

"Open your eyes," the voice ordered.

"I see nothing," Mitch said.

"Embrace the dark," the voice said. "And respect it, for it is your life. Darkness has two sides; the bad and the good. As does light. "But you must choose what you are going to do. You stand now in the gap between light and dark."

"What do I do?" Mitch asked.

"Open your eyes," the voice said.

"I don't understand," Mitch said.

"Open your eyes and find the door."

Mitch tried to take a step forward and discovered that there was no floor in front of him. He flapped his arm in an attempt to find his balance. When he had righted himself, he discovered that he was on a square platform four feet wide.

"What the hell!" he yelled.

"Close your eyes," the deep voice said. "And all of this will end for now."

"Where am I?" Mitch asked.

"Close your eyes," the voice said.

Mitch obeyed. A few moments later, he heard Eli. "Open your eyes," Eli said.

Mitch opened his eyes and found himself in a light gray room with white grids running from behind him to in front of him, and black grids running from left to right. Eli was standing next to Mitch and Mitch was laying on a table. Eli was leaning on a walking stick.

"Welcome to the simulator," Eli said. "Within a few minutes, you will use your gear to shoot down drones that will be able to shoot you.

"Shoot them with what?" Mitch asked.

"Check your holster," Eli replied.

Mitch put his hand on his hip and found a handgun.

"Your lesson starts now," Eli said. He hit the floor with a stick and as he did so, all the lights went out. A bean bag flew past Mitch's head and Mitch heard it but did not see it. He whirled and shot blindly at the sound. Another bean bag zoomed past and Mitch turned again to shoot. He did not know what was going on and his heart rate was increasing. One bag hit him on the thigh and knocked him to the floor. A woman's voice said "End simulation." And the lights came back on. Eli was still standing in the same spot.

"That's enough training for today," Eli said.

"But I didn't learn anything," Mitch said.

Eli said, "You did, now expect another lesson tomorrow. Eat, shower, and sleep. There is much for you to learn."

Eli turned and walked away. Mitch turned to Demsi. "Did Leroy train like this?"

"Not exactly," Demsi said.

Mitch looked down and Demsi lay an arm over his shoulder. "It always gets worse before it gets better," Demsi said. "Come, let me show you to your quarters.

Demsi led Mitch through a hidden door. Mitch saw a room full of computer screens, people were holding joysticks and wearing virtual reality headsets.

Mitch stayed silent as he walked through but thought 'What a waste,' to himself.

"In the wrong hands, this can all cause more damage than good. We must not be quick to take to voices.

"How do you deal with them?" Mitch asked.

"Jesus."

"Jesus?" Mitch looked incredulous.

The only thing that shuts up the voices is my Savior."

"I don't hear voices," Mitch said.

"You will," said Eli. "You have two sets of sense, including the five liars. The only way to see is with your heart and not your eyes."

"I don't understand," Mitch said.

"When you shoot, you must first shoot with your heart and then with a gun."

"How do I do that?"

"Clear your mind and trust your heart. It will show you the way. Time to sleep. Follow me," Demi said.

"I still have questions," Mitch said.

"Ask them tomorrow," Demsi said.

"Fine," Mitch said with a little attitude.

They walked down a narrow hallway for a little while. Demsi stopped in front of a white door, opened it, and said "This is your room."

Mitch looked in. There was a mahogany armoire, a metal rack, and a green twin size bed.

Demsi pointed at the armoire. "This is where you will put your uniform when you get it. The drawer has your PT uniform inside it." Demsi pointed at a rack. "This is for your stilts. It's the only place you may take your stilts off. I left some ointment for your blistered feet next to the rack. Rest well. I'll see you in the morning."

Demsi swung the door closed but Mitch yelled, "Wait!"

He pulled the same door back open but saw nothing but an empty hallway. He shook his head as he sat on his bed. Then he took off the stilts, removed long black socks, and grabbed the ointment. Soon he was curled up in bed, asleep.

"Open your eyes," the dark voice said.

Mitch opened them. He was in the black hole with his stilts on. He tried to stand but stumbled.

"What the hell!" he yelled.

"Open your eyes, pass through the straight and narrow, if your heart is true it will lead you true."

"Where do I start? What do I do?" Mitch asked.

"Listen to your heart, the voice said. Find the straight and narrow."

Mitch looked in every direction but saw nothing. He stepped off the edge of the platform he was on and fell. "When he landed he opened his eyes and saw that he was on a training ground."

Eli stood with his legs apart. "Shoot the drones before they shoot you."

Eli slammed the concrete ground twice and the lights went out. Mitch began to hear bean bags whizzing past his head. He panicked, ducked for cover, and began to shoot frantically in every direction. The bean bags pelted him. He closed his eyes tight and they stopped.

When he opened his eyes, he was back in his room lying down on the twin-size bed. He sat up, examined himself, and saw that his whole body was now one giant bruise.

Eli appeared from the shadows. "When you shoot your first shot, you give away your position."

"Yeah, thanks for the heads up," Mitch said with sarcasm.

"You're stuck in the moment," Eli said. "You still don't use your second set of senses. That's why you still don't believe. It's why you fail."

"I don't understand what you want from me," Mitch complained.

"What do you want for yourself? It's not about me, I can continue without you and not lose sleep. But I'm here teaching you."

"More like trying to kill me," Mitch said.

"Maybe making amends with Monica will put you in a better mood."

Eli walked into the shadows and Monica showed up where he had been standing. She tucked her hair behind her ear and said, "Hi."

Mitch did not acknowledge her.

"I miss talking to you," Monica said. "Do you want to talk?"

Mitch lay down and turned away from Monica.

"Why have you stopped talking to me? I'm real." She sat on the bed next to Mitch and the bed creaked as she sat.

"You're not real," Mitch said.

"So you hear me," Monica said. "Why do you hate me now?"

"I don't hate you," Mitch said. "I just can't afford to lose another person close to me. You almost died. I can't live knowing you're in danger, or that you died because of one of my stupid decisions. So I choose to believe you're not real. Now go away."

Monica chuckled. "I know what I signed up for. I volunteered to protect you at any cost. I just didn't think that I would…" Monica stopped talking and pressed her lips together.

Mitch turned. "Would what?"

"It is forbidden," Monica began, "For an angel to fall in love with a human. We cannot be together because we were not created to be together. The last time such a thing happened, God sent a flood to kill everyone. It was also a part of the reason why Sodom and Gomorrah were destroyed by fire."

"I didn't know that," Mitch said.

"I will die for you if it comes down to that," she said.

Mitch reached up and kissed Monica. Monica, stunned, kissed Mitch back. He rested his forehead on hers and said, "I missed you."

"We can't do this," Monica said.

"Why not?" Mitch asked.

"I've told you why," Monica said. "You know why. Plus, your heart belongs to someone else."

"It's not fair," Mitch complained.

"We don't get to choose who we are. But we can choose who we love. It would not be fair on Nissi if I stole your heart. It wouldn't be fair to you either. If you love Nissi, stay fair to her. I will not be unfair to Nissi or even you, but I love you and I will always love you.

Monica stood up and walked backward, still looking at Mitch. "Tara sue nostus tu brack ta darosc ni tara sin nostu tu fi ta lan." I have loved you since the beginning and I will love you at the end. She stepped into shadow and was gone. Mitch turned around and touched the wall beside him thoughtfully.

CHAPTER 18

Fort pierce, Florida. Night fall.

A lady in black armor runs into the café. She is frantic. "Ten ves any." They took her!

Taavet responded calmly. "An truve yen." It's about time.

The young lady is dumbfounded. "Sho be tu fend eb ma be?" What do you want us to do?

Taavet smirked. "Nutren. Fewdren ta Zarnors ma sordren madru." Order the Zealots to stand down.

The lady hesitates before she turns to leave. She looks back at Taavet for a moment and then runs off.

Taavet turned to Basheer. "Well, it seems we don't have a waitress and I'm tired…" Taavet signals for the Zealot to come. "This nice man will show you to your quarters."

"This city won't be here for much longer," Basheer said.

"We will see," Taavet said. "Anything is possible."

The Zealot escorted Basheer out of the café. In a poorly lit corner of the café, twenty Shadows reveal themselves. "Sindres sho nir tun fewdren?" General, what are your orders?

"Ta mandren nir vian, ten oshnes eb. Shanor ta Zarnors ni ta

Shandru." The ghosts are coming, they found us. Prepare the Zealots and the Shadows.

The men tap their chest and say "Re clande." My captain.

A young man rushes into the café. "You are needed at the front lines."

"I'll be there," Taavet says. He stands, walks into the shadows, and touches something that opens a silent door. Then he walks out on to a platform that leads down to a submarine. He sits in a chair among Shadows. "Re clande," each one says. The sub launches to the north through a natural underground water tunnel. Taavet nods at them all.

Five minutes later, they have arrived at the front line. The top of the submarine folds open and Taavet sees a young man standing in a full Navy Admiral's uniform. The man taps his foot impatiently.

"Are you in a hurry?" Taavet asks.

"What the hell are you thinking?" the admiral demands. "Sending her out, of all people, and without backup!"

"She knows how to take care of herself," Taavet says. "Plus, she will take my place soon."

"And that is why she needs backup."

Taavet turns to look at the admiral. "If you send backup, McCoy, you may ruin this mission."

McCoy scowls. "This is stupid."

"I know my place," Taavet says. "Do you?"

"Yes," McCoy says. "I am your superior."

"Not according to Amendment 105 of the Freedom States: 'The shadows are not, nor will ever be governed by a government for the safety of the world.' She is under my protection. We spoke about it and she felt that she was ready, and I concur."

"She is just a child," McCoy laments.

"Back off. Or the Shadows will leave you to fight this battle alone."

"Leave," McCoy glares. "We can handle this."

"Like you handled the massacre of Norfolk."

"That was different…"

"Okay. How many people did you lose?"

McCoy drops his head. Taavet continues, "I am not here to take over your operation. I am not here as a weapon. I am here to save the lives of our countrymen and our people."

"What are your orders?" McCoy asks.

"Get the sub-jets ready," Taavet instructs.

"Done."

"Prepare mine also."

"Is that wise? We already have one behind enemy lines."

"I have calculated the risk," Taavet says. "You will be in charge of the surface attack."

McCoy salutes. Then he turns to a young man who has just run up to him and whispers in his ear. The boy nods and runs out of sight. McCoy turns back to Taavet. "Everything is being prepared."

"Thank you," Taavet says. "Where is your canteen? I'm starving."

McCoy lifts his arm and an extremely lanky fellow comes running up. "Take him to the canteen," McCoy instructs.

The young man nods and turns to Taavet.

Taavet takes a few steps forward and asks McCoy "Who is he?"

"A slave," McCoy says. "I took him out of prison."

"Who is greater?" Taavet asks. "A slave or his master?"

"The master," McCoy replies.

"Not in the eyes of God," Taavet says. "All men are created equal and free and they remain so if they stay true to the word God has put down for us to follow. Be careful that you don't think yourself higher than what you are because your fall will be great."

McCoy looks hard at Taavet, but nods. "Thank you for your words of wisdom," he says.

Taavet turns to the man again. "This way?"

The man nods and takes Taavet to the canteen.

The canteen is a beige tent with a pitched roof held up by ropes. When Taavet walks in, the tent is well lit. There are three rows of five wooden tables and benches that can fit twenty men per table. But the room is empty. In the back of the tent, a partitioned room is reserved for the leadership. The man tries to lead Taavet to that room.

Taavet shakes his head at the young man. "No thank you, son," he says. Then he sits down at the table closest to the door. "I'll sit right here. Can you grab me something to eat? I'm really tired."

The man bows and leaves the tent. A few moments later, he reappears with plates of fried chicken, mashed potatoes, gravy, baked beans, and a biscuit. He lays the spread before Taavet gently and steps back. Taavet has just folded his hands to pray when he hears the young man's stomach growling.

Taavet finishes praying and motions to the man. "Sit," he says.

The man shakes his head, no.

"Please," Taavet insists. "You must eat something."

The man continues to shake his head, but Taavet grabs him by the arm and pulls him down.

A soldier walks in at that moment and sees the young man sitting. "What are you doing?" he barks.

The man moves quickly to stand but Taavet grabs his arm and holds him. The man looks frantically from the soldier to Taavet and struggles to stand.

"I asked you a question!" the soldier barks again.

"Calm your tits," Taavet says. "I asked him to sit."

"Who the hell are you?" the soldier asks Taavet.

"Son, you don't want to go there," Taavet responds.

The soldier approaches the young man. As he reaches to grab him, Taavet intercepts his lunge and pulls the young man to the side, causing the soldier to fall forward on to the table. He lands on his nose.

The soldier grabs his bleeding nose and bellows, "That was a mistake, old man!"

"Go cry outside and leave this man alone. As long as I am here, no one lays a finger on him unless it is to help him."

Taavet signals and two Zealots grab the soldier and drag him out kicking. Taavet splits half of all his food and says to the young man, "This is too much for me, but it is enough for both of us. Please eat with me."

The man hesitates, but soon grabs a piece of chicken and begins to devour the meat.

Taavet eats slow and steady. "It is good for a man to eat," he says.

The man responds in a thick middle eastern accent. "Why are you feeding me and treating me with kindness? I am your enemy. If you were my prisoner, I would beat you harder than they beat me."

Every man, woman, and child deserves respect and a chance to live. You are indeed my enemy, but I don't have to hate you."

"You are still my enemy," the man responds between bites.

"As you are mine. But that does not give me the right to abuse you."

"It does in my country."

"I know," Taavet says as he stands. "It was nice talking with you. Take care."

The man bows "As-salamu alaykum."

"Alaykum as-salamu." Taavet responds. The man is stunned by Taavets flawless accent. He stares after Taavet as the old man walks away.

Taavet meets with two Zealots right outside the tent and asks, "Where do I go?" The Zealots walk him to a hidden staircase disguised as a giant tree. They stand on a platform that takes them down a dimly lit shaft.

Taavet says "Fas un ta mandren a ta shandru?" Who is the Ghost in the Shadow?

The Zealots look at each other and shrug their shoulders, then point their weapons at Taavet. Taavet spins, grabs both weapons, and pulls both soldiers close to his body; one behind him and the other in front. As they shoot, their bullets strike each other in the stomach, just below their bullet proof armor. One Zealot releases his weapon and it drops to the floor. Taavet twists the arm of the second Zealot and jumps, breaking the arm as he comes down. Then he places his foot on the knee of the other and bends the leg back, shattering it. A few moments later, the platform reaches the bottom and is welcomed by a battalion of troops who all have their guns aimed at the mouth of the elevator. The elevator doors open to reveal one man lying in a pool of blood with a makeshift bandage around his torso, and another clutching his arm close to his body with a sling. Taavet stands between them, leaning on his cane.

McCoy pushes through the crowd of soldiers. "Hold your fire! Hold your fire!" he orders. He sees Taavet and the two injured men. "What happened?" he asks.

Taavet looks at him and says "Please stop sending me bodyguards." Then he steps out of the elevator.

"But they were Zealots!"

Taavet looks at a shadowy area of the room and says "Ten nir a, ta mandren a ta shandru un ba" They are in, the Ghost in the Shadow is here. Then he turns to McCoy, "Those men you sent me are spies."

Mccoy recoils in shock. "How do you know?" he asks.

Taavet finds a different shadowed corner and speaks to it. "Bastro abent fi ell kin." Defend him at all costs. The mask of a shadow prophet emerges from the darkness and startles McCoy.

"Re clande." The Shadow says.

McCoy continues to press Taavet. "May I know how you knew?"

"Every true Zealot speaks Arcadic, for one. Two, they were wearing the armor of our fallen Zealots from the battle of Kazan." Taavet makes it to the subjet and settles into its slender cockpit.

"But how do you know?" Mccoy insists.

"No more questions," Taavet says. "The submarines are ten miles out from the shore. We will talk later, if you survive." He chuckles at the look on McCoy's face and puts on his shadow helmet. Then he plugs a thick, black, beaded wire into his helmet as the cockpit closes and the sub submerges. "Freedom one," Taavet calls into the radio. "Freedom one, this is Shadow Doyen. Do you copy?"

A voice sounding like it belongs in a radio station replies, "Good copy Shadow Doyen. Welcome back. We have a massive invasion. We see fifty submarines and a countless amount of ships."

"Thank you Freedom One. Good copy." Taavet switches his comms. "Hello. This is Shadow Doyen speaking. I am in command of this underwater operation. There are many targets, but try to focus on the submarines, aim to disable, and if there is no other choice, then destroy. If you don't like prayer, switch channels for two minutes." Taavet begins to pray. "In the name of Jesus, we pray for these brave men going into battle. We ask that you keep us and protect us in the battle. If we are to pay the ultimate price, please take us to your perfect place, in Jesus' name. Amen."

A voice yells out "Hell yeah!" and another says "Time to have fun." A third voice chimes in. "I love this part."

"Remember your training," Taavet instructs. "Be visual."

The sub-jets shoot off like rockets through a narrow water tunnel underground. At the end of the tunnel, they shoot straight out toward the fleet. From a safe distance, they see a sea of ships as well as one hundred and fifty submarines moving as a unit. Voices pour through the headset in a mixture of excitement and fear.

"Focus," Taavet orders. "And take them one at a time."

As they get into firing range, a barrage of underwater cannons come out of the sides of the submarines and begin to fire on the sub-jets. The sub-jets break formation and split into twenty different units. They try to find an area of weakness in the enemy's formation but the enemy seems well-fortified. Sub-jets begin to drop like flies.

"Shandru mell," Shadow fall, Taavet says. "Men, fall back to second position."

Taavet hits a button that turns him invisible, then he jams all signals and shuts off his engines. He drifts silently, and the wall of submarines pass by him without detecting him. Taavet whispers into the radio, "Are you in position?"

HQ responds. "In position."

"Finta." Attack, Taavet orders.

Taavet and fifty other hidden sub-jets launch a hell storm of small torpedoes on the enemy fleet, instantly taking out ten submarines. The submarines search frantically for source. Choas builds and the foreign submarines begin to slam into each other. Taavet screams "Attack!", and a second wave of sub-jet ammo streams through the water. They hit the sides of the foreign submarines and destroy five more. The submarines shoot their weapons in desperation and begin to sink their own ships. The sub-jets continue to pick off the enemy one by one, but despite the chaos, the foreign fleet pushes on.

"Fall back," Taavet suddenly orders.

"Why?" Someone asks. "We have them on the run."

"Fall back!" The sub-jets fall back to the mouth of the tunnel.

Taavet says to HQ, "Now."

An electric magnetic pulse shoots through the water, knocking off all of the ISA's electronics and leaving most of the ships stranded.

Taavet says to McCoy "Can you finish up?"

"Of course," McCoy responds.

"Good," Taavet says. "I'm heading back."

Taavet heads back to the hidden dock with his troop. As they step off, McCoy meets them clapping. "That was good work boys."

Taavet glances at McCoy. "I suggest you find your own bodyguards now." Five prophets, three pastors, and an evangelist emerge from the darkness, dragging two men.

Taavet continues. "You're going to need it. Tan un ratran." That is enough.

McCoy, shocked, asks in a shaky tone, "Can I just borrow some of yours?"

Taavet gets into the transport submarine and sits before he answers. "No," he says, right as the hatch closes.

Taavet makes it back to Fort Pierce. As they dock, Taavet says to his team, "Thank you all for your help. Tomorrow morning, bring me Basheer. But tonight you must rest. We shall see what tomorrow brings us."

One of the Shadows stands and puts his arm on his chest as Taavet makes his way out out of the submarine and yells "Re clande!" The rest follow, all doing the chest salute. Taavet turns and does a small bow to acknowledge their respect. Then he treks to his beach house a quarter of a mile from the café. As he walks through the front door, he begins to cry. He leans back into the front door and slides down to the floor.

Taavet cries, "Lord forgive me! I tried to save lives, but I had to take them."

He cries for half an hour out loud until a knife hurtles out of the dark hallway and embeds itself an inch away from his head. Taavet does not react, and a woman moves out of the shadows toward him.

"I'm sorry you had a bad day. How can I help?"

"I need sleep," Taavet says.

"Okay." The woman says, and she helps him up.

"Thank you, honey," Taavet says.

The woman helps Taavet to his room, changes his clothes, and tucks him in. Taavet asks, "Would you sleep with me tonight?"

The woman answers, "Always."

She strips down to almost nothing and lays next to him.

CHAPTER 19

Time is bending together; I can't tell how much of it has passed. I thought that, by this time, I would be finished with training. But I no longer understand what Eli wants from me. I'm doing everything by the book but I still don't understand.

All I hear is open your eyes and hit your target in a pitch-black room. I have tried everything, but nothing is working. But what I really wanted to tell you is that I love you. I miss the smell of your brown hair. And the way you smile as if the sun will rise forever in a cloudless sky. I need your help to teach me how to fly. I know with your help I can reach beyond and grab a hold of the moon. I hope to take us on adventures one day, to unknown places. But alas, I must go, for training is at hand. I hope to see you soon and hold you one last time.

Yours truly,
Mitch

Fort Pierce, Florida. Sunrise.

The sun is just rising from the water.

Taavet is sitting at the table Basheer found him, holding a letter. Basheer is escorted into the café by two Zealots wearing plain white t-shirts and black sweatpants.

Taavet says, "Welcome back, are you hungry?"

Basheer scowls, "Just cut the crap and tell me where Sitch is.

"Hey, cook" Taavet yells. "Two batter pancakes for us, please."

"Two cakes and two weiners," the cook yells back. "Coming right up.

"You're out of your mind," Basheer says.

The Black Hole

Mitch walked up to Eli. "How do you do the impossible?"

"It's only possible if you believe," Eli responded.

"I've gotten nowhere, and you're not helping," Mitch complained.

"Stand next to me and don't move," Eli said.

Mitch stood beside Eli.

"We're doing this at the most difficult setting," Eli said.

"It's impossible," Mitch said.

"Close your eyes," Eli instructed.

A few moments later, Mitch was startled by an incredible amount of gunfire. He ducked down and put his hands over his head, trying to find cover. After about five minutes, the noise dwindled to nothing and Mitch unlaced his intertwined fingers. He opened his eyes and saw Eli leaning on his cane. He was surrounded by destroyed machinery.

A voice came in over the speaker. "All clear. Wow."

"See? Aim with your heart and it will never fail you if your heart is pure."

"How is that possible?" Mitch asked.

"Sell out," Eli said. Then he walked out the door and shut it behind him.

"How am I supposed to sell out to something I don't know?" Mitch muttered.

"It's called faith," Demsi replied. "Faith is for the unknown - you hear 'jump into the dark', and you can either ignore it and stay with what you know, or you can have faith and jump."

"That's impossible," Mitch said.

"The only thing that's impossible is impossibility."

Mitch looked up at Demsi. "Albert Einstein?"

"No, Phineas Flynn."

Mitch was confused. "Who?"

Demsi chuckled. "It's from a TV show way before your time. Come on, it's time to rest."

"No," Mitch replied. "Set up the simulator."

"We can't," Demsi said.

"Why not," Mitch asked.

"Because Eli destroyed all the drones," Demsi said.

Mitch folded his legs under him and got into a comfortable sitting position. "Then I'll sit here until they've been fixed."

Demsi shrugged. "As a bad tailor would say; suit yourself."

Mitch sat with his eyes closed for some time. Then he heard a familiar voice.

How far will the mighty fall?

"Holy Spirit," Mitch said under his breath.

Hi Mitch.

"It's been a while," Mitch said.

I have not left you, I only gave you your space.

"Thank you," Mitch says. "I need your help."

I can help you see through the dark with your heart.

"Okay, what's the first step?"

Empty your mind. What do you see?

"I see... Darkness."

That's a good start.

"I see the mountain of drones surrounding me."

Without moving your body, move your spirit through the walls. What do you see?

Mitch walked in spirit through a wall and said, "Am I in a janitor's closet?"

The Holy Spirit laughed. Yes. Wrong wall. Walk through the adjacent one.

Mitch walked through the adjacent wall and said "I see a room full of computers. I see one, two, three.... fifty men inside. Now I see Demsi talking to Eli."

What are they saying?

"I don't know," Mitch says.

Focus and listen.

Mitch took a deep breath. "Demsi is saying 'Are you sure?' and Eli is saying; 'The one who has lost it all, must now lay his life to save the last generation.'" Eli turned and looked right at Mitch's spirit as if letting Mitch know that he knew Mitch was there. Mitch was dragged back into his body and snapped out of his vision.

Do you remember the map?

"Oh my God, yes. What happened to it?"

You dropped it just before your last battle. It immediately turned to dust to protect its information.

"Can I have another?" Mitch asked.

"No. There was one, and you used it for the wrong reason."

"I did what was asked of me, to protect the dot that was shown."

How come there were two then? If every other time you looked at the map there had only been one? Mitch remained quiet as the Holy Spirit continued. *The map shows you what needs to be done, but the holder can get greedy and influence the map with their desires.*

Mitch became angry, "So it was my fault?"

Yes.

"Then I must make things right," he said.

Finish what you have started, then everything will be clear.

Mitch nodded. "Alright, what do I do now?"

Go to your room and rest. Tomorrow I will show you how to do things you thought you couldn't do.

"Okay."

Instead of going straight to his room, Mitch turned left to the closet he had seen in his spirit. He opened the door and confirmed that it was a janitor's closet. Then he continued to his room, rubbing his temple in disbelief. As he walked, he pondered on what Eli had said. When he walked into his room he found three angels standing in their white togas and golden armor. Each one had a flaming Claymore mounted on its back that did not seem to be burning anything around it.

One angel spoke, and its voice was like rolling thunder. A pale white glow came out of its mouth, but the light was not overwhelming. Mitch froze as the angel spoke. The power of its presence and its voice dropped Mitch to his knees. He felt a hand touch him on the shoulder, and it gave him the strength to stand. A massive angel stood beside him, seven feet tall. His eyes were like blue fire, but soothing to look at. He was holding a ten-foot wooden staff. On either side of him, the angel had two winged cherubs that seemed almost glass-like. The angel gestured to someone behind Mitch and Mitch looked to see that it was Monica who had given him strength to stand.

Monica followed the angel, and Mitch remained rooted to the spot. When the angel left, so did his entourage, leaving Mitch alone in his room. Mitch lay on his bed and waited for Monica for hours. Monica came back into the room looking like a giddy girl.

Mitch swung his feet to the floor. "What was all that?" he asked.

Monica, struggling to contain her excitement, said, "That was Michael the Archangel. He has asked me to join his troop."

Mitch scrambled out of bed. "That's incredible! When do you leave?"

"When I have finished my mission," Monica said.

"No one deserves this more than you."

Mitch hugged Monica tight. They both closed their eyes. "Thank you," she said.

When Mitch opened his eyes, he was in the black hole. Unfazed, he asked, "What now?"

Remember your training from yesterday, a small, still voice said.

Mitch sat, closed his eyes, and began to scrunch up his face.

What are you doing?

"Trying to focus," Mitch said.

Empty your mind.

Mitch relaxed and took a deep breath.

Where is the opening?

Mitch looked around him in the spirit and saw a crack in the wall. "About fifty feet up," he replied.

Now find the path.

Mitch began to spot the pieces of an obstacle course and found the outline of the path. "Okay," he said. "I found it."

Good, now do it.

Mitch stood, turned around, and stuck his foot out. He expected to fall on his first step, like every other time. To his surprise, he stepped on something solid and began to walk across what seemed like a beam. At the end of the beam, Mitch knew there was a drop-off, but about five feet away there was a rope, so he jumped, grabbed the rope, and climbed onto a platform.

Good start.

Mitch smiled and side walked to his left where he knew there was a climbing wall. He followed the strange pattern of hand holes and made it to the other side. There, he discovered five, fifty-foot-tall poles that were separated from each other and only two inches wide. He realized that he must jump across them. He felt like he was still trying to find his balance on stilts, but he attempted a jump and fell. When he picked himself up, he saw Eli observing him and leaning on his cane.

"You have come a long way. I see that you have opened your eyes. Now let's see how much." Eli struck the floor and the lights went out. Mitch began to panic, but then remembered to empty his mind. He took deep breaths and began to shoot as bean bags flew at him. He never moved an inch, but he was not hit by a single one. The lights came on.

"You missed one," Eli said.

A drone appeared behind Mitch and shot a bean bag. The bag knocked Mitch to the ground.

"It's not only about seeing your target; it's about finding the best way to accomplish your mission. You must widen your view to truly see. But welcome to the land of shadows. Now we can truly begin your training. Sleep. I will teach you to truly open your eyes." Eli walked away.

"I know enough to avenge Leroy," Mitch said to himself.

That is a very bad idea, the small voice said.

Back in his room, Mitch spirit walked to the intelligence center. There, he saw the blue holographic image of a man and heard the low growls of familiar Morse code. He listened. "Spetsnaz located in Yaksha." Then he looked around and found a map highlighting the location. The Spetsnaz was in the mountain, ten miles southeast from the Pechora Ilych Nature Reserve in Russia.

Mitch saw that he was about thirty miles away. He left the room and walked through the hallways, peeking into doors and trying to find the armory. After half an hour of searching, he found it near the drone training area. He looked around some more to see if he could find transportation. As he searched the room, he found that there was a door he could not walk through. He skipped the door and moved to the next. There he found a modified F35 Lightning also known as The Archangel. It had all the bells and whistles – cloaking, silent vertical takeoffs, and the capacity to contain seventeen people.

He ended his spirit walk, snuck out of his quarters, and used what he had observed and learned. Shadows were to his advantage. He successfully snuck into the armory. There, he took black armor and a scary-looking prophet helmet with blacked out eyes and a missing nose plate. It looked like a skull.

Mitch wasted no time getting on to the plane. He flicked a few switches to turn it on. Then he buckled in and hit full throttle. He shot through a tunnel that spat him out the side of a beautiful, snow-covered mountain. Then he pulled up a holographic map and found Yaksha. Mitch got there in a few minutes and found the auto-land feature. He landed quietly, half a mile outside of the city. Then he got out of the plane through the open hatch of the cockpit.

Mitch found his way as the day dimmed to nighttime. He found the city and decided to hide inside a tree. There, he began to meditate and was soon able to spirit walk out of the tree and into the town. In a matter of minutes, he had scouted the whole city and found no one.

Frustrated, he headed back to his body. But at the outskirts of the city, he saw a faint figure in a tree. Mitch looked through his helmet and saw that it was the man from the hologram. He returned to his body and stepped out of the tree, trying to move subtly as he attempted to get a clear shot. He took a deep breath and stepped forward. He slipped. As he fell, he pulled the trigger and let off a barrage of bullets.

He hit the floor flat on his back and got the wind knocked out of him. But a few minutes later, he heard a thump. He scrambled for his gun and pointed it in the direction of the thump. He held his breath and walked slowly in that direction. When he saw a pool of blood forming, he knew that he had killed his first Spetsnaz.

He left the body lying there and got back on the plane to head home. He engaged auto-pilot as he approached base and the plane flew through the tunnel and onto the landing pad. Mitch snuck back into his room and hid his armor, then slept.

Everyday Mitch learned more and more. After training, he would go out and assassinate a Spetsnaz. Each time, he was more efficient than the last time. Eventually, he got to the point where he stopped spirit walking and began to walk into cities himself. When it came to the time for him and his armor to be named, Mitch snuck his armor back into the armory.

"Just because you get a name and armor does not mean you are ready to fight," Eli said. "You must learn to use every inch of your armor, your weapons, and your judgment. Just because you have the shot does not mean you have to take it."

Eli walked into the armory and there was a table set up with five helmets. "Each one of these represents a different branch of the Shadows," he said. He grabbed one that looked like his without any paint on it and said, "This is the helmet of an apostle. They lead certain groups of people. Some may lead five, ten, hundreds, or even thousands of people. No one is less than the other, and all share the same goal: salvation."

Eli grabbed another helmet and it looked like the one Mitch had stolen. "This is the helmet of a prophet. They are the first into battle, and second in command under the apostles. They must see the battle before it happens and guide people.

Eli put the helmet down and grabbed another one. It looked like a leader's helmet but had a little more definition on the brow, with two accented triangles down the center that made it look almost bug-like. In both eyes, there were three small lenses in a cylinder. Eli held it up. "This is the helmet of an evangelist. They are scouts and assassins, hitting their targets from a mile and a half away. They infiltrate enemy lines and are never seen, never found."

Eli moved on to the next helmet. It was blocky, with deep-set eyes and a big jaw plate. "This is the helmet of a pastor. They defend an area, making sure it becomes a fortress for its citizens."

Eli moved to the last helmet; it was slender with a beaded metal faceplate and big eye lens. "This is the helmet of a teacher," Eli said. "They are the most powerful of all Shadows."

Eli put the helmet down and said, "Every man, no matter how good or how humble he is, is likely to change and abuse power to get ahead when he is given too much of it. A great leader learns that even with all that power, no man is better than the lowest man on the totem pole. Be yourself but stay humble, for the day your pride takes over you will find yourself standing alone with nothing."

CHAPTER 20

Shadow HQ. Three weeks later.

Mitch mastered the black hole and the shooting range, hitting everything that moved. Eli soon taught Mitch advanced spirit walking techniques like Walking the Line – moving through a place between the spirit and the physical world. A place where you were completely invisible to most.

Eli moved to the next phase of field training and taught Mitch how to become one with his surroundings. He showed Mitch old-fashioned camouflage, multiple camouflage techniques, and the new vanishing armor.

He showed Mitch how to move and fight in the dark, teaching him that darkness was only the absence of light and how, in the same way, a lack of knowledge left him in the dark. "Just because you have a shot does not mean you have to take it," he said. For reasons he could not fully explain, those words angered Mitch every time Eli spoke them.

Soon enough, Mitch had progressed far enough in his training to be taken out into the field. Eli took Mitch to the front lines to defend a small rural town called Grachyovka. The Shadows had received intel that a troop of Spetsnaz was planning to infiltrate the town as revenge for false information.

The Shadows built a small tent city in the trees in two hours. Night fell and Mitch began to pace back and forth in Eli's green and beige tent. The only pieces of furniture were a black cot and a small wooden chest. Eli entered his tent and saw Mitch pacing. "What's wrong with you youngin?"

"I've been waiting for an hour to have my lesson," Mitch said.

"I've been busy helping people, like everyone else. And you're supposed to be at your post."

"You said to meet you every day at nightfall and it is well past that," Mitch said stubbornly.

Eli stopped and looked at Mitch. "We're trying to protect lives and save a city from destruction."

"But they're the enemy. Shouldn't we just leave them to make their own decisions? Since it's their country."

"It doesn't matter if it's their country or not. These people are innocent, and because of us, they are going to be slaughtered. We have someone who is killing everyone instead of helping us, and he has exposed us. The United States government only knew us as a myth before now. Now that they are convinced we exist, they will try to weaponize us and use us to do their dirty work.

"But why can't we do the dirty work?" Mitch asked.

"Why do you act like a child? Questioning everything? Every life is precious, and every time you kill someone, their spirit goes into you."

"I will pay the price," Mitch said.

"It's easy to make a decision when you're not directly involved. But when you fight out of a need for revenge, you become blinded by rage and hatred. Hatred is the precedent of fear and unforgiveness."

Mitch raised his voice at Eli. "And what is wrong with revenge?! The Bible speaks of loving your enemy, but how can you kill something you love?"

"Life was not made to be taken," Eli said quietly. "It was made to be preserved. When you fight, you must have a clear mind and a clean spirit. Learn to save a life instead of taking it."

"Your passive nature will get more of us killed," Mitch said.

"Learn your place," Eli warned.

"I know mine," Mitch said. "It is to save my country and serve my people."

"Who are your people?" Eli asked.

"My fellow countrymen."

"To truly win this war, we must first win over the people," Eli advised. "I make those decisions daily, and if I have to take a life I will. But there is always a chance we can save them."

"Why do you get to decide who lives and who dies?"

"Somebody has to," Eli said.

"But why can't we just choose one side?" Mitch asked.

"We must choose what is right."

Mitch smiled. "You taught us to kill."

Eli shook his head. "No, I taught you to survive and to save others in need."

"America needs us right now!"

"Mitch, America is using us. This town needs us."

"Aren't they the same thing?"

"No! America is trying to make us do their dirty work, but you will understand soon enough."

"But–"

Eli, angry now, cut him off abruptly. "Enough! No more buts! Go to your post."

Mitch stormed off in a rage. Eli watched him storm off and shook his head in disappointment. Then he turned around and walked into the giant tent that had been designated as a war room.

On a spirit walk, Mitch heard "Spetnaz located in Podkolki." Podkolki was a newly developed city that had been destroyed when the United States swept through the South. Mitch snuck away at daybreak, taking the archangel and a .50 caliber with a whispering death silencer. Flying over the supposed target location, all he could see was a demolished city covered in ash. Charred remnants of buildings and houses were surrounded by thick forest. It seemed like it would be almost impossible to get any tanks through. Yet, only a tank could have done the kind of damage Mitch was seeing.

He landed a kilometer from the edge of the city, in a small opening in the forest, and as he landed, he kept the cloaking on. Then he moved a dead tree close to it, to remind him of its location. Mitch went on into the town, making his way through the forest surrounding it, swinging quickly from tree to tree with the help of his grappling hook. As he approached the edge of town, he spotted the lone bell tower of a half-standing Catholic church, about two hundred yards away from the forest's tree line. The church was a dirty white, with bullets and explosive holes in it. The tower seemed unsafe to even be close to. Mitch snuck his way through five different patrols and past one sniper on top of a mountain of rubble. The sniper was hidden, but Mitch knew how to see past the Russian's attempts at cloaking.

As he made it to the bell tower, he found five men positioned throughout the structure. One by one, Mitch took the men out. He noticed that the troops were wearing a unique looking uniform that looked neither Russian nor American. It was black and brown camouflage with three lens night vision goggles flipped back over the shoulder. Their helmets were United States issued helmets, which was strange, because no one except the United States knew their helmet's full design. Mitch set the information aside for later and set up shop just below the top of the tower. He set his sights through a small hole facing the center of town and waited for his target.

A few hours went by and Mitch had only seen a handful of people. He grew restless and had just considered abandoning the mission when the rubble around the tower suddenly began to move. Men stepped out of the rubble like ants, and he saw his target appear with a Shadow Pastor style helmet. As the target approached the other soldiers, she took her helmet off. Her long black hair fell and the wind caught it, making it whip and flow like a palm frond on a windy day in the Caribbean. She was coming from the forest behind him and walking toward the town square about a hundred yards away from the tower. Mitch could not see her face because her back was to the tower. Regardless of his hate, Mitch felt that assassination was a demoralizing action that could only be done with honor if the target was shot in front and never from behind.

The Spetsnaz stopped and spoke to many people, and Mitch tried not to fidget. It was as though she knew he was in the tower with his sights on her, and she was taunting him. After an hour, she started to turn toward him. The turn was slow and graceful, she moved like a ballerina and had the posture of a soldier high in rank. Mitch aimed.

As her face peeked around her flowing hair, Mitch's grip on the gun and trigger grew stronger. It felt like she had been turning for an eternity. A gust of wind blew at the last minute and obscured most of her face with her hair, leaving only her eyes and the top side of her nose. She was looking right at him. Before he pulled the last inch on the trigger, he hesitated. Her eyes were so familiar he blurted out 'Nissi', loud enough for some men close to the tower to hear him. He shook his head, not knowing he had said anything out loud. At that moment, he spotted a second sniper in a building across from him. He swung the archangel and took the shot, taking out the sniper with a headshot. Too late, he realized that he had not set up the whispering death silence properly. The sound of his gunshot rang out.

He ran to the top of the tower and jumped off, leaving the archangel behind. As he glided toward his aircraft, a massive explosion went off and blew him into a tree. The explosion had come from the tower.

He realized he no longer had a quick escape and that he still had to make it back to Grachyovka before the Shadows moved out. He heard soldiers approaching from both above and below him. As he swung through the trees, he looked back and saw someone catching up to him. The figure moved swiftly and quietly, gliding between trees as though they had Shadow training and a lot of experience.

Mitch missed a step and fell into a bush. He didn't move. Four tree runners and ten ground trackers went past. A fifth tree runner stopped right above him. It was the black-haired lady. This time, she had her helmet on. The camouflage pattern confirmed to Mitch that it was a Shadow helmet.

The black-hair lady looked around and moved closer to the bush. Mitch held his breath and curled himself up as she drew close enough to look through the leaves of the bush. Suddenly, a whistle went off. As soon as she heard it, she was gone.

Mitch waited a few minutes, breathing very slowly. Then he let out a sigh of relief and made his way back to his cloaked ship. He headed back to Grachyovka covered in mud and leaves. His uniform was ripped from head to toe.

Mitch made it back close to mid-day and tried to sneak into his bunk, but just as he was halfway through the door, a familiar voice spoke up. "Did you learn your lesson?" it asked.

Mitch froze, then turned to face the owner of the voice. "You knew about this?" he asked Eli.

"You thought I would not catch on to where it is that you keep disappearing to? By the way, how many lives have you taken in your vengeance?"

"You should know, since you know everything," Mitch replied.

Eli shook his head. "I thought you were ready." He turned his back on Mitch and looked over his shoulder at him. His voice was calm but downcast, like a father speaking to a disobedient son. "You've disappointed me. Too many innocent people, dead." Then he walked away.

A heavy feeling of shame fell on Mitch. He went into his room, fell on his cot, and cried himself to sleep. Hours went by. Suddenly, Eli walked into Mitch's tent, grabbed a chair close to the entrance, and dragged it to the side of Mitch's cot. Mitch stayed lying face down in his cot. He knew Eli was sitting next to him but did not react.

Eli leaned against the cot with his elbows and begins to speak softly. "Ervin, Sandra, Josephine, Jeremy, George, Francisco, Jeremiah, Hilton, Cortez, Anna. Just a few of the names of people we've lost, thanks to you. I know you thought you were helping by eliminating the Spetsnaz, but what you were really doing was killing Shadows. You've killed without remorse, without proper intel. Even though you had one ear in HQ."

Mitch sat up in shock.

"You are a gifted Shadow, but you are wrathful and you nurse hatred. I never told you to forget your loved ones, just to never use them as justification for revenge. Making decisions is hard, but it's even harder when your decisions affect others. Your decisions have caused the loss of many lives. Starting with the death of Prophet Isaiah. He was the first Shadow you killed. He was tracking a tyrant known as The Liquidator."

"The day Isaiah found him, you killed him. Today, the city we were supposed to defend was flattened without warning. They came through a hole that you left. For that, I am suspending you for ten days. You leave for the black hole in an hour. No detours. You go straight there. I have my best men escorting you, including Demsi. I have convinced the other Shadows to not kill you. But if you mess up again, I cannot guarantee your safety."

Mitch could not look at Eli. "I understand. Thank you for giving me another chance."

"Take this time to heal," Eli said, "and we will finish your training when you are done." Eli stood and walked out of the tent. He paused at the exit as if he was going to say something, but left instead. An hour later, two Zealots appeared. Mitch stood and walked to the tent door. His escorts were armed to the teeth, as though transporting a prisoner.

Demsi walked up to Mitch. "Please listen to everything we say, because the Zealots are under orders to shoot you if you don't cooperate. You are not under arrest, because Shadows are not under any government. But you have made many enemies for yourself within the Shadow Order. Lay low, do your time, and breathe. You still have the chops to be a great leader. Maybe one day, but not just yet."

Another Shadow walked up to Mitch wearing a Pastor's helmet. "Mitch Walker. Please follow me."

Mitch nodded and followed the man to a cloaked archangel. He sat with one Zealot to his left and another to his right. An hour and twenty=one minutes later, they arrived at the black hole. The Zealots stood and Mitch stood with them, but his movement startled one of the Zealots, who immediately pointed his weapon at Mitch. "Hold!" Demsi yelled. The Zealot's M-16 was inches away from Mitch's face. Mitch looked down the barrel, too shocked to be frightened.

"Lower your weapon now," Demsi ordered.

The Zealot lowered his weapon slowly, and a Shadow Pastor spoke. "Follow orders and don't deviate. Understood?"

"Yes sir," Mitch responded.

They walked him to his old room.

The Shadow Pastor said, "You will stay in this room and nowhere else.

There will be two Zealots posted at your door at all times, so if you try anything funny, you will be shot."

"Understood," Mitch said.

The door closed.

For five days, Mitch prayed and cried. On the fifth day, Monica appeared to try to comfort him. "God has forgiven you, Mitch. Paul was a killer of Christians before he became known as the father of Gentiles for the Christian faith. It is never too late to make things right. Starting with Nissi."

"Alright," Mitch sniffed. "I'll write to her."

Pain flickered across Monica's face and she turned her face away, but Mitch put a finger under her chin and turned her face back to him. "I know. You still have a special place in my heart, but we must hold fast and know that God will help us."

A tear trickled down Monica's cheek. "Thank you. You have helped me in ways you may never know of."

"Thank you for checking on me. I will never forget you," Mitch said.

Monica stood and kissed Mitch on the forehead. "I will see you soon."

"Okay," he said. "Until then."

Monica smiled. "Until then. God bless you."

"God bless you too," Mitch replied.

After Monica had left, Mitch spent some time thinking. Then he picked up a pencil and a piece of paper and began to write.

Dearest Nissi,

I'm so sorry... I lost my way. I have filled my heart with rage and hatred. You were keeping me alive, but anger and fear helped me kill. I did not know I was killing my people; I was blinded by my desperate need to find justice and peace at the end of my barrel, instead of truly giving my pain to the Lord. My sin calls to me. The cries of the innocent haunt me in my dreams. I am tormented by the ghosts I have created. I have become a ghost in the shadow. A murderer and a lost cause. And worst of all, I almost lost you in my fury. In Podkolki, I found myself in a conflict between finishing the job by pulling the trigger and losing myself or abandoning my foolish pursuit of self honor and self-justification. I thought getting rid of the Spetsnaz would fill a gap within me, and I almost lost you for a foolish decision because of the evil within my heart. The very evil I've been running away from... It's time to face the music and take responsibility for the lives I have taken. I beg God for forgiveness every day, and I pray beyond prayers, that you will forgive my stupidity and my immaturity. I will work on myself under the guidance of the Holy Spirit. I miss you and think about you daily. I miss the way your eyes shimmer in the sun like a glassy sea. I pray to see you again soon.

Yours truly,
Mitch.

CHAPTER 21

Fort Pierce, Florida. Mitch's Landing Café.

"Change is inevitable," Taavet says. "But what direction we go is entirely up to us."

A man walks into the café and whispers something in Taavet's ear. "Take them to purgatory," he replies. "But not him," he says, looking at Basheer. "After we are done, take him to the Captain's Quarters. Then you know what to do." The man salutes Taavet and stalks off.

"What's purgatory?" Basheer asks.

"It is a city of prisoners. A place they will live in until the war is settled. We give our prisoners a chance to live a somewhat normal life instead of treating them like slaves. Only the worst criminals are taken to the last level of purgatory. A place of regret known as luminescence, where Lumite always shines. Some men have gone mad there, because there is no escape from the pure white light."

Basheer scoffed. "You Christians are truly stupid, gathering an army. I would not waste my time on prisoners or their comfort. My enemies will fear and respect me."

"Fear is the absence of respect, for a man who fears will one day turn against you. Someone who truly respects you is loyal till the end. Fear does not even prevent betrayal. Instead, it is the fuel that leads to it."

Basheer shook his head. "That is not true. Some of the greatest rulers operate by fear."

"Rulers like?"

"Xeroxes, Julius Caesar, and Hitler. To name a few."

"Xeroxes was assassinated by his priest. Julius Caesar was assassinated by his counsel members and Hitler killed himself after he had lost control. They were betrayed by those closest to them. All except Hitler, who was betrayed by his own mind."

"That is one view, but no one ever looks at how the country grew in peace and prospered during his rule."

"Actually," Taavet corrected, "that was the start of the fall of the nation. It caused revolts, poverty, and unnecessary fights they could not finish. The United States was one of the greatest nations of the modern world, but look what happened. They started one too many fights."

"The United States has been the biggest sign of plague and blasphemy on this earth."

Taavet smiled. "A plague that was at one time, a beacon of hope to the world."

Basheer waved a hand in dismissal.

"Let us continue the story," Taavet said.

The Black Hole, Russia.

Ten days passed with no sign of life; but Mitch continued to get visits from Monica. On the tenth day, Zealots open his room door. Mitch stood and Eli walked slowly into the room. When he had come face to face with Mitch, he began to speak.

"All life is precious," he said. "And taking a life out of revenge is the worst way to live. One who lives by the sword will die by the sword."

"I know that I did evil," Mitch said. "I was blinded by hatred and revenge. I did not want to deal with the hurt within me and I was looking to make the world hurt through my retribution. Looking for the wrong kind of justice. I know that now, and I am sorry to whoever is suffering in the wake of my destruction. I am not looking for forgiveness. I just want to make things right."

"Is your mind right?" Eli asked.

"Not yet," Mitch said. "But I'm working on it."

"I can work with that. You still have two areas to complete before you can be called a true Shadow."

For the next six months, Eli fought alongside Mitch, teaching him every step of the way.

After six months, Eli said, "This is the last step of your training. You must find someone to teach. Someone of your choice, who you will keep under your supervision. Train them as you like, with little to no guidance. Are you ready?"

"I am," Mitch said.

"Choose wisely."

A month later, Mitch and Eli went off on a mission that led them north to a town called Norilsk - an industrial city that was filling fast with Russians who were trying to escape the Americans still lingering in the south. Intelligence came in from one of the younger Shadows, an Evangelist called Rebecca Sparks. Although Mitch had never seen her, he had heard of her legendary skills with bladed weapons and her accuracy with anything she held in hand. Her intel suggested that a group of refugees were walking into a place where all the men would be killed and all the women raped - a place oddly known as the Rape Hotel.

The Shadows arrived at Norilsk an hour and a half before daybreak, and the first thing they did was set up a small microphone next to rooftop snipers, which they used to record their voices and call signs. With that information, they began to eliminate the snipers. The recorded voices and call signs were kept in HQ's database and generated when needed.

Eli, Mitch, and seven other Shadows placed themselves in strategic locations on the rooftops. A Shadow principle was that orders were not to be executed until the target was either about to commit the offense, in the act or had just committed it. While Mitch waited, he noticed that there was some movement in a lake nearby. Navy Seals came out of the water and began to rush toward the nearest ten-story building. Seconds later, they heard gunfire and explosions. Eli whispered through the radio; "Shadows, move in and take your shots."

Eli and Mitch set up an entrance through the roof with a device called a flame cord. The flame cord was like a detonating cord, but instead of exploding it would become molten and melt rapidly through any material except Lumite. Eli set the flame cord in a small circle, just big enough for one person to enter, and he jumped into the first hole, closely followed by Mitch. As Eli and Mitch walked down hallways, they saw an army rushing through. They looked like Navy Seals but wore ball caps instead of helmets. Eli showed himself for a moment and the soldiers began to shoot and give chase. Eli took the men down the hallway to where Mitch waited. When the last man had run past him, Mitch began to make quick work of them with a sword. He ran through the hallway, cutting through the men and jumping from wall to wall.

After clearing the floors, Eli and Mitch put a special weapon on the roof and floor called 'the bush'; a small half-domed device that would shoot tiny needles to pierce through any kind of armor. The needles were coated with a synthesized paralysis serum that lasted six hours and could paralyze a human being in three seconds.

Mitch had learned how to spirit walk without having to be in a trance. He checked the hallways and saw nothing. Then he moved to a divide where the Holy Spirit told him, Don't shoot. He checked the hallway and saw nothing. Moments later, he turned into the intersection and came face to face with a Navy Seal who fired two shots at Mitch's chest. Mitch quickly disarmed the man and swept him off his feet. Then he stood over the man and said "Friendly."

The man slowly holstered his gun and apologized. "I'm sorry, he said. "I just lost five of my men two floors down."

"I'll help," Mitch said, "but we do things my way, understand?"

The man nodded and together they began to clear rooms. After clearing the floors Mitch said, "Don't go back, keep moving forward." The man did not ask any questions and kept moving.

They fought for five hours, going door to door. When they were finished, Mitch knew this man was the one.

After the raid was over, Mitch and the man walked to a building the Navy Seals had turned into a field hospital. The hospital was swamped with victims, prisoners, and Navy Seals. The man collapsed in a corner, exhausted.

"You fought well today," Mitch said.

"Thank you, sir, but I would have been a goner if it wasn't for your help." The man took his cloth mask off and Mitch recognized him. He was Hispanic looking, five feet and eleven inches tall. He had a round face, a goatee, and dark brown eyes. "David," Mitch said, "You have to give yourself more credit."

David was shocked. "How do you know my name?"

"I've known you your whole life. Find me in the city called Tolka." And then Mitch vanished.

Back at the café.

"Wait," Basheer says. "Are you telling me that David, Mitch's stepbrother, was a Shadow?"

"David is a Shadow, yes," Taavet says.

Basheer ponders that for a moment. "So our former leader was a Shadow who learned under Mitch."

"Yes," Taavet says. "That is why he was sent to kill Sitch. Even though he was not fully trained, he caught on quickly. Mitch taught David to be a killer, and he didn't have a hard time teaching David because David was a natural in the physical and the spiritual. Mitch did not realize that David was surpassing him, but Eli, who had been quietly observing them, did. Eli did not teach David because he belonged to Mitch, but Eli would try to advise Mitch in teaching and warned Mitch to pay more attention to David instead of their missions. Unfortunately, most of Eli's advice fell on deaf ears. Mitch would teach most of the Shadow's principles, leaving out some important information to save time. He thought if he showed David instead of teaching him verbally, David would catch on. As David learned, he began to feel that something was missing in the information Mitch was giving him, which was true. Mitch would say in his teachings 'To hide in darkness, you must become darkness.' What he failed to teach David was the second part, which is Shadow work in the darkness known as the unknown - the same place where Moses met with God daily."

"I don't understand," Basheer says.

"There are two types of darkness," Taavet explains. "There is the evil darkness, and it is the known darkness, the one portrayed in every movie and every book to be evil. But the Bible speaks of a darkness that God the Father works in. It is a place man cannot comprehend by looking into."

"I still don't understand," Basheer says.

"Then you are not supposed to know. We can sit here all day going around in circles, or we can continue talking about your former leader."

"So be it," Basheer says.

Taavet continues.

"Mitch trained David on the field because he believed that he had wasted too much time in the black hole. And he felt that David would learn on the go. But Mitch did not know the lasting effects he would leave on David."

"You mean helping him become the greatest leader in the ghost origination?"

"Actually, the greatest was the unintentional founder and the one who tried to end it."

"David was not the founder?" Basheer asks.

"No," Taavet says. "The true founder was Mitch, who unintentionally became the first Ghost in the Shadow, then it was David. David did not know that Mitch was the founder until much later. Eli taught Mitch how to save lives, but Mitch taught David to be a killer. The big difference between Mitch and David is that Mitch killed everything and anything, but David tried not to kill at all."

"What does that mean, Ghost in the Shadow?" Basheer asks.

"The Ghost in the Shadow is the leader of Ghosts who were trained to be Shadows but use their knowledge to kill their own. That is why there is only one entrusted with all five Shadow styles and that is why David was the most cowardly man to be called the Ghost in The Shadow."

"That's not true! David was the most feared and loved leader of the Ghosts."

Taavet shakes his head. "David killed when he needed to, but if he could save a life, he would do that instead. Either way, there is something worse than death."

"What?"

"Life," Taavet says. "Everyone will die at one point or another. It is easy to die for a cause or for what you believe in, but it is harder to live for it. Life is worth fighting for."

"Then why do you take life?"

"There is no way to justify a killing. The only time I kill is to defend innocence, but my life is not more precious than the next man. That is one thing Mitch forgot to teach. Mitch would tell David that life was precious and that 'We as Shadows hold the power of life and death.' But because of his youth, he forgot to mention that we are all equal."

"No we are not," Basheer says.

"If I were to order this Zealot to shoot you, what do you think would happen?"

"I would be worshiped as a hero."

"How about if I have her shoot you?"

"Who?" Basheer asks.

At that precise moment, a stiletto blade grazes past Basheer's face and embeds itself in the wall behind him. Basheer groans and grabs his ear in horror. He looks around frantically but sees nothing.

Taavet smirks and then says "The darkness holds mysteries that you can only wish you knew."

"Where did that come from?" Basheer asks.

"From a place forbidden to talk about, the shadows." At that moment, five Shadow masks appear in five dark areas of the room, then vanish back into the shadows again.

"I know more than you think," Taavet says. "I may be Christian, but I am not a fool."

Basheer attempts to compose himself. "I never said Christians were fools."

Taavet gives Basheer a sarcastic look but continues talking. "The Shadows are based off a Christian foundation."

"Can you tell me more about the Zealots?"

"The Zealots are Shadows who have gotten older and slower but cannot retire because of this endless war. Back to David. David learned so fast that at one point he left Mitch behind in training. Mitch saw this, and knowing that David could not become a full Shadow without training someone else, decided to bend the rules. Instead of instructing him to find someone to teach, Mitch came up with a plan to become David's student. In which case, David could become a Shadow faster and Mitch could bounce ideas off David to help develop the Shadows. David began to feel used. Eli liked the idea but he did not like that Mitch could use David's gift for the wrong reasons. David began to speak more to Eli, and Eli became like a father to him."

CHAPTER 22

Fort Pierce, Florida.

Taavet looks at a terrified Basheer almost curling up into a ball in his chair. "You should not be scared, so long as you do not attack the innocents."

"No one is innocent," Basheer says. "We all make choices and we all support a cause. Once you have put your hand to it, you become just as guilty."

"So don't make a choice. I'm getting close to what you want to know. For two years, Mitch and David learned and developed new attack procedures, new hiding techniques, and new methods of surprising by ambush. They perfected them all. Many times, David clashed verbally with Mitch. Somehow they always found a compromise. Until the day Mitch turned."

Yeyka, Russia

An airplane took off. It was carrying a new, experimental, radar that could shoot ultrasonic sound waves at a perfect frequency. These sound waves would penetrate solid rock and make a three-dimensional map of an entire bunker with one hundred percent accuracy. After flying over some mountains near Kislokan, they found an anomalous bunker, a location not shown in any of the maps the Shadows currently had. Eli sent Rebecca to investigate the bunker. Two days later, Rebecca found that it was a hide-out for a highly ranked Spetsnaz leader. The intel put Eli on high alert and the Shadows developed a realistic VR simulator that would provide an accurate model of the bunker and its surroundings for them to practice in.

For two weeks straight, David and Mitch rehearsed in the simulator, going through different scenarios with different people. But the best results, with the biggest success and lowest impact, were from when Mitch and David attempted the mission alone.

It was soon D-day. The sun had just fallen and Mitch, David, and Eli were getting ready to leave when an urgent call came in. There was a troop trapped in Kodinsk.

"I have to help a troop trapped in Kodinsk," Eli said. "But you guys know what to do. Remember your training, keep a clear head, and bring him in alive."

"Yes sir," Mitch said.

Mitch and David entered the archangel alone, strapped themselves in, and launched. On the way there they received confirmation that the leader was on location, and an update on guard positions. Mitch landed the archangel less than a quarter of a mile from the front of the bunker. Then they made their way to the back entrance, knowing there were only two entrances. Mitch took position by some trees just beside the camouflaged entrance, while David approached the door very slowly.

"You're all clear," Mitch said.

But something caught his attention on the top side of the cliff. When Mitch looked, it was a patrol of four Spetsnaz with old cloaking technology.

"Hold position," Mitch said.

David stopped in his tracks and lay down. Mitch aimed. When two of the Spetsnaz were aligned, he took them out with one bullet, and then quickly eliminated the other two with two more shots. One of them fell off the cliff and landed next to David.

"All clear," Mitch said.

David moved to the secret entrance and placed a specially designed bar on the armored door. The bar embedded itself into the ground, completely jamming the door. Mitch and David now made their way around to the front side, the only way left to get in or out. They spotted about ten men patrolling different sections of the forest and took them all out. When they arrived at the front of the bunker, they discovered two giant camouflaged armor doors and a small door to the left. Mitch and David spirit walked through the doors and found five cloaked Spetsnaz guarding it. They continued through the bunker, traveling in the Line so they could not be seen spiritually or physically. They went room to room, and found their target in the last room, behind a door on the left. They left the Line and cracked open the front door of the bunker, then rolled a new and improved 'bush' through the crack in the door. The bush went off, immobilizing the five guards and allowing Mitch and David to sneak in. As they entered, David put the special bar on each door they passed. They arrived at the room they had scouted and began to fire, trying to flush out the leader. In the simulation, only ten Spetsnaz came out to face them; five troops from one door and five from another. But, intel had failed to tell them that the last door on the right led to a barracks. Forty men rushed out, guns blazing. They took cover behind door frames as bullets whizzed by.

"Oops," Mitch said. "I forgot about the barracks behind the last door on the right."

David shook his head and rolled his eyes. The storm of bullets prevented them from moving. David spotted the Spetsnaz leader as he came out and ran into a tunnel that seemed to lead toward the secondary entrance. David said "Target spotted," and began to push towards the 40 men, guns blazing. He threw a second bush into the middle of the troop. The needles knocked out ten of them before one man landed on top of the bush. Mitch and David began to run and bounce off walls until they came in sword range. Then they pulled out their swords and began to slice through the men. The Spetsnaz, overwhelmed, retreated into their barracks. Once they were all inside the barracks, Mitch put a metal bar on the door and trapped them there. Then he and David went after the leader and his entourage. As they caught up to them, the entourage began to shoot. David threw his last bush into their midst and knocked all of them out cold.

"Good thinking," Mitch said.

"Thank you, I thought you were going to kill them all."

"I was only going to kill the people around him."

"I guess you don't get the consent of a target before you capture him."

Mitch chuckled. "Thank God you were here. It's time to move the prisoners."

"Amen to that," David said. "I just want to head back and take a hot shower."

"Alright, let's get a move on."

Mitch and David stripped the men down to their underwear and then zip-tied their hands together. The noise of the Spetsnaz trying to break out of their barracks filled the hallway. Mitch and David moved four men before moving on to the leader. Mitch turned to the leader, and when he saw the mask, he had a flashback of the moment Leroy was killed. When the head of the Spetsnaz had stabbed Leroy, this man was there. As soon as David removed the man's helmet, Mitch whipped out his handgun and fired a shot just that grazed past David's ear and entered the leader's head through his left eye.

"WHAT THE HELL DID YOU DO?" David yelled.

"I passed judgment," Mitch said.

David looked down at the dead Spetsnaz. "No, you just murdered a target we were specifically ordered to bring in alive."

"They were going to kill him anyway," Mitch said.

David closed his eyes. "They were going to interrogate him, then put him on trial."

Mitch shrugged. "Too late."

"Who made you judge, jury, and executioner?"

"I did," Mitch said. Then he turned around and began to walk to the archangel.

David grabbed a brick and threw it at the back of Mitch's helmet, making Mitch stop in his tracks. David yelled, "I am SICK and tired of your self-pity and self-justification. You are nothing but a murderer and a tyrant!"

"And you are just an orphan and a cursed child. You're the real reason mom is dead."

David marched toward Mitch as if he was going to attack him. "Don't you dare try to turn this around on me."

Mitch turned as David grabbed a metal pipe to swing at Mitch. He grabbed it at the last minute and held it tight. "You said it yourself," he said. "Everyone you care about dies."

David kicked Mitch away then attacked by thrusting the pipe toward Mitch. Mitch deflected the thrust. David used his momentum to swing the pipe around his head and down. The pipe hit Mitch square in the face and knocked him to the ground. David twisted the pipe and tried to hit Mitch again, but Mitch flipped himself up and jumped out of the way.

Mitch grinned and said, "Now this, is a fight." David yelled and swung the metal pipe, but Mitch ducked, and as he turned, he grabbed the pipe from behind, stopping David's momentum. David pushed the pipe and it hit Mitch in the chest, almost lifting him. Mitch noticed that David was trying to get his back against the wall and pushed the pipe away at the last moment. The pipe dug into the wall instead.

Mitch chuckled, and David became even angrier. He pulled the pipe out of the wall, but Mitch jumped and flipped over to David's back. David tried to hit him with a backswing but Mitch used his momentum against him and flipped him to the ground. As David hit the ground, Mitch grabbed the pipe and pinned David to the floor with it. "You still have a lot to learn," he taunted. "But the next time you come at me you better be ready, because I know who you really are."

At the precise moment Mitch finish speaking, shots rang out. Mitch yanked David up and yelled, "Run!" Then he grabbed the dead body and ran for the archangel. They dumped the body in the aircraft and David began to return suppressive fire. Mitch quickly got the archangel in the air and they first set off in a random direction before they circled back for base. Both men were quiet all the way back to base. When they landed, they found Eli standing on the launch pad. Mitch walk straight out of the cockpit and went past Eli without a word.

"What happened?" Eli asked David.

"Mitch just snapped and shot the leader."

"He did what?!" Eli exclaimed.

"He just took one look at him and shot him in the face."

"What about the others?" Eli asked.

"I knocked them out before Mitch could kill them."

Eli walk to the plane and saw the dead body, then he looked at the rest of the prisoners. He walked back and said "Mitch didn't kill the leader, the leader changed his mask. Good job."

"Thank you sir."

"Go have a hot shower, a hot meal, and some rest. You've earned it."

"Yes sir."

"From that day forward," Taavet said, "David started a campaign to eliminate the Shadows. He was convinced that deep down, all Shadows were like Mitch. First, he sent an anonymous email to the Shadows:

The Shadows have fallen. They have fallen into a self-justification that makes them judge, jury, and executioner. Today I have seen the weakness of the leadership. The upcoming leaders have lost their way. We cannot have this wild justice come into our country and infect our families. To preserve the true nature of the Shadows, we must become better. Each one of us must become a Ghost in the Shadow. There comes a day when we must do what is right, regardless of history or glory. We must do what we have learned all these years to do - stand up for the innocent. We have all seen or done things that we did not agree with, but it was done in the name of doing what is right. But what is right? Who determines what is right?? The men who believe they are above all others claim that they hear a divine voice. I say we walk in what we know is right. We must stop depending on a man to do the work of God, for, in the Dark Ages, kings would attack countries in the name of God. But all they did it for was the glory, using God to manipulate the people to do their bidding.

There is a time for peace, but now is a time of war. A time to protect our people. Now I ask you, will you stand under the thumb of a singular leader doing everything at the snap of their finger, or do you want to fight for what we hold dear, for freedom? Freedom is not free. If you stand with me, you will have a voice and a choice to come and go as you please, learning whatever you want. I leave it to you. If you want to stand with me, paint a single red line in the blacks of your helmet. I will find you.

In a month, David had convinced ten percent of the shadows that the Shadow Order was corrupt. He began to eliminate Shadows who pretended to join the cause. David then turned to the United States and warned them about the Shadow Order. The United States asked how David intended to handle the situation, and David responded, "I will take them out from the inside."

"How?" he was asked.

David had made a small group loyal to the United States. "Plus if you eliminate us all," he told the American government, "the country will surely fall." The government thanked him for his loyalty.

Two months later, the Russians attacked the United States, and the United States sent an order out for all American troops in Russia to return. On the 13th day of August, a Friday, the United States sent out an order for all Shadows to be eliminated. David told his second in command, a cryptographer named Teacher Simon Jacobs, and he relayed the information to the rest of the newly established Ghost organization. The Mission was called Ghost in the Shadow, in honor of David, who is now known as the Ghost in the Shadow."

CHAPTER 23

Friday, August 13. 2 A.M.

The news reached the Shadows, but the Russians had already infiltrated the United States. In retribution, American troops still in Russia were going from city to city, destroying everything in their paths. Meanwhile, Russian troops were going from city to city, destroying any that had supported, or were rumored to have supported United States troops.

Eli, troubled, called for a mandatory debriefing of all Shadows. A black three-dimensional camera sat on a stick in the center of the room and there was a computer screen up against the back wall. The room was filled. Shadows who could not be there had joined through video screens that were projected on to the walls.

Eli began to speak over the noise. "Friends, we have a situation. The homeland was just hit." The entire room went completely quiet. "The remnants of Russian troops are wreaking havoc on cities that supported or were rumored to have supported United States troops. We cannot leave this country desolate and in shambles. We did not want this war, but we cannot leave in this way. Today, we must defend the people we are fighting and bring stability. But do not try to take power, we are only here to oversee the transition of power. Understood?"

Everyone said, "Yes sir!"

Eli divided the Shadows into groups of twos and threes, and Eli put David with himself.

David went up to Eli and asked, "Why didn't you pair me with Mitch?"

"I need you for a special assignment," Eli said. "You have a clear head and a pure heart."

"I believe I can do a better job keeping Mitch from losing it."

"I need you right now, David. I thought Mitch was going to be the next leader, but I see you are a much better choice and I need to show you one thing before we go home."

David conceded. "I still don't like your decision, but I would like to assign two Shadows of my choosing."

"Which two?"

"I want Leon and Ralph assigned to him," Mitch said.

"That's an odd match; an evangelist and a prophet... but okay. Mitch!"

Mitch heard Eli calling him and approached. "Yes sir."

"You have a new assignment; you are to go to Kazan."

Mitch frowned. "Kazan?"

"Yes, Kazan. We need your prior experience with the city, and you are taking Leon and Ralph."

"Alright, when do we leave?"

"Immediately."

Mitch saluted and left for his room. Moments later, Eli walked into Mitch's room, closed the door behind him, and locked it. Mitch looked at Eli but did not react.

"Mitch, I have to tell you something."

Mitch turned back to his bag and continued to pack, glancing at Eli occasionally. "Yes sir."

"Everything is not as it seems," Eli said.

"Okay?" Mitch said.

"I have taught you many things, but to grow you must put old knowledge away and learn from your mistakes." Eli walked up to Mitch and looked him in the eye. Mitch stopped packing.

"There is one thing I taught you long ago," he said, and then he hugged Mitch tight. Mitch was shocked, but hugged Eli back. Eli began to sing softly in Mitch's ear.

Be gentle, be kind, don't look for a fight…

Mitch jolted a little, remembering the song. He started to sing along.

But if one finds you, you do what is right…

Eli released Mitch and walked to the door.

Stand straight and upright, with God by your side…

He stepped out and closed the door behind him. Mitch ran to catch him but Eli was already gone. Mitch finished softly.

… that is the way you live your life.

Mitch walked back to his bed, dropped to his knees, and began to pray.

"Oh Lord, I'm sorry for my stupidity. I'm sorry for being quick to shed blood. I did not want to be full of hatred and anger, and I did not want to kill for killing's sake. I ask for your forgiveness. Keep my mind right and clear. Help me do what I have to do. Help me Lord, to save at least one person today. In the name of Jesus. Amen."

The call came in for Mitch's group to depart, so he grabbed his bag and headed to the launch bay. There he saw the all too familiar modified C-17. Mitch, his group, and at least a hundred more shadows boarded the C-17. The plane was quiet. The only sounds that could be heard were the running engines. Group by group, the jumpmaster called on them to jump.

"Orca up," the jumpmaster called. Mitch and two Shadows stood.

The jumpmaster tapped his shoulder and said "Check equipment." They checked and gave the all-clear. Then the plane came to a halt and the doors opened. A red light turned green and the jumpmaster yelled "Go, go, go!" Mitch jumped first, closely followed by Ralph, then Leon. They free fell to about a thousand five hundred feet before pulling their parachute, then they glided to fifty feet where they released their parachutes and landed on a tall building right in the middle of Kazan. Mitch, Leon, and Ralph scanned the area for threats. Not finding any, it seemed as if they had got to the city before the Russians could. Mitch took command. "This is where we will stand. Fight strong, and stay aware. Now let's pray." Mitch dropped to one knee, as did Leon and Ralph. They all took off their helmets as Mitch prayed. "We thank you, Lord, for this opportunity to defend the innocent. Help us shoot straight and save a life. If we are to pay the ultimate price, we ask you to take us to your perfect place. In Jesus' name amen."

Leon and Ralph repeated, "Amen."

"Leon," Mitch said. "You are in charge from the north to the west. Ralph, you take from the north to the east. I'll take east to west, facing south. Remember your training and we will get through this."

The men said, "Yes sir!"

An hour went by without any sign of an attack. Everyone was in the process of checking their sections when Mitch saw someone moving in strange darts as if trying to find cover or get into position.

"I see something," Mitch said into his radio. "A man." Mitch slowed his breathing and started to pull the trigger when he heard that small, still voice. Listen.

Mitch listened and heard the sound of a knife being pulled slowly out of a sheath. He turned around quickly and found Leon coming down on him with a knife. Mitch crossed his arms and blocked the knife but did not see Ralph also attacking from his right side. Ralph plunged his knife into Mitch's side. Mitch kicked Leon away, turned, and pushed off a wall, causing Ralph to lose his grip on the knife. Mitch pulled out the knife from his side and grabbed his from his boot. "So you want a fight," he said.

Just then, an explosion rocked the city close to its center.

Leon grinned. "Now you have a dilemma. Either fight us or save the people."

Ralph tried to sneak around Mitch. He grabbed a rebar, jumped, and tried to come down on Mitch, but Mitch quickly dove out of the way. Leon was on Mitch fast, with a series of jabs and slices. Mitch blocked, bobbed, and weaved through the barrage. Ralph joined in, and Mitch seemed to be holding his own until Ralph hit Mitch in the chest, knocking him back on his butt. Mitch rolled and at the tail end of his roll, threw a knife right into Leon's lens. The knife only went as far as the lens.

Leon quickly took off his helmet and shook his head. "You're going to regret that," he said.

Mitch grasped his knife in one hand and held his wound with the other. He backed up to the edge of the building as Leon and Ralph split and slowly approached from two different angles. Mitch, now at the edge, looked down and saw the tail end of a troop rushing the building. Leon and Ralph charged at the same time. Ralph got to Mitch first. He thrust the rebar at Mitch but Mitch flipped, grabbing Ralph's helmet in the process and yanking it off. He landed behind Ralph and Ralph turned quickly, trying to knock Mitch off the edge. But Mitch deflected the swing with Ralph's helmet. Mitch then grabbed a sticky grenade and stuck it on Ralph's armpit, then kicked Ralph to the open door, sending him back against the troops that were coming up the stairs. The bomb exploded.

Leon continued to thrust and slice as Mitch countered every attack. They fought until Mitch disarmed Leon by grabbing the knife. He hit it out of Leon's hand mid-air, then snatched it and plunged it deep into the top of Leon's skull. Leon stood still for a moment, then dropped to his knees, fell over, and died.

Mitch sat, lightheaded from blood loss. He took off his helmet and chest piece to examine his wound. Then he cauterized the wound with a device from his medkit and bandaged himself. He wore Leon's chest piece and dog tags, and grabbed Ralph's helmet, putting that on too.

When he looked over the edge, he saw about nine hundred troops rushing into the building. He looked in Leon's satchel and found about fifty grenades and a rope. He quickly tied it to the door and jumped off the edge, throwing grenades into every window as he ran down the wall. One of the grenades hit a gas pipe and the explosion flung Mitch a hundred feet away. Rattled, Mitch found cover and sat. Then he turned on his radio to debrief HQ.

Screams and chaos from Shadows all over Russia blasted through. Then the radio went dead. Mitch's ears were still ringing when he heard a lone voice speak. "The light has been shown in the shadows and they are no more. If you hear this, Eli is dead. So is Mitch. If you are a Shadow, you can run, that's the way we like it. We will find you and you will have a choice; join us or die."

Mitch sat and reflected on what was going on. He searched Leon's satchel and found a piece of paper that said "After your mission, go to the hole. There you will find your way out."

Mitch considered his options and decided to go to the nearest airfield, one in the city of Ufa that had been taken by the United States at the beginning of the war.

Mitch snuck his way through town and found a car with keys in it. He made it to Ufa in four hours. There he saw United States troops lining up, so he did the same, trying to blend in. Down the line, a soldier grabbed a man dressed in Shadow uniform. "You belong to the Shadow Order," the soldier said.

"Yes," the Shadow said, not knowing that all shadows were to be shot.

Two others who had been patrolling the line ripped off the man's helmet and shot him. Mitch quickly cloaked himself and weaved through the crowds of people to the tarmac. Before he could step foot on it, another man ran onto it. As soon as the man's feet touched the tarmac, he was shot.

Mitch took a closer look and found that the asphalt was riddled with tiny seismic sensors that could alert the guard. He saw a truck approaching the tarmac and hitched a ride, still fully cloaked. The truck got close to a military plane that was about to take off, close enough for Mitch to run on to it without triggering too many sensors. Mitch dropped from the bottom of the truck and ran as fast as he could. He made it to the landing gear. When he looked back, seven more men were running on the tarmac and heading for the landing gear he was on. Still cloaked, he reached out to try to grab the men and pull them in, but just as he touched fingertips with one of the men, all seven were gunned down. In shock, he crawled up the landing gear and into the cargo hold. Two hours later, he snuck upside and hid among the troops.

Back at the café.

"I wish I never revealed the Shadows," Taavet said. "I wish I forgave Mitch. Eli would still be alive now… We are children that were forced into a life of war. He was just trying to do his best." Taavet sighed. "In the end, I became the one thing I hated most, a tyrant."

Basheer stared. "Who are you?"

"I was the Ghost in the Shadow," he said. "I am David."

Acknowledgements

To my Lord and Savior Jesus Christ for giving me the drive to start and finish this book.

To my parents for supporting my craziness and believing in me.

To Yaneli, Hector and Felicity for creature ideas, character names and comedic relief.

To Liani, Justin, Sebastian and Lilah for inspiring the languages and being there at the beginning.

To Arial and Dory for showing me what to fight for and for the stories.

To Dale L. Roberts for helping me and showing me that writing a book is not impossible.

To my aunts Tata and Tita, thank you for the food and support.

To Aca thank you for the love and making my life interesting.

To the people I based my characters off; Emmanuel, Alejandra, Erika and Sarah, thank you for being an inspiration

To my team Tochi, Jessie, Yuri and Alina, thank you for all the work and help. I can't wait to continue working with you.

Special thank to Tochi for going above and beyond and being a great friend.

Flashlight Lidice for being a constant source of inspiration and support, she is the real reason I wrote this book.

I.R. VASQUEZ

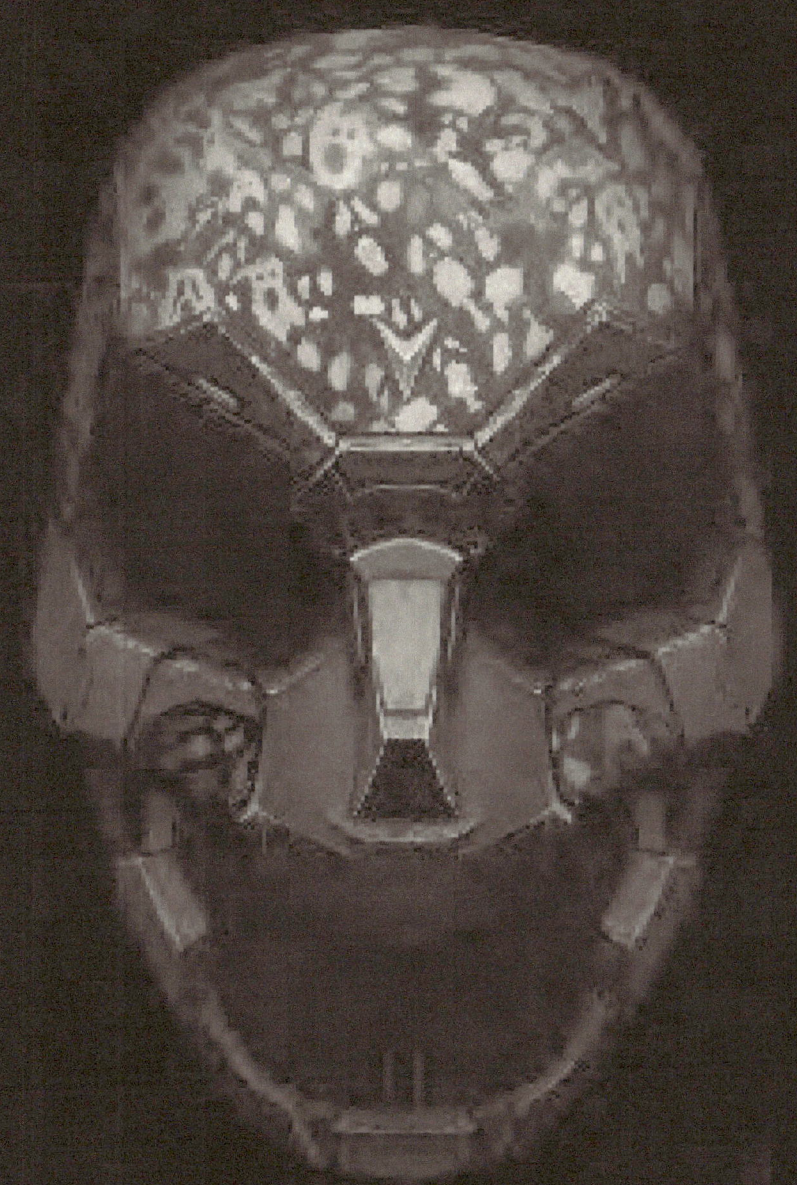

SITCH
CONFLICT OF SOULS